A REQUEST TO DANCE

Annabelle noticed Thorne's body swaying to the strains of the waltz emanating from the ballroom. She felt herself caught up in the music, too. She stood and extended her hand.

"Come. Dance with me, Thorne."

"Annabelle . . ."

"Miss Rhys said you once danced beautifully."

"That was before—"

"I know. But you cannot have forgotten how to waltz. No one will see if you stumble and I promise not to tell a soul."

He shook his head, but he stood reluctantly, leaned his stick against the bench, and opened his arms.

"Do you *always* get your own way?" he murmured.

"Nearly always." She laughed nervously and knew the instant he touched her that she had gone too far. This had been a mistake—if only because it felt so wonderful and so absolutely right. . . .

Books by Wilma Counts

WILLED TO WED

MY LADY GOVERNESS

THE WILLFUL MISS WINTHROP

THE WAGERED WIFE

THE TROUBLE WITH HARRIET

MISS RICHARDSON COMES OF AGE

Published by Zebra Books

MISS RICHARDSON COMES OF AGE

Wilma Counts

ZEBRA BOOKS
Kensington Publishing Corp.
http://www.zebrabooks.com

ZEBRA BOOKS are published by

Kensington Publishing Corp.
850 Third Avenue
New York, NY 10022

All Kensington titles, imprints and distributed lines are available at special quantity discounts for bulk purchases for sales
promotion, premiums, fund-raising, educational or institu-
tional use.

Special book excerpts or customized printings can also be
created to fit specific needs. For details, write or phone the
office of the Kensington Special Sales Manager: Kensington
Publishing Corp., 850 Third Avenue, New York, NY 10022.
Attn. Special Sales Department. Phone: 1-800-221-2647.

Zebra and the Z logo Reg. U.S. Pat. & TM Off.

First Printing: November 2001
10 9 8 7 6 5 4 3 2 1

Printed in the United States of America

I daresay every writer has unpayable debts to those who have offered help and encouragement. I would like to acknowledge some of my indebtedness here.

Jane Toombs
has been a source of inspiration and encouragement from the very beginning;
Dee (Emily) Hendrickson
has been more than generous in sharing her expertise and knowledge of the Regency;
Jane Jordan Browne
managed to sell that first book for me and she continues to offer great advice and to work on my behalf;
Members of my Critique Group
continue to keep me on my toes as a writer.

One

Very early in her third Season, Miss Annabelle Richardson had not one but three proposals of marriage.

"Good heavens!" Harriet, Countess of Wyndham, exclaimed after the third one. "You are sure to best last year's record."

"I think she already has," the Earl of Wyndham said. "I managed to discourage two others."

The three of them were enjoying a rare evening at home together. They sat in the family drawing room of Wyndham House, lingering over after-dinner tea.

"And I thank you, Marcus," Annabelle said. "You undoubtedly spared me two more fortune hunters. Would that you had spared me the Viscount Beelson and Mr. Ferris as well."

Marcus's eyes twinkled with amusement. "I did try to discourage them, but it is well known that Miss Richardson has a mind of her own and will not be directed in the choice of husband by her guardians."

Annabelle smiled. "For which Miss Richardson is very grateful to said guardians." Her teasing tone turned serious. "I truly am grateful that neither of you has ever seen fit to be overly controlling in my life."

"I am thankful," Harriet said, "that it was never necessary that we be so."

"You have—usually—shown uncommonly good

sense," Marcus noted, "as in your rejection of those two."

"Many girls would be taken in by the fact that Beelson and Ferris are extremely handsome men of considerable charm," Harriet noted.

"Handsome is as handsome does," Annabelle said airily, pleased at the approval of these two whom she loved so dearly. "I doubt either of them cares two figs for *me*. I would wager that each of them knows to the last shilling what my fortune is worth."

"And young Wainwright?" Marcus asked.

"Mr. Wainwright—Luke—is a sweet person, but he is very young, is he not?"

Harriet laughed. "I believe he is exactly your own age, my dear."

"Well, he *seems* younger." Annabelle knew she sounded defensive.

"What he *seems* is very intent on winning your affection," Marcus said. "He is likely, though, to be ruled by his brother. Rolsbury takes a keen interest in matters involving family members, and he controls the younger Wainwright's purse strings. Still, Luke is quite smitten, and I doubt your refusal discouraged him overmuch."

"I know." Annabelle felt both regret and impatience at this idea. "But at least Luke took my refusal in stride. Lord Beelson and Mr. Ferris both seemed terribly affronted, especially Lord Beelson."

"Beelson is not accustomed to failure in dealings with the fair sex," Marcus said. "His first wife was swept off her feet early in her only Season on the town."

"I remember her as such a shy, sweet little thing," Harriet said. "She died within a year of the marriage."

There was a moment of relative silence in which the only sound was the clink of teacups against saucers.

"I did try to be diplomatic in telling him I could not love him as I thought a wife should love her husband."

"That alone would have inflamed his anger," Harriet observed. "He sets great store by having women fawn over him."

"That he does. My diplomacy was wasted on him. He simply dismissed my explanation," Annabelle went on. "He insisted love is unimportant in marriage in our circles."

"Did he just?" Harriet's tone was indignant and she exchanged a knowing look with her husband.

"I think," Marcus said, his tone utterly serious now, "you should be careful around him, Annabelle. Beelson *is* a ladies' man, but he can be vindictive when he is crossed. Your refusal of his suit will not have been palatable news to him. And he and Ferris are birds of a feather."

"What can they possibly do?" Harriet asked.

Marcus shrugged. "Hard to tell. But I should expect some sort of retaliation from one or both of them."

"Can you do nothing to forestall such, Marcus?" his wife asked.

"I tried to discourage them from offering at all, but they were both determined and each knew very well it would be up to Annabelle herself in the end."

"So their resentment will be directed at her."

"Yes. And it is difficult to say what form it might take."

"Oh, dear," Harriet murmured.

"Still, I could do naught but refuse them." Annabelle raised her chin. "And I would do so again."

In the next few days any worry over the actions of Lord Beelson or Mr. Ferris was lost in a flurry of acting on invitations arriving at Wyndham House. Some were sent directly to Miss Annabelle Richardson and others included her along with the earl and his countess. The

Season this year was especially hectic. An unusually large number of the nation's notables had already arrived and would stay through July for the king's coronation. The residents of Wyndham House were high on many a guest list.

At these affairs they often encountered the three erstwhile suitors. Annabelle was wary of Beelson and indifferent to Ferris, but, mindful of Marcus's cautionary words, she maintained a polite demeanor around them. Viscount Beelson continued to seek Annabelle's partnership for at least one dance when such activity was on the hostess's program. Mr. Ferris remained cordial.

"I do hope I may still change your mind," he said. He had stopped her as she returned from the ladies' withdrawing room during an intermission at a musicale.

"Mr. Ferris—" she started in an admonishing tone.

He put up his hands to forestall her continuing. "No. No. I shall not press you now, my dear."

"Good." She took his arm. "Now if you will just see me back to my chair, I believe Signora Margoni is about to perform."

She slid into her seat beside Harriet, who raised an eyebrow at seeing the gentleman who accompanied her. Annabelle, her back to Ferris, rolled her eyes slightly and shrugged. She was thankful there was no empty seat nearby for Ferris to claim.

Harriet leaned closer to whisper, "Do not take any notice now, but young Wainwright is leaning against the wall over there. He keeps watching you and looks not unlike a puppy lost in a rainstorm."

Annabelle sighed. "I think he views himself in the same light as the poet Byron."

"Byron?"

"You know—melancholy and misunderstood. He even writes *poetry* to me! Bad poetry, I might add."

"I noticed he has called on you several times of late," Harriet said.

"He does not take 'no' for an answer. I think he hopes to wear me down. And, to be truthful, he means well and can be amusing."

At this point their hostess introduced her featured performer and further conversation would have been rude.

Later, as Harriet and Annabelle prepared to leave, a light drizzle was falling. Luke Wainwright suddenly appeared at their side and snatched an umbrella being held by a footman.

"Do allow me," he said.

Rather than make a scene, Harriet and Annabelle thanked him as he accompanied them to their carriage. He handed Harriet into the vehicle first, then lingered over Annabelle's hand.

"Thank you again," Annabelle said, regaining possession of her hand.

"My pleasure entirely. I would do anything for you. Anything," he said fervently.

As the carriage moved away, Annabelle saw Luke still standing there, gazing after the vehicle and seemingly oblivious to the rain.

Despite Ferris's assertion that he would not press his suit, he did exactly that the next day. He had arrived for a morning call and invited Annabelle for a drive in the park, extending his invitation in front of others and in such a manner that she could not refuse without appearing woefully arrogant.

He called for her later in a brightly painted green-and-gold curricle drawn by a pair of matched white horses. On the seat in the rear sat a small boy in livery to match the vehicle. Ferris was dressed in elegant day wear, his wine-colored coat cut to show off a perfect male body. It occurred to Annabelle that with his black hair, brilliant blue eyes, and even features, the man epitomized the word *handsome*. Why was it that she simply could not warm up to him?

They chatted amiably as he negotiated city traffic. Once they reached the park, he seemed determined to have others acknowledge the two of them together. Annabelle was already less than wholly comfortable when he stopped the carriage in a secluded spot and instructed his tiger to jump down from his post in the back to hold the horses' heads.

Ferris turned to Annabelle and grasped her hand. "I have been a patient man, my dear, but I simply must renew my suit. Please say you will be mine."

She tugged at her hand, which he refused to relinquish. "Mr. Ferris! Please. Did you not just last evening promise not to press me on this matter?"

"George. You really must call me George, my darling Annabelle."

She felt a flash of annoyance. "I am not your 'darling' anything, sir. I gave you my answer on this matter."

"Of course you did—and quite properly so." His tone was condescending. "No young lady accepts a proposal on its first being offered. We gentlemen are willing to play the game by established rules."

Finally, she jerked her hand away and made no attempt to hide her anger. *"This* young lady, Mr. Ferris, is not 'playing a game.' As I said before, I appreciate the honor you do me, but I simply cannot accept your offer."

He drew in a deep breath and suppressed fury turned his normally beautiful eyes into hard blue stones for a moment. He quickly masked this expression. "As you wish. We shall continue to play the game." She thought his smile was intended to be indulgent.

"No. We shall not. This 'game,' as you put it, is over. Now, I would appreciate it if you would take me home."

Taking up the reins, he motioned the tiger to return

to his seat. Both were silent on the return trip, but Annabelle knew her companion's frustration was tinged with anger more than regret.

She did not discuss the incident with Marcus and Harriet, but mulled it over herself at some length. She knew she was passably pretty, but she doubted Mr. Ferris was overwhelmed by her personal attributes. Perhaps he was in more desperate financial straits than they had realized. Ferris turned distantly polite when they met at social functions thereafter.

Soon, however, Ferris's attitude and feelings paled in comparison to the actions of Lord Beelson and young Wainwright.

The Patterson ball was a grand affair to introduce Miss Melissa Patterson to Society, its grandness clearly intended to show the extent of the dowry that would accompany the rather plain Miss Patterson to the altar. Annabelle, standing on the sidelines with her friend Celia Hart, observed that Ferris pursued the young woman with some vigor.

"Hah!" Celia said in a low but sarcastic voice. "As Frederick would say, that dog will not hunt." Frederick was Celia's husband, who had gone for refreshments.

"Why? What do you mean?"

"The Baron Patterson is not likely to shackle his precious darling to a man so lacking in prospects."

"I suppose you are right."

"Of course I am." Celia laughed with mock superiority, then said in a more serious tone, "Frederick and I were quite relieved when his pursuit of *you* cooled."

"No more so than I, I am sure," Annabelle said, "but—tell me—what do *you* object to in him? I confess I cannot put my finger on my own reservations."

"Well, for one thing, Frederick knows him to be a frightful gamester. He is said to have squandered his entire fortune."

"Marcus intimated as much."

"Apart from that, I just do not feel he is truly sincere . . . I mean, he often seems just too glib, too polished. Do you understand what I am trying to say?"

"I think so." Annabelle thought Celia's view of the man paralleled her own.

"Such a shame," Celia went on. "The outer packaging is so very pretty there."

Any reply Annabelle might have made died on her lips as she observed the approach of Viscount Beelson.

He gave the two ladies an exaggerated bow. "I believe the next dance is mine, Miss Richardson."

She had been dismayed earlier to see him signed up for a waltz, but she made no show of reluctance as they took to the floor. They had gracefully executed a complete turn around the ballroom when Beelson waltzed her through the tall French doors to the terrace.

"Lord Beelson! Whatever are you about?" she asked in some alarm.

There were three or four other couples on the terrace and heads turned with casual interest in their direction. Beelson pushed Annabelle into an unoccupied, but far from secluded, area of the terrace.

"Just this, my dear." He wrapped his arms around her and lowered his mouth to hers, his tongue immediately seeking entrance.

Momentarily shocked, Annabelle soon became aware of giggles and smothered guffaws from the other couples. Trapped in the viscount's embrace, she nevertheless struggled to be free. He tightened his hold. She went limp and opened her mouth ever so slightly. She heard an appreciative grunt from him just before she gripped his lower lip with her teeth and bit down—hard. He immediately jerked his head back from hers.

"Why, you—" It was a murmur of pure fury. "You

go too far in this ploy of being hard to get, my love."
He touched his fingers to his injured mouth.

She jerked away. Despite being angry and embarrassed, she did not raise her voice, but neither did she
bother to keep it unduly lowered. "No, my lord. *You*
have gone too far. I never—never!—gave you leave to
take such liberty with my person."

"Oh, come now, my dear." His placating tone—
adopted, no doubt, for the benefit of their now avid audience—belied the fury in his eyes. "A lover's quarrel,"
he explained in an aside to their public and reached for
her again.

She sidestepped his grasping hand. "Why, you insuf-
ferable boor!" Without pausing even a second to think
of her reaction, Annabelle doubled up her fist, slammed
it into his face, spun on her heel, and returned to the
ballroom. Behind her she heard shocked squeals from
the ladies, even louder guffaws from the gentlemen, and
Beelson's surprised outrage promising that she would
be "sorry for this."

Annabelle immediately sought Harriet, who sent a
servant in search of Marcus. He arrived with a concerned look on his face. "I just heard. Are you all right,
Annabelle?"

"Furious, but intact," she replied. "The very nerve
of that man!"

Marcus grinned. "I think your quick action precludes
the necessity of my calling the fellow out." His wife
shot the earl an alarmed look. "Yes, my dears. Public
humiliation is probably sufficient retribution." Marcus
chuckled. "Bested by a woman—and a slip of a girl at
that! Beelson will never live this down in boxing circles."

"Come," Harriet said to both of them. "We had better
take our little pugilist home. She is attracting far too
much notice."

Annabelle's anger with both Ferris and Beelson festered. They continued to frequent social affairs she attended, though neither accorded her special attention any longer—and for that she could only be grateful. However, she had twice observed Beelson eyeing her in a rather calculating manner. She dismissed such observation, thinking he was probably still fuming because his puffed lip and swollen nose had required that he absent himself from Society for a couple of days.

Her third would-be suitor, Luke Wainwright, continued to seek her out and she tried to be patient with his youthful posturing. She liked Mr. Wainwright. He was an amiable fellow, although often too intense, tending to take himself far too seriously. A well-featured young man, he possessed gray eyes and wore his brown hair slightly longer than most men did—and in a style that was clearly a studied imitation of his favorite poet. He dressed in the fashion of a veritable pink of the *ton* with colorful waistcoats, high shirt points, and elaborately tied cravats.

Wainwright had been sending her his own poetic offerings on a nearly daily basis. Although they occasionally took the form of an epic or a painfully contrived sonnet, these were usually only a few lines of doggerel accompanying a bouquet of flowers.

One afternoon, however, Annabelle and Harriet attended the Baroness Oglethorpe's elaborate "at home" affair when Wainwright happened to be there. Also in attendance were Lord Beelson and Mr. Ferris as well as nearly three dozen other people, most of whom were high-ranking members of the *ton*.

Annabelle felt Mr. Wainwright's gaze dwell on her as she moved about the room, greeting other guests. Celia, who had arrived before Annabelle, beckoned her to a seat on a settee in the center of the room. The two young women were engaged in idle conversation when

Mr. Wainwright suddenly fell on his knees before Annabelle. Guests in the immediate vicinity paused in their conversation at this unusual behavior. Annabelle drew in her breath apprehensively. Luke put his clasped hands over his heart and began to declaim,

> *All the world is contented well*
> *When one is able to behold*
> *The eternal beauties manifold*
> *Of the goddess Annabelle.*
> *Her doe eyes and sunlit hair*
> *Denied a lover bring despair*
> *To a heart that ever desires*
> *But to be made whole by such fires.*

Taken aback by the abruptness and the public forum in which he chose to present this latest offering, Annabelle noted muffled laughs and curious gazes directed their way. Despite being embarrassed by the intensity of his emotion and annoyed at his singling her out in such a fashion, she was struck by the humor of both the situation and the sentiment. She began to giggle.

Celia immediately joined in and the two of them fed on each other's mirth until they both had tears in their eyes. Others seated or standing nearby were infected by their merriment and their section of the room now rang with laughter. Annabelle suddenly caught sight of a stricken look on Mr. Wainwright's reddening face.

"You . . . you do not like it?" He sounded plaintive as he struggled awkwardly to his feet.

She looked up at him and, striving for a more seemly expression, she tried to think of something that might be both truthful and comforting. "I . . . I am flattered—"

"No, you aren't," he interrupted. "You are laughing at me." He turned abruptly and left the room.

"Oh, dear," Annabelle murmured into the uneasy silence that followed his dramatic exit.

She had a fleeting impression of Beelson watching the young man's departure. The viscount had a speculative look on his face, but then her attention was distracted by Celia's renewed giggles.

" 'The *goddess* Annabelle?' Oh, my. There will be no living with you now."

This comment lightened the mood left by Wainwright's departure. There were a few comments about inferior poetry and the pretensions adopted by Byron's imitators, but Annabelle refused to encourage these and talk among the company soon turned to other matters. Annabelle was torn between being exasperated with Luke's behavior and remorseful over his embarrassment. Surely she could have done something to forestall his humiliation. But it had happened so quickly. . . . Well, perhaps she could find a way later to smooth the young peacock's ruffled feathers.

Before she could do so, however, social disaster struck.

Two

The first inkling that something was amiss came when Annabelle paid a morning call at the Hart residence. Ostensibly, she called on Celia, but she never failed to visit the Hart nursery as well.

"I must be assured that you are treating my godchild properly—that is, according her all the privileges to which she is entitled."

She knew the Harts were besotted with their tiny daughter—as was the child's godmother.

Celia laughed as she handed the babe over to her friend. "Honestly, Annabelle! One would think you had enough of babes in the Wyndham nursery. I know how much time you spend with their son. I vow, you need one of these of your own!"

"Yes, I probably do," Annabelle said absently. She cuddled the babe, nuzzling her soft cheek. Little Annie, at six months, smiled and cooed happily. Her small hands reached for Annabelle's hair and the sparkling brooch at her neck. "No, no, no, sweeting." She sat down on a windowseat and bounced the baby on her knee as Celia discussed the child's care with the nursery maid. Finally, they gave the babe over to the maid and the two friends made their way to the Harts' rather modest drawing room.

"Would it not be wonderful," Annabelle said with a laugh, "if your daughter and Wyndham's son made a match of it one day?"

Celia rolled her eyes as she reached for the bellpull to order up tea for them. "Annabelle! You cannot be making a match for those children already!"

"It was just a thought."

"I was serious earlier," Celia said. "You should have a child. You are so good with Annie."

Annabelle laughed. "Are you not omitting an important detail?"

"Oh, pooh!" Celia waved her hand in a dimissive gesture. "You know very well you could be married in no more time than it takes to read the banns!"

"*If* I were interested in having a husband merely to father a child, that might be true—but, honestly, Celia, how can *you,* of all people, suggest such a match for me?" Celia looked a bit chagrined and Annabelle added softly, "I want what you have—I want to be madly, wildly in love with the man I marry."

"I—I am not sure that is always possible—or even an absolute necessity for a successful marriage."

"I will not have mere 'success.' I want real happiness, too! You and Frederick have it. Letty has it with Winters. Harriet and Marcus do as well. I will not settle for second best!"

Celia smiled. "All or none—is that it?"

"Something like that."

"Well, my dear, if you are to discover this elusive love, you cannot keep refusing invitations."

"Refusing invi—? Why, whatever do you mean?" Annabelle was genuinely puzzled.

"You were not at the Mertons' breakfast on Wednesday last. You missed Lady Henley's 'at home.' And you were absent from the Paulsons' ball just last night."

"I—I—" Annabelle felt her face growing warm with

embarrassment. "I did not know of these events," she said quietly.

Celia sounded indignant. "What? Are you telling me you did not receive invitations for them? You?"

"I am sure I did not."

"How very strange . . ."

Annabelle shrugged. "A hostess cannot invite *everyone* to every gathering."

"Perhaps . . ." Celia then changed the subject.

In the next few days, Annabelle, who had heretofore enjoyed uncommon popularity, found fewer and fewer invitations coming her way. At affairs she did attend, she often encountered an abrupt silence followed by a babble of changed topics when she came into a room. On entering a modiste's shop one morning, she was given the cut direct by a certain Mrs. Phigby, wife of a baronet.

Harriet stared after the departing matron who had at least nodded to the countess. "What was that about?"

"I have no idea," Annabelle answered. "But I know who will. Letty. I shall call on her this very afternoon."

Lady Letitia Atkinson Castlemaine was the daughter of a duke and wife of Jonathan Castlemaine, Marquis of Winters, who would one day inherit a dukedom himself. The Marchioness of Winters was accounted one of the leaders of Society, though she, like Annabelle, had a few months yet before reaching the age of majority. The two young women, along with Celia Berwyn Hart, had been school friends. Celia, too, had married well, though Celia's beloved Frederick was a mere mister, being the son of a younger son of an earl.

Annabelle was a frequent visitor to the Winters's house, but the splendor of Letty's drawing room always took her breath away. Done in burgundy and gray with touches of silver here and there, it was one of the most elegant of London's drawing rooms. When Annabelle arrived, she found Celia there also.

"When I received your note, I sent one around to Celia to join us." Letty gestured to a place on a settee next to Celia, reached for a bellpull, and instructed the footman who answered to bring up a tea tray.

"Good. I should have called upon you later anyway, Ceel," Annabelle said.

"We saved you the trip then," Celia replied.

"You know why I have come?" These were her dearest friends, but Annabelle felt embarrassed about bringing up the subject of her apparent fall from grace.

"We think so," Letty answered. "We were just discussing the rumors." Letty nodded her head of deep auburn curls in Celia's direction.

"What rumors?" Annabelle demanded, sorely afraid that she knew. After all, that scene with Beelson had occurred in a rather public place.

"There are some very unpleasant rumors flying around about you," Celia said.

"I thought it must be something like that. What is being said?"

A long pause ensued as the footman brought in a large tray laden with a teapot, cups, and pastries. Annabelle wanted to scream with impatience as he fussed over the arrangements. When he left, Letty busied herself pouring tea and Celia took over the thread of conversation.

"We have no idea what the source is, but the tales say you are no better than you should be, and that you have been toying with the Wainwright boy."

"Toying with him? Why, I tried for three weeks and more to be rid of him!"

"We know that." Letty looked at Celia, who nodded her agreement. "However, there is more. You are also

held to have been rather free with your favors. You were seen in the park in a *tête à tête* with Mr. Ferris, and then kissing Beelson at the Patterson ball."

"Being kissed, you mean. He took me by surprise." Annabelle hated sounding defensive.

"Annabelle, you need not explain to *us,"* Celia said.

"So who is spreading these stories—and to what end?" Annabelle set her untouched tea back on the table and rose to pace impatiently.

"There is no absolute proof—there never is with something like this," Letty said, "but my guess is that Beelson and Ferris are behind it. *And* they seem to have enlisted the support of young Wainwright."

"H-how do you know this?" Annabelle asked.

Celia rose to pat her friend's shoulder. "Frederick was playing cards at White's. Beelson and Ferris were there."

"They were bandying my name about?" Annabelle was appalled. She allowed herself to be guided back to the settee.

"No. I gather they were allowing others to do so as they strategically kept silent on the matter, only raising an eyebrow now and then."

"That is not all," Letty added. "Winters saw them at play with Wainwright at Watier's. Young Wainwright was drinking and playing too deep. Seems he was also rather vocal about his losses at Cupid's game, too."

"Oh, good heavens!" Annabelle exclaimed.

"Winters said it appeared that Beelson and Ferris were egging him on in his injured sensibilities—at least they did so until they realized Winters was taking notice of what they were doing."

"And now the ugliness has spilled over from gaming tables to drawing rooms." Annabelle's shoulder slumped disconsolately. She felt her eyes grow moist, but she refused to allow the tears.

Letty shrugged. "Some men do not take rejection well, it would seem."

"Do not worry, Annabelle," Celia assured her. "The worst is probably over."

"How can you say that?" Annabelle hoped, though, that it was true.

"Well, if the aim were to discredit you, it has not worked terribly well," Letty said. "*I* have no intention of dropping you from *my* invitation lists—yet." Letty's impish grin told Annabelle just how preposterous that idea was. "Nor do the patronesses of Almack's intend to deny you vouchers to their assemblies."

"You have talked with them?"

"Yes. And they agree this is in the nature of a tempest in a teapot."

"There! You see? Nothing to worry about," the ever-optimistic Celia declared.

"I wonder . . ." Annabelle mused. "Still—I do most sincerely appreciate your efforts on my behalf."

"What are friends for?" Letty asked with a smile.

"And—" Annabelle went on, "I am not without resources of my own."

"The Wyndhams are likely to be powerful allies as well." Celia seemed to agree with Annabelle.

Yes, Annabelle thought, but her resources included not just Marcus and Harriet. She had it in mind to enlist the aid of Miss Emma Bennet.

Three

Thorne Wainwright, Earl of Rolsbury, reluctantly and clumsily climbed the steps of his London townhouse.

"Welcome home, my lord," his unflappable butler said.

"Thank you, Perkins. Is my brother here?" Thorne leaned heavily on his walking stick. Five years since Waterloo, yet three days in a traveling coach and his leg stiffened up painfully.

"Er . . . yes, my lord, but I think he has not yet arisen."

"Not yet—Good God, man, it is nearly noon!"

"Yes, my lord."

"Send word that I shall see him in the library in half an hour."

"Very good, my lord." The butler snapped his fingers at a hovering footman to tell him to see to it.

Thirty minutes later an obviously hurriedly dressed Luke Wainwright entered the library to find his brother seated behind the huge mahogany desk that dominated the book-lined room. The desk was already strewn with papers.

"Gads, Thorne, you might have sent some warning you were coming." Luke sounded youthful, petulant, and defensive.

"I was unaware of needing permission to visit my own house—any of them." Thorne rubbed his leg, carefully concealing the action from his brother.

"That is not what I meant. And what is it you want from me?"

"Sit down." Scowling with both discomfort and displeasure, Thorne gestured to a chair in front of the desk. "Now—just what in the hell have you been up to?"

"I . . . I have no idea what you're talking about."

"For starters, there are all these duns from creditors." Thorne held up a sheaf of papers. "Do you never bother to check the post for anything but perfumed notes from some lightskirt? Some of these are weeks overdue."

Luke ran a finger around his neckcloth, which appeared to have suddenly tightened. "I . . . uh . . . well . . ."

"Come on. Out with it. Why have you not paid these accounts?"

"I meant to. But I've had uncommonly bad luck at the tables lately, you see, and . . . well . . . a debt of honor comes first, as you know."

"Gaming debts? Besides these bills from tradesmen, you have amassed gaming debts as well?" In his annoyance, Thorne made no effort to control his voice. "I did not encourage you to come to town to create a load of debt in gaming hells!"

"It—it is not as though I *meant* to do so. After all, anyone can have a streak of bad luck—"

Thorne snorted in contempt. " 'Bad luck' usually translates to lack of skill or too much drink—or some other distraction."

Thorne saw a slow flush creep over his brother's countenance.

"Yes. Well . . . if you could perhaps give me an advance on next quarter's allowance . . . ?" His voice trailed off and there was not much hope in it.

"Yes. Well." Thorne deliberately repeated Luke's words. "How much have you lost?"

Luke's mouth worked and his neckcloth moved up and down as he swallowed and named a figure.

Thorne felt his eyebrows climb upward. "Good God, boy! Have you no sense at all? I leave you on your own for a few months and you amass debts like the king himself!"

"Oh, now, it is not quite *that* bad . . ."

"Damned near! And I'll not have it—you hear? There's nothing wrong with a bit of gentlemanly play, but this is ridiculous." He paused, letting his words sink in as he deliberately shuffled through some of the papers again. Finally, he held Luke's gaze and said, "Very well. I shall pay them—but if you perform another such idiotic stunt, I swear, Luke, I'll see you rot in debtors' prison before I do so again. Now—to whom do you owe all this blunt?"

"Some to Rhoads. A bit to George Ferris. Mostly to Viscount Beelson."

"Who?" Thorne fairly shouted the word. "Did you say Beelson?"

"Y-yes."

"You idiot! You confounded idiot. That sorry jackanapes was probably cheating you right and left without your even knowing it!"

Luke leapt to his feet. "Here now, Thorne. I ain't such a flat as all that."

Thorne gazed at his brother and tried to control his anger which, in truth, was directed more at Beelson and even himself than at Luke. Finally, he softened his tone. "No, I doubt you are. But Beelson is clever—he rarely gets caught in his knavery."

"He . . . he has been a capital fellow to me," Luke insisted, beginning to pace in agitation. "I did not know you were even acquainted with him. 'Taint like you to judge another on hearsay."

"Nor do I do so now. He was only a year ahead of me in school."

Luke halted in mid-stride, a look of surprise on his face. "Is that so?"

"You thought him younger?"

"Um . . . well . . . yes. As a matter of fact, I did." Luke abruptly sat down again.

"You might ask yourself why a man of his age and experience would choose to befriend someone with whom he has so little in common."

"I am sure you are eager to enlighten me."

His brother's resentment was clear and Thorne wondered how he might have presented his own views differently. Lord! Had he no recollection of the tender sensibilities of youth?

"You are not the first young buck to be fleeced by someone older and less scrupulous than you. And certainly not the first to be had by Beelson! But I would surmise that he took special satisfaction in subjecting *my* younger brother to his schemes."

"What is that supposed to mean?" Luke's resentment was overwhelmed by curiosity.

"Let us just say there is bad blood between the two of us."

"But you are not telling *me* the whole of it—is that it?" Resentment was back in full force.

"No, I am not, for it involves another as well."

"Until you can offer a more substantive reason for me to cut the connection, I see no reason to give up Ralph's friendship."

"*Ralph* is it?" Thorne was silent for a moment. "Well, I have no intention of choosing your companions for you. However, Beelson is not welcome in my house. I will thank you not to invite him here."

"As you wish," Luke said stiffly. " 'Tis your house and you hold the purse strings."

"Yes, I do. And know this, Luke—" Thorne held his brother's gaze. "I will advance you the money to pay all these debts—including your gaming debts—this time. You will repay the exact sum when you come into your own fortune."

Luke sneered. "And when might that be? You control that, too."

"You know very well the terms of Mother's will. When you are twenty-seven or when I deem you responsible enough to handle your own affairs."

"And I suppose you find it to your advantage to prolong that event."

Thorne drew in a deep breath and struggled for patience. "No," he said with studied calm. "At the moment, though, it would appear to be to *your* advantage."

"Hah!"

Thorne's patience snapped. "Believe what you will. But know this, little brother—I will not advance you another farthing after these debts are paid." He waved the sheaf of papers at Luke. "You *will* learn to live within your rather generous income."

"And if I do not?"

The peevish bravado of this response annoyed Thorne even further. "Then I shall simply cut your allowance entirely and you can rusticate at Rolsbury Manor."

Silence reigned as Thorne wrote out a bank draft for the sum Luke had named.

"There." He handed the draft to the younger man. "We will speak no more of this."

"I insist on giving you an IOU," Luke said, sounding very stiff.

"That is not necessary."

"I think it is."

Luke rose and reached for paper and pen to scratch

out the note of indebtedness. Thorne hid both his surprise and his approbation.

"Now. Is that all?" Luke asked, still standing.

"No. Sit down, please." Luke sat on the edge of the chair, his hands on his knees, and waited for Thorne to continue.

Thorne deliberated, wondering how best to approach a more sensitive subject. Head-on, of course, he answered himself. "I want to know about this chit you have been making a cake of yourself over."

"How did you know—? Ah, I know. Aunt Dorothy. I suppose she couldn't wait to tattle to the family patriarch."

"So, it is true, then?"

"How am I to know if what you heard is the truth?"

"Try not to equivocate. Did you offer for the girl knowing full well you would need my approval for such an action?"

"Well . . . yes. But in six months I will not require your permission to marry. I shall be of age then." There was a note of triumph in Luke's tone.

"You think to support a wife—*and* maintain your manner of living—" Thorne gestured to the bills on his desk—"on the allowance you receive as a bachelor?"

"I thought . . ."

"You and your ladybird thought I would be forced to accept a *fait accompli*—is that it?"

"Not exactly. And she is not my ladybird."

"Well, what is she then? Aunt Dorothy reports that your Miss Richardson has been on the town for three Seasons, and now she seeks to attach a green boy? You *will* eventually come into a comfortable fortune."

"It is not like that at all. Lord! You really should come to town once in awhile. Ever since Waterloo you have been a recluse at the Manor. You need to get out more, brother dear."

"Perhaps I do—if only to keep you from making a fool of yourself. However, you forget—I was here just last autumn for the Queen's trial." Had it really been less than a year, he wondered, since the king had tried to enlist the aid of Parliament in ridding his royal self of his estranged wife?

"Only because all peers were required to be here—or pay a huge fine."

Thorne made no reply to this. It was, after all, the truth.

Luke went on, "And even then, you never went out. Why, you even went back home during that recess they had between the king's accusation and her defense. I would wager you came this year only because you are required to take part in the coronation."

"Well, that would be yet another wager you would lose."

Luke colored slightly at this none-too-subtle reminder. "Then why *did* you come now? It is a good two months and more until the coronation."

"There are a few other matters of concern to the country besides celebrating the accession of the fourth George to the throne."

Luke gaped at him openly. "You came to town to take an active role in Parliament?"

"Partly. *And* to ensure that you are not bamboozled into an ill-advised marriage."

Luke's color deepened. "Well, you need not concern yourself with that. She turned me down."

Thorne raised his brows at this. "Did she now? Well, that is a common ploy of females. Unusual in a fortune hunter, though."

Luke, apparently fuming over the entire conversation, simply gave him a tight little smile and did not respond verbally. There was a moment of silence during which

Thorne wondered what was *really* going on in his brother's mind.

"Will that be all?" Luke finally asked.

"Yes. You may go. But do think twice before you propose again."

"I *told* you she refused me." Luke quickly made his escape.

Thorne sat back in his chair and again rubbed his thigh where a French musket ball had put an end to his military career. Perhaps it had been a mistake to allow Luke such a free rein in the last few months. He was, after all, a mere boy. A mere boy? Thorne shook his head ruefully. Only in the eyes of a brother nearly a decade older. Had Luke himself not pointed out how close he was to the age of majority? Besides, he was already older than Thorne had been when he joined Wellington's forces in the Peninsula.

Numbers on a calendar do not equal maturity, Thorne reminded himself. Still, the lad's insistence on signing that IOU had been a responsible step. But proposing marriage to some female who was looking to advance her material or social advantage? That smacked of immaturity—not to say muddy thinking.

Well, any woman seeking to entrap the younger Wainwright would find herself contending with the older brother! Had he not always protected persons for whom he was responsible, be they either of his siblings, soldiers in the field, or tenants? He would hardly avoid that self-imposed duty at this stage of his life!

Thorne's first decision in dealing with the problem of the troublesome female followed closely on Luke's departure from the library. The Earl of Rolsbury had come to town largely to take some sort of role in political matters that were directly affecting his people in

Lincolnshire. Now he would himself have to appear on London's social scene in order to learn firsthand what this scheming Richardson woman was up to with his brother. First, though, he would call upon his Aunt Dorothy.

Lady Dorothy Conwick welcomed him the next day. She was a tall woman with iron-gray hair and a no-nonsense approach to life. Thorne had always thought she liked her pet dogs—two Welsh terriers—better than she did people. She held one in her lap now, stroking it frequently. "How very agreeable to find you have finally come to town without a government edict as your only incentive."

"Your last letter was rather insistent, was it not?"

She gave a decidedly unladylike snort. "My insistence never persuaded you before—and I doubt it did so now."

"I had no family member courting disaster before," he said.

"Your brother is certainly doing that from all that I hear." She proceeded to give him an account of Luke's deep play at gaming hells—a surprisingly accurate account, Thorne thought, judging by what Luke had revealed the day before.

"Yes. I know about those activities and I have taken steps to curb them."

"Well, what about his foolish behavior with Miss Richardson?" she demanded.

"Is it really so very bad? I rather think he fancies himself in love with her."

Her ladyship snorted again. "Love! What does a green boy know of love?"

Far too much—and far too little, Thorne thought ruefully. But he did not voice his opinion and only half listened as his aunt related what she knew of Luke's troubled courtship. Unfortunately, Aunt Dorothy herself rarely went into Society. She therefore relied on others as her sources.

"—and then there was that business of his reciting some silly poem at the Oglethorpe do—" She finally caught his attention.

"He *what?* Poetry, you say?"

She repeated the tale of the scene in Oglethorpe's drawing room.

"Oh, good grief." He shut his eyes, but could not erase the image of Luke's humiliation.

"She probably encouraged it, if you ask me!" his aunt said. "Such adoration would be a feather in the cap of any young woman. And that Richardson chit seems to like collecting feathers. Why, I am told she has had dozens of offers already."

"You mean she has played this game with other young men?"

"Well, maybe not such *young* ones. Mrs. Ferris told me Miss Richardson quite shamelessly chased poor George—who has nearly thirty years—and at the Patterson ball she was seen *kissing* Lord Beelson."

"I question her taste in partners, but a mere kiss is fairly innocent."

Lady Conwick sniffed. "There may have been more."

Thorne was all the more determined to protect his brother from a woman who readily displayed such questionable taste and shocking behavior.

Indeed, there *was* more as he heard when he dropped into his club later. The men there occupied themselves with tales of the Richardson woman's indiscretions, speculating at length as to who had or had not enjoyed her favors.

Thorne was annoyed with himself for engaging in or merely listening to gossip as he had on this day. However, in a fight to protect a member of his family, he would use any weapon available. At the moment, information seemed his best weapon. Maybe he would be able to talk some sense into his lovestruck brother.

On his return from visiting his solicitor one afternoon a few days later, Thorne was surprised to find that a number of invitations had arrived for him. One was to a dinner party at the home of his old comrade-in-arms, Captain Frederick Hart, late of His Majesty's army.

He knew Hart had sold his commission and married some two years and more ago, but the wedding was rather private and took place in the dead of winter when road conditions as well as distance from Lincolnshire to Somerset made travel unattractive. Thorne had had only occasional communication with Hart since the marriage, though the captain had visited Rolsbury Manor from time to time before that. Thorne admitted to some curiosity about the woman who had brought the elusive Frederick Hart up to scratch.

The first guest to arrive at the Hart dinner party, Rolsbury found himself in a modest house located in a respectable, but not fashionable, neighborhood. His early arrival was by design. Though he walked well enough, he felt awkward at having to use the walking stick and always strove to avoid "making an entrance."

Hart and his wife received him in their drawing room. In appearance, at least, he thought them well matched. Hart's sandy hair and freckles formed a contrast to his wife's dark hair and pale complexion. After a bit, he thought them equally well matched in temperament as well.

In the course of initial conversations, he learned that the party was, indeed, rather a small one as promised on the invitation.

"There will eventually be but twelve of us," his hostess said, "and I believe you will already know most of the gentlemen at least, my lord, for Frederick was insistent on seeing his fellow warriors." Celia smiled up at her husband in a teasing manner that told Thorne much regarding his friend's happiness.

"Really?" Thorne gave Frederick an inquiring look.

"Rhys and Berwyn will be here," Frederick said.

Thorne addressed Celia. "I seem to recall that Berwyn is your brother, Mrs. Hart?"

"Yes, he is," she replied. "And *his* wife Charlotte is the sister of Harriet, Countess of Wyndham. Are you acquainted with the Wyndhams, sir?"

"I met *him* several years ago and sat in the same chamber with him during that unseemly trial of the queen—but to answer your question, no, madam, I am not."

"Well, I am sure you will find them agreeable company. And I do think we may drop the formality between us, Lord Rolsbury. As you are one of Frederick's oldest and dearest friends—or so he tells me—I insist you call me 'Celia' as *my* friends do."

"Your wish is my command, Mrs.—uh, Celia. I am 'Thorne' to family and friends."

"Thorne is a very interesting name," she said. "I do not ever remember knowing anyone of that name before."

"It is a family name," he explained. "The story is that my maternal grandfather would not sanction his daughter's marriage until my father agreed to give their firstborn son the old man's surname." He shrugged. "And since my mother came to the marriage with a very considerable dowry . . . well, you see the result—Thorne, it is."

"Or 'Thorny,' if one is a former schoolmate." Frederick grinned as he handed Thorne a glass of wine. "And believe me, my love, he earned that sobriquet."

"Oh, I cannot believe that," Celia said, but then she

was immediately distracted by the arrival of additional guests, including the Berwyns and former cavalry captain Charles Rhys with his sister, Miss Helen Rhys.

Thorne found himself inordinately pleased to see his old friends again. His pleasure was enhanced with the arrival of the next guests, Lord and Lady Winters.

"Winters!" Thorne exclaimed, offering another old school chum his hand. "It has been years."

"Yes, and I must say, Thorne, having heard you were in town, I had expected to see you before this."

"I would have liked to oblige you in that, but I had certain other matters that required my attention first."

Winters nodded, with a look of sympathy. "Luke."

Thorne was uncomfortable at this reminder that his family name had been bandied about London drawing rooms so freely. "Yes. Luke," he admitted, and then added, "but I am in town also because I felt it was time I took a more active interest in what you fellows are doing in Lords."

Winters gave a visible start of surprise and clapped him on the shoulder. "Do not say you are really taking your seat in Parliament?"

"I think so. Yes."

"Good. You know, you need to come to town more often instead of hiding away up north."

"My brother said the same thing. He—and you—may be right."

A lovely, auburn-haired woman approached and placed her hand on Winters's arm in a familiar manner. Winters introduced his wife to Thorne and it was readily apparent that Winters, too, had made a fortunate choice in his bride.

"Lady Winters," Thorne acknowledged the introduction.

"Lord Rolsbury. I have heard much about you and I am ever so happy finally to meet you."

Thorne flashed his friend a mocking grimace. "My dear Lady Winters, I do hope you were not misled into believing all that your scapegrace spouse might have told you of me."

She laughed. "Not *all* of it—but there was something about filling a certain headmaster's office with crumpled papers? And putting vegetable dye in his fish tank? You must tell me the whole of those tales."

"I shall be happy to do so, my lady. Those were, after all, two of Winters's better—well, most successful—plots against that abominable man."

"You must address me as 'Letty,' " she said. "I mean to say, all of us here tonight are friends of long standing and we really cannot have you be the only one among us 'my lording' and 'my ladying' everyone."

Thorne covered his surprise at this, for he knew Winters's wife was the daughter of a duke and of course Winters himself would one day inherit a dukedom. Most women of such pedigree would be extraordinarily aware of their rank. Then he immediately chastised himself. Jonathan Castlemaine, Marquis of Winters, leading prankster in their school form, would hardly have chosen a wife with a puffed-up sense of pride.

Thorne was warmed by the reception his friends' wives had given him. Truth to tell, he rather envied Hart and Winters, if first impressions of their ladies were anything by which to judge.

A few minutes later, Thorne stood conversing with the Rhys brother and sister and Berwyn. All four of them had been in Belgium just before Waterloo. Thorne remembered dancing with Helen Rhys at the ball given by the Duchess of Richmond on the eve of the great battle. Miss Rhys had been barely out of the schoolroom at the time. He wondered why she had not been snapped up on the marriage mart, for she was quite a lovely woman—tall, with silvery blond hair and blue eyes. His musings were interrupted as the butler intoned the names of the last arrivals.

"Lord and Lady Wyndham. Miss Richardson."

Richardson? Thorne immediately stiffened but hoped he appeared casual as he turned to observe the new-comers and brace himself for the inevitable introductions.

"I see Celia chooses to ignore all that talk about Miss Richardson," Helen Rhys observed quietly.

"My sister is nothing if not loyal to her friends," Berwyn said. "She was even so as a child."

"And that takes a certain degree of courage sometimes," Charles Rhys said.

Yes, I suppose it does, Thorne thought, admiring Celia all the more as she greeted the newest guests. Lord Wyndham was a tall man—in his mid-thirties, Thorne surmised. Both he and his wife were attractive, well-dressed people with dark hair. The woman accompanying them—for this was no mere girl—came as a shock to Thorne.

She was breathtakingly beautiful. He had to admire Luke's taste in appearances, at any rate. Annabelle Richardson was of medium height with a nicely proportioned figure. She possessed a crown of hair the color of dark honey and well-defined brows, darker than her hair. As Celia brought the three to meet him, he saw that she had brown eyes; a slightly upturned, straight nose; and a generous, kissable mouth. Now, where on earth had that thought come from?

Mesmerized by the woman who had captured his brother's heart, Thorne paid scant attention to her companions, but as Celia made the introductions, he roused himself to be properly polite. He thought Miss Richardson seemed slightly nervous at meeting him.

"Lord Rolsbury," she said when introductions were finished. She sounded very serious, but a distinct twinkle danced in her eyes. "Would that be the bravest of soldiers, the smartest of men, and the absolute paragon among older brothers?" She smiled at his mildly puzzled expression and hastily explained, "I am acquainted with your brother, you see, and he sings your praises."

"Is that so?" He was surprised, especially as he recalled the scene in the library with Luke and the nearly monosyllabic conversations they had had since. "Family loyalty and all, you know."

"More in the nature of hero worship, I should say."

This line of discussion was cut off as Winters approached to tell Wyndham of Thorne's plan to take his seat in Parliament. Thorne fully expected Lady Wyndham and Miss Richardson to excuse themselves when Lord Wyndham introduced the subject of child labor, a topic being bandied about the halls of Parliament these days. Instead, both women not only stayed, they also offered their own views which—in both cases—were more studied than sentimental.

"I say, Rolsbury," Lord Wyndham said, "did you not touch on this topic in an article some months back in *The London Review?*"

"Oh, of course!" Lady Wyndham said in a tone of discovery. *"That* is why the Rolsbury name is so familiar to me. You write for the *Review."*

"Only occasionally, madam." He turned to Wyndham. "I am surprised you remembered that bit—it was, after all, but part of an article on labor problems we are having in the midlands." In fact, he was rather surprised these people even knew of—or remembered reading—his writings, though he acknowledged a certain degree of pride that they did so.

"I read the article," Lady Wyndham said. "You did, too, Annabelle. I remember your commenting on how well written it was."

A sudden blush heightened Miss Richardson's beauty.

"I . . . yes," she said, looking distinctly uncomfortable. "I do recall having read it now, but I confess that I did not note the author at the time. I was touched by your description of women who work in the textile mills."

This was the female with whom brother Luke was enamored? Luke, who rarely voiced an idea that did not involve horses or hunting and sport—or some new sartorial splendor in waistcoats and cravats? And what did *she* see in Luke—other than a potential fortune?

Well, that alone would certainly be enough for most females.

However, later in the evening, he had to revise this view, too. When the gentlemen rejoined the ladies after dinner, they found the women discussing—of all topics!—slavery in the former colonies.

Miss Rhys had apparently just read—and been greatly taken by—a sentimentalized account of how plantation owners provided for and took loving care of their slaves.

"I cannot approve the institution of slavery," she said, "but such workers are not merely valuable property. In their simple innocence, they are naive and gullible and need to be taken care of by those who are better qualified to make responsible decisions for them."

"Nonsense! Utter nonsense!" Annabelle Richardson said forcefully. "All people should be allowed to decide matters of their lives for themselves! And that goes for women in this country, too."

Thorne found himself standing near Miss Richardson's chair as she made this expostulation. "Are you likening the status of women in England to that of negro slaves in the Americas?" he asked.

"Uh-oh," Berwyn said. "Please, Thorne, do not get her started—she will hold forth for hours." Berwyn grinned at Annabelle, but Thorne thought others seemed to share this view of Miss Richardson's inclination to speak out on such matters.

Annabelle slanted Berwyn a look of exaggerated hurt, but addressed herself to Thorne's question. "No, not precisely. For the most part few English women have horsewhips taken to them on a regular basis. However—"

"However, my dear Annabelle," Celia interrupted as she stood and extended her hand to Miss Richardson, "we all know that you not only freed your Jamaican slaves these two years and more ago, but you provided settlement on them to allow their relocation—*and* you sold that plantation. Now, come. Helen promised to play for us. Those of us who feel so inclined will lift our voices in song—not social issues."

Jamaica? Selling a plantation? Providing settlements to freed slaves? Although he joined his baritone to the singing, Thorne's mind reeled with Celia's comments. He felt somewhat abashed at the discovery of Miss Richardson's apparent wealth. Any woman with those kinds of resources would have no need of his brother's modest inheritance.

Four

Annabelle had heard that Lord Rolsbury was in town and she remembered vaguely that he had been a commanding officer in Frederick Hart's cavalry regiment. Therefore, she was not overly surprised that he should be present at Celia's entertainment. She *was* surprised at the man himself.

He was much younger than she had expected. She had assumed from the respect Hart accorded him that he was a man of more mature years. Also, despite his case of hero worship, Luke had chafed against his brother's advice and strictures in terms other young men used for their fathers.

Lord Rolsbury was not only younger than she expected, he was also disconcertingly attractive. Images of nature and the outdoors leapt to mind with him. Despite the necessity of the walking stick, there was something solid and earthy about him. He had dark brown hair and heavy dark brows. He was smooth-shaven, but a firm jaw showed a hint of the beard he might have allowed. When he smiled, even white teeth flashed against a complexion that suggested much time spent in sun and weather. His most arresting feature, though, was his eyes. They were a deep gray-green, the color of a cloud-draped forest.

A tall man, he carried himself with military erectness. Most people requiring a walking stick would be somewhat stooped from leaning into that tool. Not this man.

At dinner she had been seated across the table from him. Since rules of etiquette required that she confine her conversation to persons on either side of her, she had not actually talked with him beyond the merest polite exchange. However, she felt his gaze directed her way from time to time. Whenever she caught his eye, she felt a confusing warmth suffuse her body. They *might* have had a substantive discussion later, but of course it had been diverted by the music and singing.

Still, she had been extraordinarily aware of him from the moment Celia introduced them. She found this rather strange, for Annabelle Richardson rarely reacted in such an elemental way to another person. Moreover, she knew she had not imagined his gaze on her from time to time. What had Luke told him?

Annabelle had been irritated with Luke over that miserable poetry presentation in the Oglethorpe drawing room. But she also knew Luke's feelings had been hurt not only by her laughter, but by the fact that the entire company had found the incident amusing. She had hoped for an opportunity to speak with him and smooth things over with an apology. However, when they did chance to meet at social affairs afterward, Luke avoided her and refused even to look at her. He was often seen laughing and joking with Lord Beelson and Mr. Ferris. She knew from their sly looks and occasional gestures that she was often the chief topic of their discussions. This, in turn, raised her hackles.

Then the destructive nature of the gossip campaign had hit and Miss Emma Bennet was called upon to help control the damage by turning the tables on the perpetrators of this smearing of Miss Richardson.

Very few people knew that Emma Bennet, author of

several popular novels, and Annabelle Richardson, sometime darling of *ton* society, were the same person. Harriet and Marcus knew and had approved her. literary endeavors early on. Mr. Murray, the publisher and editor, had been sworn to secrecy. Certain of her friends probably remembered she had once been enthusiastic about writing, but they were—even then—not privy to the name she used as a *nom de plume*. Annabelle was content to allow her friends to think writing had been only a passing fancy of youth—even though it remained a driving force of her life.

Miss Emma Bennet's latest offering was a slim volume—hardly more than a pamphlet—that presented a scathing satire of the mating practices of the *ton*. It centered on two experienced rakes and a naive young man just up from the country, all of whom pursued an heiress through drawing rooms and balls. The portraits were somewhat disguised, but the principals of the tale were readily identifiable. Certain minor characters were apparent as well, but Miss Bennet dealt more kindly with the nervous debutantes and anxious mamas trying to manage the intricacies of the marriage mart.

The motivating factor for the would-be suitors was, of course, the fictional heiress's fortune. The rakes—called Brewster and Franklin—needed her wealth to continue their profligate lives in gaming hells and brothels. The young man—Lester—had come to town on the advice of his older brother to seek a rich wife. "Lester" explained in detail his brother's instructions on how to conduct the courtship—instructions by which Miss Bennet depicted an ignorant country bumpkin trying to ape his betters.

Annabelle had delivered the manuscript to the editor two days before Celia's dinner party. It would hit the streets the following week. Even before the story was copied in its final form, the author had had second thoughts about it. She had produced it in a fit of pique. Yet, in the last few days, Luke had begun to make conciliatory overtures. She had an impression of his not being quite so agreeable to the tales Beelson and Ferris had spread. Perhaps, she reasoned, Luke's anger had cooled enough that he saw how truly vicious the rumors were.

However, she had promised the work and had struggled to meet the due date for it. So, despite her misgivings, she delivered it as promised.

Then she met the real brother at Celia's party and her vague misgivings became a raging case of apprehension. The man was a far cry from the country clod she had depicted! Moreover, he was a writer whose work she admired. She tried the next day to call the manuscript back, but it was too late to do so. She would just have to weather it through and hope no one—least of all the Wainwright brothers—discovered that Miss Annabelle Richardson and Miss Emma Bennet were the same miss.

By the end of the following week, Miss Emma Bennet's story, *Innocence Betrayed,* was the primary topic of conversation in London drawing rooms. Annabelle cringed whenever she happened to overhear others discussing it. She did not concern herself with the possible reactions of Beelson and Ferris, for she was still angry with their attempts to blacken her name in Society. She had forgiven Luke's role and harbored no ill will toward him. Now she worried about how he had reacted to the piece. And—even more—she wondered how the Earl of Rolsbury might have taken it.

Marcus reported that the story figured heavily in conversations in the gentlemen's clubs as well.

"Beelson and Ferris can hardly show themselves,"

Marcus said one evening as he, Harriet, and Annabelle awaited the announcement of dinner. "Of course, Luke has not been seen so much in their company since his brother arrived in town."

"The story has become a much bigger sensation than I expected," Annabelle said. "I . . . I wish now I had shown it to you before sending it off to Mr. Murray."

"Well, the tone may be a trifle strident," Harriet said, "but it is wonderfully funny—and those two, especially, deserved a comeuppance."

"That they did," Marcus agreed. "But really, Annabelle, you were rather harsh on poor Luke Wainwright, were you not?"

"Perhaps—in retrospect—I was," Annabelle agreed. "But I was so angry at his going along with them, you see. And I *did* try to soften it a bit by showing that his innocence, too, was betrayed."

"I doubt either he or Rolsbury will see it that way," Marcus responded.

"Oh, once he gets over the initial shock, Luke will come around." Annabelle tried to believe this was true. "He does have a good sense of humor."

"Yes, but does his brother?" Harriet asked.

"We shall see," Annabelle said, but she felt an inkling of apprehension. Rolsbury did not strike her as the sort to ignore a direct insult.

"We had best not 'see' too closely," Marcus warned.

"Why? What do you mean?" Annabelle looked worriedly at Marcus.

But it was Harriet who answered, "Let us hope that Miss Emma Bennet remains the anonymous entity she has been heretofore—at least for a while. If it gets out now that you wrote that story, the gossip will be renewed a thousandfold."

"And," Marcus added, "there is no telling *what* Beelson might take it in mind to do."

Throughout dinner, though they talked of other matters, Annabelle's mind kept returning to the concerns Marcus and Harriet had expressed—and to her own second thoughts on the matter.

Well, there was little that could be done about it now.

In another part of the city, the Wainwright brothers sat in their own drawing room, each with a glass of wine at hand, and considered Miss Bennet's tale. One was embarrassed; the other was furious.

"Who *is* this Bennet woman?" Thorne demanded, waving the pamphlet under his brother's nose. "Are you acquainted with anyone named Bennet?"

"N-no. At least . . . that is . . . I don't think so. Jeremy Kenton says ladies often take a false name when they write stuff."

Thorne snorted disdainfully. "And rightly so with this sort of drivel." Trying to calm himself, he took a fortifying sip of wine. "Hmm. Well, we know this much—*she* knows you fairly well—and she is sympathetic to Miss Richardson."

"It could be a man writing under a woman's name," Luke ventured. He clenched a fist on his knee. "And would I ever welcome a chance to give him a facer!"

Thorne gave this conjecture serious thought, then said, "It *could* be a man, but somehow I doubt it—it seems so definitely a female viewpoint."

This appeared to take the wind out of Luke's sails. He slumped back in his chair, a picture of dejection. "I think maybe I should return to the country for a spell. Just until this thing blows over."

"You will do no such thing!"

"But, dash it, Thorne! It is embarrassing to walk into a room knowing people have been laughing behind your back!"

"Yes, it is. But you might have considered that before you became a party to bandying about a lady's name as you did."

Luke's face reddened. "How did you—? I did not—"

"I doubt you actually told any of those scurrilous tales—I grant you that much. But you apparently did nothing to quell the gossip either—as a gentleman should have done."

"I don't see how you came to that conclusion." Luke's voice was full of petulance and injured youth.

"For starters, I asked around. Obviously, this . . . this *thing* was written in reaction to some perceived abuse. The writer makes that point quite clear."

Luke apparently did not want to examine *that* idea too closely. "I still think I should leave town for a few days."

"Turn tail and run? Absolutely not! That is not the Wainwright way—and you well know it!"

"But—"

Thorne held up his hand. "No buts. You will stay here. And, we will accept every invitation that comes our way. We will ride or drive in the park at the most fashionable hour. And we shall make calls on the most notorious gossips in the *ton.*"

"Oh, Lord—" Luke groaned.

"What is more," Thorne added, "we shall ask Miss Richardson to join us on occasion."

"Why?" Shocked surprise forced out this single word. "She will never agree. She hates me."

"Because doing so may help divert the talk. And she did not seem to 'hate' you when I met her at the Harts' party."

"What if Annabelle refuses? And what if she is privy to who did this?"

"She may well be. I would not rule out that possibility. However, I doubt the current talk redounds to her credit any more than it does to ours."

"So that's it? That is all we do? We just smile and pretend all is well? I cannot like this at all." Luke sounded rebellious.

"No, that is not all we do." Thorne's words were all the more menacing for the soft tone he adopted. "I intend to find out precisely who this Emma Bennet is. No one subjects me or a member of my family to public humiliation and gets away with it."

In his usual manner of attacking a problem head-on, Thorne's first step was a visit to the publisher of the questionable pamphlet. The man invited Rolsbury to a seat in his office.

"I am sorry, my lord." Mr. Murray was polite but unhelpful. "I cannot give you the information you seek."

"*Can*not?" Thorne raised a skeptical eyebrow.

The publisher looked away. "I am bound by contract, sir."

"I am willing to make it worth your while. No one need ever know." Thorne watched the man's expression turn decidedly cold at this suggestion.

"I have explained that I have a contractual obligation to the writer." Murray sounded offended.

Thorne nodded and stood. "So be it. In truth, I am sorry not to obtain the information I seek, but I am glad to make the acquaintance of a man of your principles." He offered Murray his hand, which the publisher took without hesitation.

Thorne's next stop was the printer. Publishers usually sent their work out to independent firms for the actual printing. In this case he encountered a stroke of luck, for the same printer had been listed for the last three of the Bennet books Thorne had found in a bookshop.

Here, too, however, he initially met a blank wall. The printer was a harried-looking man of middle age with thinning black hair and thick eyeglasses. He stood behind the battered counter of his shop and Thorne could hear the slap of presses in a rear room.

"I honestly do not know the identity of the writer," the man said, wiping ink-stained hands on a canvas apron. "I hardly know Mr. Murray. He just sends the stuff over with one of his clerks, we print it, and send it back to Murray."

"What if you have questions that need to be answered?"

"Have to go through Murray."

"That seems rather inefficient in terms of time." Thorne hoped he sounded sympathetic enough to the printer's problems to soften the man to persuasion.

"Well, it is, but Mr. Murray, he sets the rules—and pays the bill." The man paused, then added, "But we don't often have questions with this writer. She has a very neat hand, you see."

Thorne had started to leave, but turned back, latching on to a grain of hope. "Does she now? Would you happen to have a sample that I might see?"

"Might have." The printer rummaged around, in, and on a messy desk in the corner. "Ah, here we go."

The sheet of paper contained only the title of the story, *Innocence Betrayed,* the author's name, Emma Bennet, and three sentences of printing suggestions. Thorne saw that, indeed, the script was very neat—and the Bennet woman had decided ideas about how she wanted her work to appear.

He fished a coin from a pocket and said, "Would you be willing to part with this sheet?"

"Well, now, I just don't know." The printer eyed the coin and shook his head.

Thorne mentally measured the man's greed, then

fished out another coin and the man nodded. The exchange was made and Thorne left, pleased that he had a start at least.

"Annabelle," Celia challenged, "are you *sure* you have no idea who this Emma Bennet is?"

Annabelle, Letty, and Celia sat around a tea table having a "comfortable coze" in Letty's private sitting room. It was a well-appointed room, done in Letty's favorite shades of blue. Sunlight spilled in through opened draperies.

"Well, I have *ideas,* of course," Annabelle hedged. "I think we all do." She reached for another biscuit, then thought of the cream-colored silk she intended to wear to the Bradleys's ball next week. She pulled her hand back. She wished these two would find another topic to discuss.

"Well, *I* think *you* may be Emma Bennet," Letty announced with a penetrating look at Annabelle. "You were ever the best writer among us."

Annabelle groaned. "Oh, Letty! We go through this every time Miss Bennet publishes something new."

"Yes—and everything she writes has a certain sound of Annabelle Richardson to it."

"Sheer coincidence, I am sure. I do hope you are not voicing that opinion abroad," Annabelle added in some alarm. She hated deceiving her friends so, but right now it seemed more necessary than ever.

"Well, of course not. I am not such a ninny as *that.* You *are* my friend, after all."

"For which I am most grateful."

"So—tell us. *Did* you write *Innocence Betrayed?*"

Annabelle sighed. "Letty, you must know that even if I *had* done so, it would be better if you remained ignorant of such."

"She is right," Celia said, setting her teacup down with a clatter. "You never could lie very well, Letty."

Letty gave a little pout of protest.

Annabelle patted Letty's hand. " 'Tis probably best that none of us professes too much interest in public about the author of this particular piece."

"I suppose you are right," Letty agreed reluctantly. "It is rather a naughty piece—but deliciously so!"

Celia laughed. "I loved the passage where Brewster was bragging about his 'swordsmanship.' So did Frederick."

"Celia!" Letty's tone gave an exaggerated impression of a shocked matron. "Do remember that we have an unmarried woman with us!"

"An unmarried woman who—while we were still at school—told *us* about the birds and the bees," Celia reminded them.

"Speaking of which, I have some news." Letty paused dramatically.

"Speaking of what?" Celia asked.

"The birds and the bees," Letty explained patiently.

Celia and Annabelle exchanged puzzled looks, then seemed simultaneously to grasp the import of Letty's announcement.

"You are increasing!" Celia said with a low squeal of delight.

"A babe," Annabelle breathed. "How wonderful. When?"

Letty blushed. "Late autumn, we think. I shall be able to finish out the Season at any rate."

Talk then turned to nurseries and babies. Annabelle quelled the flood of envy she felt toward both of her friends. She was determined to be happy for them—and, indeed, she truly was.

When the exciting news was at least temporarily exhausted, Annabelle gathered up her maid and returned to Wyndham House. As she and the maid walked the few blocks home, she found herself considering again her friends' domestic bliss. Well, "bliss" might be over-doing it a bit—she knew very well both couples did have their differences now and then, but that was prob-ably natural enough.

Harriet had apparently been waiting for her return, for she met her in the entrance hall.

"Brace yourself," Harriet said softly. "Rolsbury is here with his brother."

"Do they know—?" Apprehension gripped her.

"No. But they did come to discuss the latest Emma Bennet publication."

Annabelle quickly divested herself of her bonnet and cloak and checked her appearance in a large looking glass that hung above a table in the entrance. She tucked an errant curl behind her ear.

The three gentlemen—for Marcus was with them—rose as Harriet and Annabelle entered the library. Anna-belle noted empty glasses that indicated the Wainwrights had been here for some time. She wished she knew what had been said before her arrival. She greeted the brothers civilly, but with reserve, and took a seat near Harriet on a settee. Lord! How she wished now that Emma Ben-net had kept her pen free of ink!

Rolsbury spoke as he reseated himself. "We have been discussing the contretemps in which we seem to find ourselves—and how best to deal with it."

Annabelle did not pretend to misunderstand. "Oh? Would it not be best just to ignore it? After all, such a thing is usually a nine-days' wonder."

"Ordinarily, I might agree with you. But this is not likely to disappear so easily," Rolsbury said.

"I fail to see why it would not," Annabelle replied, feeling a bit defensive but trying not to appear so.

"That's what I told him," Luke said.

Rolsbury ignored Luke's echo of this idea. "Because the author of that . . . that . . . bit of drivel so clearly identified the two of you—as well as Beelson and Ferris."

The condescending tone Rolsbury used annoyed Annabelle. " 'Clearly identified'? That is coming a bit strong, I would say," she argued.

"You *have* read this thing, have you not?" he challenged, pointing to the pamphlet.

Her eyes followed his gesture. The offending publication lay like a viper on a low table. She felt herself coloring. "Well, yes. Of course I have and I just do not see—" She flashed a look of desperation at Marcus.

"Rolsbury is right," Marcus said gently. "The parties do seem to be rather clearly drawn."

"Brewster, Franklin, Lester." Rolsbury ticked the names off. "Do you know of some other heiress who has had suitors with the initials B, F, and L?"

"Well, no, but—"

"Miss Richardson, you are clearly the heiress referred to in this piece, though you are less an object of ridicule than are the gentlemen—particularly 'Lester's' older brother, whom everyone assumes to be *me*. Interestingly enough, though, she seems more intimately acquainted with the others, so I would guess that this person does not really know me as she does the others."

Annabelle could not meet his gaze. No, this person did not know you, sir, she thought, and once again wished it would all just go away.

"That portrait *was* rather unfortunate," Harriet said. "Still, would it not be better to let a sleeping dog lie, as it were?"

"I think not, Lady Wyndham, for several reasons. First, the gossips will not allow this dog to lie still. Nor will Beelson and Ferris."

"It was my understanding those gentlemen had left town," Harriet said.

"They are back." Luke's voice was rather flat.

Rolsbury added, "And Beelson is threatening a libel suit if he can determine just who this writer is. Such a suit would, of course, keep the whole thing alive for weeks—perhaps months."

"Was the possibility of a suit your most pressing reason for not ignoring the whole affair?" Marcus asked.

"No. There is a consideration more personal to me." Rolsbury paused and Annabelle squirmed inwardly. Drawing a caricature of a man she had never met had seemed harmless enough at the time. Now it was clear that he was the true innocent who had been betrayed. . . .

Rolsbury continued, directing his points largely to Marcus. "As you know, I am not well known in town circles. The army was to have been my life—the life I chose. I went directly from the military school at Sandringham to the last battles of the war in the Peninsula. Luke here would have eventually handled our family's estate matters. However, a certain French marksman and our father's early death changed all that."

"I think I understand," Marcus said, "but perhaps you should explain anyway."

"Just so. I came to town in part to take my seat in Parliament—finally. There are serious matters affecting my people directly that I hope to have a hand in. Now, I am seen as some sort of country dullard, a slow-top to be barely tolerated."

"Surely when people get to know you—" Annabelle started.

"No." He turned the full impact of his gaze on her. "That could take forever, you see, and my business is more urgent. Labor unrest in the midlands will not die away as so many in positions of power would hope."

"Labor unrest?" Harriet echoed.

"Yes." He went on. "The so-called 'Peterloo Massacre' did little to answer the concerns of workers in the mills."

Annabelle knew he referred to a disaster that had erupted over a year ago when the government sent in the militia to disperse laborers involved in a huge but peaceful demonstration.

"These are my people," Rolsbury said simply. "I own two of those mills. But I can do only so much independently. And it is most difficult to persuade people who are laughing at you to consider a serious issue you raise."

"But your writing, too—" Annabelle started.

He cut her off. "Is not enough. Come now, Miss Richardson. With all due respect, you know very well most members of Society—even those in Parliament— rarely read the kind of scholarly analyses that I usually turn out."

"How can we help, Lord Rolsbury?" Harriet asked.

"I have given the matter some thought," he replied. "It seems to me—and I have persuaded Luke—that if Miss Richardson were to be seen as being in charity with us, that might serve to deflect some of the more vicious gossip."

Annabelle choked. "H-how do you propose to manage that?"

"If Luke were to dance attendance on you as he was wont to do—stand up with you at balls and so on . . ."

"Luke is to renew his courtship?" Marcus asked.

"Maybe. Maybe not. That would be up to Luke—and Miss Richardson. But it will *appear* that he has done so."

"Annabelle?" Marcus asked.

Annabelle was embarrassed—and angry. The nerve of the man! To be pushing them around like pieces on a chessboard! She did not want to hurt Luke's feelings again, but neither did she welcome the idea of his actually renewing a suit that she would never accept.

"I—I am not sure . . ." her voice trailed off. "Luke? I cannot believe you really want to do this."

She could see that Luke was as uncomfortable as she was. "N-not really," he said, "but it does seem like a workable idea and I cannot think of a better one. I promise not to plague you, Annabelle, and Thorne thinks it important that we seem on good terms—our two families, that is."

She nodded slowly, torn between a desire to refuse the plan flatly and a persistent feeling of guilt, for her own impetuous action had, after all, instigated the situation. "Very well. As long as you put it in those terms, I suppose we may manage to quell some of the talk."

"Society thrives on dissension," Harriet observed. "The gossips will quickly lose interest where they find amicability."

"And then—perhaps—we may turn their attention—and ours—to more important matters," Lord Rolsbury said.

Five

When Rolsbury and his brother had taken their leave, silence reigned in the library for several moments. Finally, Harriet spoke, her voice gentle and concerned.

"Will you be comfortable with this plan, Annabelle?"

"I—I think so. Luke is an interesting person when he is not 'performing.' "

"I should like to see Rolsbury succeed," Marcus said. "I spoke with him only briefly at the Harts' party, but despite his being a Whig, I must own I liked what he had to say."

This comment came as a surprise to Annabelle, for Marcus rarely said anything that specifically directed her activities, and he seemed to be doing so now. Her affection and respect for her erstwhile guardian was such that she would have agreed to the plan merely to please Marcus.

However, despite her annoyance at the elder Wainwright brother's high-handed manipulation, she was also aware of having wronged him. That devastating portrait of "Lester's" brother had undermined Lord Rolsbury's position. She owed it to him to try to help repair the damage. And she would do what she could, but—Lord!—she hoped he never found out who Emma Bennet really was. The man would probably be a formidable enemy—and his view of Emma Bennet was quite clear.

Well, in a few days, it would all be over and they could all go their separate ways.

The next day Luke called as planned to take her driving in the park. Now that there was not the strain of his paying suit to her, they got on very well indeed after some initial awkwardness. He was entertaining and gallant. She found she quite enjoyed his company, though she could see that their appearance together raised some eyebrows.

"The tabbies will be busy this day," Annabelle observed nervously.

"Yes. I do believe we have given them something to chew upon."

A rider astride a very sturdy but fleet-looking black approached. It was Rolsbury. Annabelle was unable to keep her gaze from locking with his. She felt an unfamiliar tremor creep through her and quickly averted her eyes. He paused to pass pleasantries with them, then tipped his hat to her and rode on.

"Your brother is not at all what I expected," she told Luke.

"No? Well, I am sure I told you he is a great gun."

She laughed. "Yes, you did—more than once."

"You should have seen him when he first came home after Waterloo. I was away at school, but I'd come home on holidays and he'd be lying in that bed cursing anyone and everyone who came near him."

"Why?"

"Well, he could not walk, you see."

"No. I mean why was he cursing everyone?"

" 'Cause he hated it so, I think. Hated not being able to do for himself and especially hated having people feel sorry for him. Doctor told him he'd never walk again and ordered up one of those wheeled bath chairs for him. Thorne refused to have it in his room even."

"So—what happened?"

"Well—he got out of bed and walked." Luke laughed softly. "Partly just to spite the doctor, I think."

"It must have been very difficult for him."

"It was. He fell ever so many times—though no one was supposed to know about those. Hinton—that's his valet—was his batman in the Peninsula—he used to be near tears himself. Hinton was the only one Thorne would allow to help him."

"The pride of a Wainwright?" she gently teased.

"You might say that—or else just plain stubbornness." Luke was thoughtful for a moment. "Our father was ill at the time, too. So there was the Earl of Rolsbury, dying in one chamber, and his heir struggling just to walk in another. Sad times at the Manor."

"You must have hated to come home on school holidays." Her heart went out to all three Wainwright men, but especially to the man struggling so to overcome adversity.

"Strangely enough, I did not. Both of them were fighting so hard. And Thorne at least finally won his battle. Took him a year and more to do so. And by then, *he* was the earl."

"I see why you admire him so," she said.

"And do you see why that Bennet person's portrait of him is so unfair?" he asked.

She swallowed. "Yes. I think so."

Thorne turned his mount around and tried to erase from his mind the image of honey-brown-blond curls and intelligent brown eyes. Well, she was cooperating. That was all he required of Miss Richardson. He still suspected she knew more of this Bennet and her—or his!—writings than she let on. But Thorne Wainwright was a patient man.

Now that he had become somewhat better acquainted with her, he admitted to very mixed feelings. So, she was not a fortune hunter out to trap an innocent youth. But what *was* her game? She was not in the first bloom of youth—not if this was her third Season. Why had she spurned Luke's offer? She had turned down Beelson, too, he had learned—and Beelson had a title to offer. Well, rejecting a titled nobleman might be unusual, but rejecting a man like Beelson was simply a sign of good sense.

Connection with the Rolsbury title might be considered a tremendous coup in many quarters. Moreover, she and Luke seemed—at the moment at least—to get on well enough. There was still the fact that Luke was far too immature to marry. The boy deserved a chance to grow into his manhood—not just be thrust into it by responsibility for a wife and children.

Oh, you want him to gain maturity? some inner voice of cynicism asked. Then find a war to which you can dispatch him. Nothing like seeing your companions chopped to pieces to produce instant adulthood.

Another voice, equally cynical, broke in. Experiencing a little self-pity, are we, Rolsbury? You chose your life. Perhaps Luke deserves the same privilege of choice.

He does not need to be hurt by a woman, though. Thorne distinctly—and painfully—recalled another young Wainwright suffering just such hurt. Lady Diana Santee had been the reigning debutante of the Season before Thorne went off to the Peninsula. She had reveled in the attentions of every eligible male of the *ton*. Thorne had been ecstatic when she seemed to single him out to receive her favor. But he had been plunged into the depths of despair to learn that she had used *his* suit to bring the Marquis of Everdon up to scratch.

There had, of course, been other women from time to time—most particularly a certain Spanish señorita during the long siege of San Sebastian, and a Belgian woman during the occupation leading up to Waterloo. Only lately had he extricated himself from the cloying tentacles of a sometime mistress—a widow in another town in the midlands. He had vowed hereafter to deal only with "professionals."

Every man knew woman problems were simply a part of growing up. So—where did he come off, trying to keep Luke insulated from such?

Lifetime habits were hard to ignore, though. And all his life Thorne had protected Luke and their sister Catherine. He had been hardly more than a boy himself—Luke's age now, in fact—when he had rescued his schoolgirl sister from an unscrupulous fortune hunter. No wonder he had leaped to conclusions about Miss Richardson.

Well, he might have been wrong about Miss Richardson being a fortune hunter, but there was something about her. . . . And he damned well was not wrong about that pesky novelist. As an aspiring member of Parliament, he could not openly attack Emma Bennet in London drawing rooms. Doing so would keep the talk alive and serve to inhibit his efforts as a lawmaker. However, as a sometime literary critic he might find a way to do so.

Not that he had been much of a *literary* critic heretofore. During his long convalescence after Waterloo, he had begun to submit articles to *The London Review,* a high-toned magazine that featured articles on matters of government, politics, literature, and social history. At first his work had been confined to matters of military history, but then he had branched into reviewing a number of scholarly tomes.

"You want to do *what?*" Henry Watson, editor and

publisher of the *Review,* had been bowled over by Thorne's proposal.

"I thought I might do a review of popular fiction—you know, the sort of stuff women seem to snatch up at Hatchard's and other bookshops."

"I had no idea you even read that stuff," Watson replied. "Are you not the very man who turned his nose up at even that superb book, *Pride and Prejudice,* when it came out?"

Thorne and Watson were friends of long standing, despite Watson's family background in trade and Rolsbury being heir to a respected title. At boarding school Watson had been an object of ridicule and even brutality—until "Thorny" had become his champion. The two later maintained their friendship, though Thorne had gone to the new military academy at Sandringham and Watson had entered university. It was Watson who brought the injured Major Wainwright out of his deep depression following his injury. Watson simply gave him something useful to do. Thorne began to take pride in what he *could* do instead of lamenting what he could no longer do.

Thorne grinned at his friend now. "Well, I have not really changed my mind about those works in general—though I do admit to liking that particular lady's portraits of her minor characters."

"But you want to immerse yourself in such stuff?"

"My idea is to expose much of it for the sheer drivel that it is."

"Ah, I see. That Emma Bennet got under your skin, did she?"

Thorne pretended to take umbrage. "Hank, you always were too sharp for your own good!"

"Whoever she is, Miss Bennet does not know *you*—that much was obvious. But—Lord!—what a laugh that piece was!"

"Yes. Well . . ."

"If you want to write it, I will surely print it, but do you really think it the wisest course of action?"

"Why do you ask?"

"I mean, the talk will eventually die down—will this not just keep it alive?" Watson asked.

"Perhaps. But I cannot leave it unanswered."

"No, I don't suppose *you* could do so."

The plan for both Wainwrights to be seen as being on easy terms with Miss Richardson went forward. At the Bradleys's ball, Luke stood up with her not once, but twice. However, it was not dancing with Luke that dominated her just-before-sleep thoughts later. No. Her mind dwelled on Lord Rolsbury.

Standing on the sidelines, talking with Harriet and Marcus, Annabelle found herself searching the ballroom. She spotted Rolsbury in a group that included at least two hopeful misses and their ambitious mamas and was startled to realize she had been looking for *him*. He glanced her way and caught her gaze. Their eye contact sent an increasingly familiar tremor coursing through her body. Soon, he seemed to excuse himself and approached Annabelle and the Wyndhams.

In elegant evening attire, the Earl of Rolsbury was quite the most attractive man in the room, she thought. His ever-present walking stick merely added a touch of vulnerability to what might otherwise be seen as polished perfection. Annabelle had already overheard—and inexplicably resented—certain females gushing over his appearance and spinning tales of his bravery.

"Good evening." His smile included all three of them, but Annabelle surmised that it turned only her own knees to jelly. Try not to be such a peagoose, she chastised herself.

The four of them engaged in polite small talk for a few moments. Then the musicians swung into a waltz that had maintained its popularity the last few years. Harriet gave her husband a speaking look.

"Yes, dear." He spoke as a beleaguered husband, but there was a hint of laughter in his voice. "Will you excuse us?" he asked politely of Annabelle and Rolsbury.

"Do you mind, Annabelle?" Harriet asked.

"Of course not."

"Did I miss something here?" Rolsbury asked when Marcus and Harriet had taken the floor.

Annabelle laughed softly. "No. Well, perhaps. You see, Marcus and Harriet danced to that tune the night they were betrothed."

"I see." An uncomfortable silence settled on them, then Lord Rolsbury cleared his throat and said, "If you've no partner for this dance, would you mind sitting it out with me?"

"Oh, I thought you'd never ask." She gave him a nervous smile and again felt herself reacting to his very presence.

He took her elbow and steered her to a seat nearby. "It has been so long since I attended one of these affairs, I have quite forgotten how to behave." He grinned at her. "Do we discuss the music or the weather or the amazing success of our hostess?"

She laughed. "So! You do have a sense of humor."

"You doubted such?" She could tell his offended tone was a sham. "I shall have to take Luke to task for that."

"No, no, no." She waggled an admonishing finger at him. "You cannot lay blame on Luke. A man whose nickname is 'Thorny' may not hold others responsible for the impressions he leaves."

He sat back and gazed at her with amused curiosity.

"And just how did you come to know of that sad misrepresentation of my character?"

"Well—" She could not admit to having discussed him with her friends, could she? "A little bird told me?"

"Oh, I doubt that. My errant brother shall have to answer for that, too."

"Luke is innocence itself in this affair," she said and then immediately regretted her choice of words.

" 'Betrayed' innocence?" His voice still held a hint of amusement, but it was more serious.

"I did not intend—"

"I know. 'Tis I who cannot seem to let go of it." He shrugged. "And eventually I shall find this writer and take her—or him—to task for that piece of work."

Annabelle felt a shiver run through her and she prayed silently for his failure in that endeavor. Aloud she said, "That sounds needlessly vindictive. Miss Bennet has probably gone on to other things by now."

"Perhaps. But she leaves unfinished business in her wake."

"Well, I wish you luck," she said, wondering at the ease with which she told that lie.

The dance ended, Harriet and Marcus returned, and Lord Rolsbury took his leave. She stared after him. "Unfinished business" indeed!

Another trip to book shops convinced Thorne that he now possessed a complete inventory of Miss Emma Bennet's published works. He also purchased a sampling of works by other popular writers and began mentally to plan his essay on the sort of second-rate stuff that generally appealed to women. He had composed several brilliantly skewering sentences by the time he reached home.

However, it was late in the evening before he was

able to start his research. He decided to begin with a writer other than Emma Bennet. After all, he *had* read one of hers recently and he hoped that he might at least *appear* to be objective in his appraisal of these works in general. He therefore started with another Emma—the novel *Emma,* now known to have been written by Jane Austen.

He found himself caught up in the machinations of Emma Woodhouse. He laughed aloud as she tried with the best of intentions—and with disastrous results—to control the lives of those around her. Thorne was struck by the fact that he knew people exactly like the vicar's self-important wife and Emma's indolent father. It was very late indeed before Miss Austen allowed the Earl of Rolsbury to retire.

The next evening he dressed carefully for a planned visit to a meeting of the London Literary League.

"This group might help you prepare that piece you are working on," Watson had told him. "In fact, you may want to join them permanently when you are in town. The meetings are *conversazioni* held in various homes."

Thorne snorted. "What? You see *me* sitting around with a gaggle of middle-aged matrons discussing the latest Gothic novel from the Minerva Press?"

"I think you will find the League quite different from the image you have in mind."

"Very well," Thorne said. "I shall look in on one of these meetings if you can secure me an invitation."

Watson had produced an invitation for the next such affair to be held at the home of Lady Gertrude Hermiston. It was not to be an ultra-formal affair, but Thorne had no desire to appear the country bumpkin Emma Bennet had presented to the world. He donned a pair of gray Cossack trousers, a white waistcoat, and a dark blue coat. Having adjusted his lordship's neckcloth yet again, Hinton finally expressed his approval and sent him on his way.

As he was relieved of his cloak and hat in Lady Hermiston's entrance, Thorne heard voices and laughter. Well, at least he would not be the only gentleman here—and had Watson not said he would be here as well? The butler showed him to the drawing room where he discovered some twenty-five or thirty people in attendance, fully half of them of his own gender.

Watson came forward and two women turned quickly toward the door as Thorne's name was announced. He masked his surprise at seeing Lady Wyndham and Miss Richardson at such a gathering, though he did recall their interest in political matters at the Harts' party.

"Allow me to introduce you to our hostess first," Watson said, guiding Thorne over to the very group that held Lady Wyndham and Miss Richardson.

Lady Hermiston was a tall, gray-haired woman with an intelligent look in her hazel eyes. She was dressed rather fashionably in a soft green gown but wore none of the feathers fancied by so many women of her age group.

"Lord Rolsbury. How nice to meet you," Lady Hermiston said politely, but she gave him an intense look. "I believe you know my niece, Lady Wyndham, and Miss Richardson."

Her niece. Ah, that explained their presence at such a gathering. He greeted the other women politely.

"A number of people are eager to meet you, my lord," Lady Hermiston said. "One in particular—Mr. Watson, you know de Quincey."

"Thomas de Quincey?" Thorne asked in pleased surprise. She nodded and Thorne said, "I had hoped to meet him in London. I have enjoyed his essays tremendously."

"If you like essays, perhaps you know Mr. Charles Lamb's work?" Lady Wyndham asked.

"Yes, I do. Do not say *he* is here, too?"

"Over there." She nodded in the direction of a group standing some distance away. "He and his sister have been cornered by Lady Mansfield and her daughter. Annabelle, we must go and rescue the Lambs in a moment."

Miss Richardson smiled and nodded, but did not say anything. He thought it unusual for her to be quite so reticent in conversation.

Lady Hermiston continued to identify certain of her guests. "Mr. Southey, our poet laureate, is here. In a short while, Mr. Stephenson will be discussing his ideas for a new transportation system—on rails, mind you."

"I have heard of his experiments—with some sort of steam-powered locomotion, I think?" Thorne said, deeply impressed with not only the level of intellect in the company Lady Hermiston had gathered, but also the eclectic nature of their interests. Where did Miss Richardson fit in, though?

"It will never work," Watson said.

"I beg your pardon?" Thorne was annoyed at his own inattention.

"That rail thing. It will never work."

"I think it *does* work even now—in mines, for instance," Thorne said.

"Oh, yes, but only on a small scale and using horses or donkeys as the source of power," Watson argued.

The two men excused themselves to make Rolsbury acquainted with more of the company. Lady Hermiston went to attend to some hostess duty. Moments later, Thorne saw Lady Wyndham and Miss Richardson in conversation with the Lambs.

He found himself torn between wanting to linger at

this group or that and the desire to meet as many of these people as possible. It occurred to him again that Luke had the right of it—he needed to get out more. He had not realized how starved he was for just such stimulating discourse.

Annabelle had been shocked to see Lord Rolsbury turn up at Aunt Gertrude's gathering—she had not thought of her hostess as "Lady Hermiston" in years. Actually *Lord* Wyndham's aunt by marriage, the lady saw herself—and was readily accepted—as very much a member of the family of Marcus Jeffries, Earl of Wyndham. Aunt Gertrude also knew of Annabelle's relationship to Miss Emma Bennet, for Lady Hermiston had been present at Miss Bennet's "birth."

As might be expected, there were mixed reactions to Mr. Stephenson's remarks.

"It will never work," Mr. Watson repeated.

"A whole network of rails throughout England?"

"Preposterous!"

"What a marvelous idea."

"Who will pay for it?"

Annabelle had been only mildly interested in the concept of rail transportation, but she listened with increasing interest as Mr. Stephenson outlined the advantages of such. *Faster, less expensive,* and *more*—these words dotted the engineer's speech. When it was over and the questions had died out, the company drifted back into small groups to discuss the prospect of rail transport and then to push on to their own favorite topics. Annabelle found herself unexpectedly standing next to Lord Rolsbury at the refreshment table.

She hesitated only a moment when she saw him obviously considering the struggle of trying to cope with a plate and a glass—and his walking stick. "May I offer you my assistance, sir?"

He gave her a look of mild chagrin. "I seem in need of it."

She took charge. "You take the glass; I can handle both plates and my glass." She looked around. "Ah. There is a free spot at that small table over there. I shall join you as soon as I manage to snatch one of those apricot tarts before they are gone."

He did as she said and stood waiting for her to join him. As he leaned near her to push her chair in, she caught a faint scent of the woodsy-pine aroma of what must have been his shaving soap. He even smells like the outdoors, she thought.

"Here. I brought you one, too." She placed a tart on his plate.

"Thank you." He gave her a teasing grin. "Partial to apricot tarts, are you?"

"Oh, yes! They are above all my favorites."

"I shall keep that in mind."

She was amazed at how much such an innocuous comment pleased her. The room at large buzzed with conversation and they were surrounded by other people, but there was a special intimacy to their sharing this small table.

"What did you think of Mr. Stephenson's remarks?" she asked conversationally to cover her nervousness.

"I am inclined to think there is a great deal of merit in them. However, such a project as he envisions will not be easy."

"Impossible, perhaps?"

"No," he said. "We are seeing steam power put to more and more uses—in our knitting mills, for instance. But those are private entities. Mr. Stephenson's project will take a tremendous amount of interest—not to say effort and funding—on the part of public entities."

"You do not speak only of Parliament, do you?" She saw him raise his brows at this question.

"No. I do not. It must also involve bankers and businessmen. The sheer logistics will be staggering—materials, right-of-way struggles—staggering!"

They sat in silence for a moment. Then, sounding a bit hesitant, he said, "Miss Richardson, I wonder if I might enlist your aid on a project of my own?"

"If I may be of help, certainly."

"I gather you are familiar with the writers in this room—and their works?"

"Yes-s-s . . ." It was her voice that sounded hesitant now.

"Are you also familiar with the works of popular novelists?"

"Some of them." She was suddenly on her guard.

"And the authors?"

"Some of them," she repeated. "I know Mr. Scott, for instance, and Mrs. Edgeworth. Wh-what are you proposing?"

"I intend a rather scholarly analysis of the phenomenon of the modern novel."

"I see . . ." But she did not see, really, what he was about.

"I shall, of course, include in my study the works of our friend, Miss Emma Bennet."

"I see . . ." Now she not only felt foolish in repeating herself so, but she felt a twinge of apprehension slither through her. What *was* he up to?

"I shall interview such of them as I can. I would have liked to interview Miss Austen," he said regretfully.

"Her death was very untimely—not, mind you, that death is ever considered truly timely." She thought this a morose comment, so she added brightly, "But her work will continue to delight for some time to come."

"Yes. I think hers will do so."

"You—you wanted my help?"

"Yes. As you know more of London society in general than I—and apparently have some familiarity with the literary scene—I wonder if you could help me locate Emma Bennet so that I might interview her?"

Six

Annabelle was stunned. "L-locate Emma Bennet?" she stuttered.

"I thought you might have some ideas on the matter," Lord Rolsbury said.

"N-not really."

"Have you no interest in the matter at all? I should think you would bear some resentment of her high-handedness." He gave her a penetrating look.

"Well . . ." Annabelle struggled for a response. "In truth, the portrait of the heiress was not as devastating as that of the suitors."

"Precisely. That is what led me to believe you must be known to her. Though I am forced to observe that the piece does not present a very flattering view of *you,* either."

"I had not thought of it as flattering or unflattering." She realized this was the truth. She had concentrated on caricatures of the other persons in the story and just let the character of the heiress develop in relation to those around her.

"I do not see much in the way of real characterization in the portrait of the heiress in that story," Rolsbury said. "She has not your *spirit*—she is far too passive."

Annabelle knew she would find amusement in this

scene later, but for now she did not know whether to be offended or flattered. On the one hand, Rolsbury had just accused Emma Bennet of shallow character development. On the other, he apparently viewed Miss Richardson as far more likable than the heiress in the story.

She gave him what she thought must be a vacuous smile and said, "Thank you—I think. Probably the writer intended to focus on other characters."

"Probably." He sounded vague and she hoped he was tiring of the topic. "So? Can you help me?"

She chose her words carefully. "I do not see how I could possibly produce the information you need." Lord! How she hated lying. She was surely no better at it than Letty.

"In your circles, you might come across something."

"I will try to keep my eyes and mind open," she said.

They went on to discuss other matters, but for Annabelle the easy camaraderie of the first part of their conversation was gone.

Several days into his research on popular novels, Thorne abruptly realized that he was violating the first rule of scholarship. He was trying to justify a preconceived notion instead of keeping an open mind to see what he could learn about what was, after all, a fairly new literary phenomenon.

True, telling stories was perhaps mankind's oldest form of entertainment. The novel, *per se,* had appeared only in the last century, however. When he set about defining his terms and examining his primary sources, those brilliantly skewering judgments seemed no longer quite so brilliant.

He wanted to test some of his ideas, but the London Literary League was not due to meet for another two weeks. Few of his gentlemen friends possessed either the interest or expertise he wished for in such a sounding board, and Luke was a lost cause in that regard. His sister, Catherine, would be the perfect person with whom to have such a dialogue, but she was still in the country. Suddenly, the image of Miss Richardson popped into his mind.

Well, why not? It was worth a try, though he still harbored reservations about her. He had watched her carefully when he had asked for assistance in finding Emma Bennet. He was convinced she was being evasive. Was she protecting a friend? Was it possible that Lady Wyndham was Emma Bennet? Or Lady Hermiston? Miss Richardson herself? No. He had now read other of Miss Bennet's works and they showed a maturity of viewpoints that went far beyond those of someone who had as few years as he knew Miss Richardson to have. Why, she was of an age with Luke!

In fact, the other works—all predating the short *Innocence Betrayed*—showed a more polished maturity than that short, satirical piece did. Surely, there was only one Emma Bennet?

During a morning call at Wyndham House, he found a moment of relative privacy in which to ask Miss Richardson to go driving with him later.

She gave him an arch look. "I thought it was Luke with whom I was to be seen on such an outing."

He grinned. "I think our reputations will survive our being seen in a public place like the park."

"If you say so, my lord."

He was pleased at the teasing note in her response. "I do say so. And I wonder if we might assume a less formal means of address between us? I notice that it is 'Luke' and 'Annabelle.' Might it also be 'Thorne' and 'Annabelle'?"

"Why, of course, if that is your wish. 'Thorne' it is."

"Annabelle." He gave her a mocking little bow to seal their agreement. "I shall call for you later then."

Annabelle dressed carefully for the outing with Lord Rolsbury—Thorne. How easy it was to think of him in more intimate terms! She had to warn herself that she must be careful around him. After all, the man still intended to take Emma Bennet to task. She finally donned a brown-and-gold-striped day dress that complemented her coloring. A gold-colored light woolen shawl and a saucy straw bonnet were the finishing touches.

He handed her into the carriage rather smoothly, then tossed his walking stick on the floor and clambered in himself somewhat awkwardly.

"I have not mastered my technique yet," he said with an embarrassed chuckle.

"And here I was thinking you did that very well," she assured him, pleased that he felt comfortable enough with her to make such an allusion to his infirmity.

He picked up the reins and signaled his tiger, who had been holding the horses' heads. The boy climbed up behind them and Thorne concentrated on driving as they left the quiet residential street for more trafficked thoroughfares. Annabelle admired the ease with which he managed his team. She was keenly aware of his body so close to her own and the occasional contact from the swaying of the carriage.

She knew she was babbling as she made idle conversation that demanded little of his attention while he drove. Finally, they entered the park and he visibly relaxed.

"This is the first time I have driven in town in years," he admitted apologetically. "I usually have my coachman contend with all this city traffic."

"Well, I am flattered that you took on the great challenge for me," she said, deliberately trying to put him at ease.

He nodded. "I am not merely playing the role of the white knight out to slay the dragon of city traffic. I confess I had an ulterior motive in asking you to accompany me."

"Oh, dear," she said in a teasing mockery of shock. "Am I to fear for my reputation, after all?"

He chuckled. "Not yet, at least. I wanted to talk books with you."

"Books?" She wondered where this was leading.

"Yes. I have been doing a great deal of reading lately."

"I see . . ."

"By the by—have you discovered anything of Miss Bennet that might be of use to me?"

"I . . . uh . . . no. I think not."

"Pity. I have been reading her earlier works, trying to get a grip on her thinking."

"Oh?" She hoped the monosyllable sounded indifferent enough that he would change the subject.

They were detained momentarily by Lady Oglethorpe, who stopped to greet them. She rode with two other middle-aged ladies in an open carriage driven by a coachman. All three women eyed the earl and his companion with speculative looks.

When they had driven on, Thorne said, "I suppose we will be an *on dit* in certain drawing rooms this evening."

"Probably," she agreed, glad the subject had been changed.

Only it had not. "Yes. Well," Thorne said, "as I was about to say, I find Miss Bennet's work to be terribly uneven."

"I . . . uh . . . I am not sure what you mean."

He looked at her, a question in his gray-green gaze. 'Have you read her earlier work?"

"Yes. I daresay I have read them all," she replied and hoped she had not said more than she should.

"Well, then—would you not agree that the earlier works are far superior to *Innocence Betrayed?*" He pronounced the title with particular contempt.

"In what way?" She felt both defensive and genuinely curious about his reactions.

"Why, in nearly every way that matters. The characters that have *not* been drawn upon real people are, ironically, far more genuine portraits. The earlier stories themselves have more substance as well."

She felt somewhat chagrined, for this assessment of her work coincided with her own judgment—now. She was pleased that he found the early works laudable, and it was frustrating to have to conceal her pleasure. However, the implied criticism of her latest effort rankled. It was not *that* bad, after all.

"Well . . ." She drew the word out slowly, trying to think.

"You do not agree?"

"Not entirely. But perhaps the circumstances of the writing were different."

"Oh, no doubt they were." This comment had a particularly bitter tone. His attention was diverted as he manipulated their vehicle around another.

To forestall his returning to the matter of Emma Bennet again, she asked in a brightly conversational tone, "What other writers have you dealt with in your research?"

He named several and they spent the rest of the drive discussing the relative merits of the works of Mrs. Edgeworth, Mrs. Radcliffe, and Miss Austen. They found they quite agreed on Miss Austen, but argued vehemently about certain aspects of the works of the other two.

By asking an astute question here and there, she managed to keep him away from the subject of Emma Bennet. She found herself enjoying matching wits with him—and just being with him.

Only one thing—other than the Emma Bennet discussion—marred the outing. At one point, she noticed a familiar rider approaching. Viscount Beelson was almost upon them before he apparently recognized the occupants of this particular carriage. He gave them a hard stare, then in a silent and sardonic pantomime, he tipped his hat to her and rode on.

"Is it my imagination—or did Lord Beelson just give you the cut direct?" she asked in appalled surprise.

"You did not imagine it. But do not refine upon it, Annabelle. Beelson and I have an unpleasant history."

"Oh," she said in a small voice. She was intensely curious, but his closed expression suggested it would be a subject best not pursued at the moment. She would ask Luke about it later.

When they returned to Wyndham House, Thorne signaled his tiger to take charge of the horses, then descended from the carriage and turned to assist Annabelle. As she stepped down, she stumbled and fell against him. He reacted quickly to catch her, but his leg gave out and they were suddenly in the rather awkward position of holding each other up. Her bonnet was knocked askew and her hair brushed his face. She smelled of lilacs.

He heard her draw in a quick breath and she held his gaze for a long moment. His glance fell to her mouth—that kissable mouth—and he knew that if they were not standing in the street he would act on his impulse to kiss her. And he also felt that she would be receptive to such.

Then the moment was gone.

He released her and reached for his walking stick. "I am sorry," he said. "My leg—"

She smiled. "No. 'Twas my fault. My foot caught on the step. These dratted slippers match my dress, but they are not very sturdy footwear."

" 'Tis generous of you to blame female vanity instead of male clumsiness, but I cannot accept such sacrifice."

"Then we shall have to share equally." She took his arm as he walked her to the door.

He thanked her and returned to the carriage as the butler admitted her to the house. He felt a sense of loss and realized his farewell had not been empty courtesy. He truly *had* enjoyed the outing and would have gladly prolonged his time with her.

Careful, old man, he admonished himself. After all, this was the woman for whom his brother had offered. Thorne had no intention of being a party to causing Luke unnecessary pain.

While she dressed for dinner, Annabelle thought over the day. As she became better acquainted with him, she found she enjoyed Thorne more and more. He engaged in some of the same boyish teasing that she found so charming in Luke. But there was far more depth to Thorne—and Luke's mere touch did not change her pace of breathing or send her heart tumbling erratically.

In a less public place, would he have kissed her? She rather thought he would have. And she knew very well that she would have welcomed his embrace. Jezebel! She laughed at herself. Not to say want-witted. Was she forgetting his real purpose in the Wainwrights having anything to do with her? He merely intended to quell damaging gossip in order to facilitate his serious work in Parliament. And he obviously had no intention of dropping his quest for Emma Bennet.

Marcus had spent much of the last few days away from home. Annabelle knew he was preoccupied with several matters before Parliament.

At dinner, Harriet asked her husband, "Has Lord Rolsbury given his maiden speech in Lords yet?"

"Yes. Two—maybe three—days ago."

"You did not tell me." Harriet's voice was mildly accusing.

"I tried to. The other night. Remember? You had other things on your mind."

Annabelle saw Harriet's brow wrinkle in bewilderment, then it cleared and a blush suffused her face. "Marcus!"

"Yes, love?" His tone was innocence, but he wore a wicked grin.

"Oh, never mind," she said in a wifely I-shall-deal-with-you-later tone. Then she added, "So—how did Rolsbury's speech go? Was it well received?"

Annabelle leaned forward, keenly interested.

"I thought it went very well, though reactions were mixed."

"Why?" Harriet asked.

"What issues did he address?" Annabelle asked.

"He spoke primarily of labor unrest in the midlands and the need for reform to allow workers some rights to organize."

"I can just imagine the reaction to that idea in certain quarters," Harriet said.

"Right," her husband agreed. "Teslake took particular umbrage—accused Rolsbury of disloyalty to his class."

"Teslake? Is he not a particular friend of Lord Beelson?" Annabelle asked.

"He is," Marcus affirmed.

"And both have interests in knitting mills in Manchester if I recall correctly," Harriet said.

"Yes, they do, though I believe Teslake's primary source of wealth comes from elsewhere. Coal mines. So Rolsbury has made no friend in that quarter."

"I do not understand," Annabelle said, waving aside second helpings being offered by a footman. "What have coal mines to do with workers in textile mills?"

"Both employ a good many children," Marcus explained, "and Rolsbury was particularly outspoken in accusing employers of abusing child workers. He went so far as to suggest that such children should, instead of working, be in school—at public expense."

"Hmm. I am not surprised," Harriet said. She signaled the servants that they might clear the table for the next course. "His article in the *Review* contained similar ideas."

"Reading is one thing. Hearing the man speak is quite another." Marcus leaned back in his chair. "He is a very effective speaker. There will be those—more of Teslake's lot—who will not welcome this new addition to Parliament."

"I wish Annabelle and I could have heard the speech," Harriet said longingly.

Annabelle nodded her agreement.

"I believe the *Post* has printed it in its entirety," Marcus observed.

His wife gave him an arch look. "But as you say, dear, reading is one thing, hearing is quite another."

Annabelle was struck again by how much more there was to the man Rolsbury in the flesh, so to speak, than her previous image of him. Before, he had been merely a title and label, "Luke's older brother." Now, she found a caring, concerned human being—one whose friendship she would have actively sought, were it not for Emma Bennet.

Seven

What with his maiden speech in Lords and other Parliamentary matters, Thorne had found little time to put his literary ideas to paper. His discussion with Annabelle had helped him refine some points and discard others altogether.

Striving for a more focused piece, he decided to limit himself to works by women that seemed aimed primarily at a female audience. He would further limit himself to discussing the works of five authors—Mrs. Ann Radcliffe, Mrs. Maria Edgeworth, Miss Fanny Burney, Miss Jane Austen, and Miss Emma Bennet. To this end, he reread works by each of them, trying to focus on similarities in their approaches, yet he also took a mountain of notes on the unique qualities of each writer.

Finally he was ready to write the piece. He was pleased to find that it went quite smoothly. True, he had to modify some of his views on what he had heretofore assumed were the inferior efforts of female scribblers. Indeed, these women seemed as concerned with their craft as the best of male authors. Still, he intended to explore the differences in novels aimed specifically at women and those aimed at a more general readership.

As he usually did with a writing project, he wrote it quickly, referring to his notes only occasionally. He would then let it "jell" for a few days and return to revise, refine, and supply pertinent quotations. With the first draft completed, he sat back, basking in self-satisfaction.

That should put the Bennet woman in her place, he thought.

Meanwhile, his evenings—and some days as well—continued to be taken up with social engagements. There were musicales, soirees, "breakfasts"—served in mid-afternoon—routs, and balls. True to the plan he had outlined to Luke, the two of them accepted as many invitations as they could manage.

"I hear you have become a veritable social flutterby." His Aunt Dorothy leveled this accusation at him when he called one afternoon.

"I probably would not use precisely that term," he said mildly.

"Why, you have set more hearts aflutter this Season than even Lord Dixon in my day. And believe me—that is saying something!"

"I think your sources are exaggerating, Aunt."

She gave him an arch look. Dressed in her customary purple, she looked as regal as a queen despite the canine occupying her lap.

"There is no need for false modesty with *me,* Rolsbury. We both know your fortune alone would insure your success on the marriage mart. And when you add your title and your looks—you get those from our side of the family, you know—well, as I say—your success is a foregone conclusion."

"You forget the splendid showing I make on a dance floor."

She waved her hand to dismiss this petty objection. "Irrelevant in husband material."

"Well, for your information, dear aunt, I am not looking to become 'husband material.' "

"All men *say* that—right up to the time they let themselves be caught."

"In my case, it is not necessary to be caught. Luke will eventually see to the succession."

"You just wait." She reached behind her to a bellpull that was within easy reach of her favorite chair. "Some young miss will get her talons in you sooner or later. Sooner than later, from what I hear."

Her butler, whose years rivaled her own, answered her summons. "Send Leeds in with a bottle of that French brandy," she ordered and said to her nephew, "You *will* join me, will you not? Unless you prefer something more 'ladylike'?"

Thorne grinned at her. "Brandy will be fine."

When the footman named Leeds reported with the bottle and two glasses, Thorne's grin widened. The young man presented the tray to his mistress with a flourish, poured for her, and bowed extravagantly as he left.

Thorne made no effort to smother the laughter in his voice. "I see you still surround yourself with pretty things."

"Well, of course. But see you do not allow yourself any unwarranted conjecturing there."

"Never." He loved this crusty old woman. She did, indeed, like pretty things, but her morals never bent to the level of some members of the *ton* who were known to take advantage of employees in every way imaginable.

"He has something going on with one of the upstairs maids," his aunt confided. "I am not supposed to know about it. 'Tis very amusing to watch them tiptoeing around each other."

"Naughty of you to notice," he joked.

"At my age, dear heart, one lives vicariously." She sipped her brandy, then set the glass down, and said, "Now. Out with it. Why are you here?"

He shook his head in resignation. "You always did read me too easily."

The widowed Lady Conwick had been the only mother the Wainwright children knew after her sister-in-law died during an influenza epidemic when Luke was still a toddler.

"Well, you are displaying that same caged-cat manner you had when you were trying to persuade your poor, beleaguered father to allow you to go to that military school."

"Beleaguered? Arrogantly stubborn, I should say. I never did know exactly why he just suddenly decided to grant his permission. I suspect you had a hand in it."

"I did. I merely pointed out to my dearest brother that his son was equally as stubborn as he—and that if he did not allow you to go to that school, you would likely run off and take the king's shilling."

He raised his glass in a salute to her. "And thus did you spare me the life of an enlisted man in His Majesty's army—for which I extend my belated and heartfelt thanks."

She nodded. "Now—?"

"You are right. I am here to ask a favor." He paused.

"I am listening."

"I should like you to come to the Manor and act as hostess for a house party at the end of the Season."

"A house party? Me?" she squeaked, her tone stirring the dog on her lap. She murmured soothingly to it and then addressed Thorne again. "You know very well that I have been as much of a recluse as you in recent years."

"Yes. And it would probably do you as much good as it has me to stir out of that rut. But beyond that, I need your help."

"What about your sister?"

"Catherine has a brood of children demanding her attention—and she is increasing again."

"Why are you doing this—after all these years?" Lady Conwick seemed genuinely curious.

"For a number of reasons. First, I want to reestablish ties with some old friends. Also, I intend to invite certain members of Parliament in order to present some of my ideas in a setting removed from the halls of Westminster."

"I see. But that is not the whole of it, is it?"

"As I say—you know me far too well." He paused again. "I also intend to invite the Earl of Wyndham and his immediate household."

"Miss Richardson."

"Yes."

"Are you thinking of offering for her?"

"Good heavens—no! She . . . uh . . . she is Luke's friend. And I thought to give him an opportunity to find out . . . well . . . to see if they really do suit . . ."

"I thought you opposed such a match."

"Well, I did. I do. I am banking on that old maxim that 'familiarity breeds contempt.' Perhaps in such a domestic setting he will find the girl less enchanting."

"And if he fails to do so?"

"Well, then, despite his youth, I shall give him my blessing." He kept his tone casual as a cold feeling of emptiness accompanied this thought.

"I see," his aunt said again, and Thorne feared she might really see more than he intended her to.

"Will you do it?" he asked.

"I shall think on it."

But Thorne knew she would capitulate. Moreover, he truly believed she would enjoy rousing herself to doing something focused outside the limited world she had created of late. After all, one in her fifties was far too young to leave life on the shelf.

And one in his thirties? that recurring silent imp of mischief prompted.

Annabelle dressed for the Finchleys' ball with as much care as she had for her own come-out ball two Seasons earlier. Yes, she loved pretty clothes as well as the next woman, but she was rarely overly concerned with her appearance—much to the dismay of her maid. Tonight, however, she was being downright fussy. When she realized this and asked herself why, Thorne Wainwright's image floated into her consciousness.

"How ridiculous!" she muttered.

Her maid, Molly, paused in the act of setting the last pin into her hair. "Oh, miss, you don't like it?"

"No, no, Molly. The hair is fine. Do finish. I am merely out of sorts with *me*."

"You look ever so fine, miss."

Annabelle stood and looked in the cheval glass, turning this way and that. The ball gown was a soft sea-green concoction of silk shot with silver. A matching ribbon wound through her hair. Simple diamond eardrops and an heirloom necklace of diamonds and silver graced her ears and neck. A very light woolen shawl of sea-green was to be tossed across her shoulder.

"Yes, I do look quite fine, I think. Thank you, Molly. You have done wonders at creating a silk purse from a sow's ear."

Molly, who was a good decade older than her mistress, had been with Annabelle for nearly five years. The maid sniffed. "I think we had a bit more to work with than that. I am just glad to see you truly interested in how you look. There is a man, I'll wager."

"Oh, Molly!" Her impatience was plain. "Can one simply not want to appear to advantage at a grand ball?"

"There is a man." Molly gathered up the clothes Annabelle had tried and discarded and left the room.

Well, yes, Annabelle admitted to herself, there was a man and tonight she intended to examine just why this man disturbed her as no other ever had.

Having determined that their house failed to offer facilities adequate to her ambitions for elegance, Lady Finchley had secured the grand ballroom at one of the city's finest hotels. It was from here that she would launch her only daughter into the sea of Society. It was late May and the weather had been excessively warm in recent days. Annabelle noted with approval that three sets of French doors had been opened to the terrace and a garden beyond.

"I thought we were early," Harriet said. "But just *look* at the number here already."

"Yes," her husband said darkly. "And each body producing an unknown degree of heat!"

Harriet tapped his arm with her fan. "Now you know very well, my love, that no hostess would consider anything less than 'a sad crush' to be successful."

"And why *is* that?" Marcus asked. "Any *man* would provide more space at such an affair."

Annabelle turned away from this latest skirmish in a familiar battle of the sexes. Surveying the crowd even as she allowed admirers to sign her dance card, she spotted Celia and Letty and their spouses.

And then, like the parting of the Red Sea, the crowd seemed to disperse and the Wainwright brothers were approaching the party of Lord Wyndham, Luke in the lead. The brothers had similar coloring and they were both dressed in evening attire, though Luke wore a flamboyant embroidered waistcoat of canary yellow. So why was it that her breath caught in her throat at the sight of only the elder of the two?

Annabelle had arranged earlier with Luke which two dances he would have. When he had signed, she thrust the card in Thorne's direction.

"Here, Thorne. I have saved this last dance on my card for you." Already feeling nervous and bold, she observed Harriet's raised brow at her brazen use of Lord Rolsbury's given name.

Thorne looked at her with curiosity, but he smiled. "I am sure you know I no longer dance, fair lady."

"But you used to," she stated rather than asked.

"Once upon a time."

"Well, then . . ." She thrust the card at him again, knowing he had no choice but to take it.

"Annabelle," Harriet said, obviously surprised at her one-time ward's behavior.

"Never mind, my lady," Thorne said. "If Miss Richardson wishes to deny herself the attentions of an adequate partner, I shall be glad to sit with her." He examined the card, preparing to sign. He looked up and caught Annabelle's gaze. "It is the supper dance."

"Yes, I know." She held her gaze steady with his.

He hesitated only a moment, then gave a slight shrug. Handing a grinning Luke his walking stick, he braced himself to sign the card. He gave it back to her with a look of "you asked for this."

The five of them engaged in idle conversation for a few moments, then the musicians switched to a dance tune and Annabelle and Luke took the floor for a country dance.

"Well done, Annabelle," Luke murmured between figures in the dance.

"You approve?" She made no pretense of being coy about what she had done.

"Yes. He needs to be more sociable—that is, beyond mere attendance at affairs like this."

Annabelle was struck by the genuine affection with which Luke regarded his brother. It was not merely hero worship. There was a protective quality to Luke's attitude. She wondered what it would have been like to grow up with siblings.

Orphaned at the age of nine, Annabelle had been delivered to the doorstep of the ill Earl of Wyndham. The earl's wife and his eldest son had shipped the child off to a boarding school. When she was fifteen she had been expelled from the school for a series of misdemeanors, some of them involving her friend Letty. Once again she was deposited on the doorstep of an Earl of Wyndham. Marcus Jeffries had by then unexpectedly succeeded his brother to the title. Marcus had been surprised to find that not only was he this young girl's guardian, but he *shared* the guardianship with a certain Harriet Knightly.

In the way of families, the Jeffries clan had molded and evolved, and made room for yet another member. Still, Annabelle often wondered what it might have been like to grow up with a traditional mother and father and brothers and sisters.

Later, yet another partner had returned her to the sidelines where he had found her. There was Thorne, waiting for her. Her heart skipped a beat.

"You remembered," she said foolishly, feeling a bit out of breath from a vigorous country dance.

He grinned. "One is not likely to forget the only dance for which one has signed in five years and more."

She waved her fan as energetically as decorum allowed. "Would you mind if we enjoyed this dance out on the terrace?"

"Miss Richardson!" A definite hint of laughter lurked beneath his pretense of shock. "First you bamboozle me into a non-dance, and now you are luring me onto the terrace!"

She adopted a very formal tone. "Do not allow your own sense of consequence to lead you astray, sir. 'Tis beastly warm in here."

Still grinning at her, he silently took her elbow and guided her out to the terrace and down the steps to the garden. There were three other couples on the terrace, but no one seemed to take any notice of Thorne and Annabelle.

Several stone benches were scattered through the garden. Thorne steered her to one of these that offered seclusion but was within sight of the terrace and caught a good deal of light from the ballroom. The air was cooler, but it was a most pleasant evening with a light breeze—little more than a whisper of air now and then.

They sat and an awkward silence ensued, during which Annabelle searched for a "safe" topic to introduce. She dared not ask him about his research lest he bring up Emma Bennet again.

Finally, she said, "Marcus tells us your first speech in Parliament went well."

"It seemed to. In some quarters at least."

"So? Are you planning to offer a bill on labor issues?"

"Not this session." He folded both hands over the head of his walking stick which was planted between his feet.

"Why not?" she challenged. "I gather the issue is one about which you feel strongly."

"Precisely because I do feel strongly about it." He chuckled at her apparent confusion at this answer. "The time is not yet ripe, Annabelle. I want any proposed bill to have at least a prayer of passing."

There was silence again. She noticed his body swaying to the strains of the waltz emanating from the ballroom. She felt herself caught up in the music, too. She stood and extended her hand.

"Come. Dance with me, Thorne."

"Annabelle . . ."

"Miss Rhys said you once danced beautifully—"

"That was before—"

"I know. But you cannot have forgotten how to waltz. No one will see if you stumble and I promise not to tell a soul," she wheedled.

He shook his head, but he stood reluctantly, leaned his stick against the bench, and opened his arms.

"Do you *always* get your own way?" he murmured.

"Nearly always." She laughed nervously and knew the instant he touched her that she had gone too far. This had been a mistake—if only because it felt so wonderful and so absolutely right.

Despite some awkwardness, he managed the steps at least as smoothly as a few of her less-practiced partners of the past. She was lost in the music and his nearness, the warmth of his body, the scent of his shaving soap, the flash of his smile.

"Not exactly a dancing master's performance, eh?" he said, executing a turn somewhat less than smoothly.

"Well, no," she said honestly, "but you, sir, are a fraud."

"I beg your pardon?"

"You are doing very well. I begin to suspect you have used your infirmity to hold off eager females."

He laughed. "It did not hold you off."

"I am made of sterner stuff."

"Are you now?" he whispered, pulling her closer. He stopped moving and tightened his arms around her. "Annabelle . . ." Her own name had never sounded so beautiful to her. He touched his lips to hers gently, tentatively at first then with greater urgency. He held her even closer and her arms were around his neck, her hands in his hair.

She returned his kiss fervently and thrilled to the feel of her breasts crushed against his chest. His hands caressed her shoulders and back feverishly.

The music from the ballroom had stopped and couples began to pour through the open doors onto the terrace and into the garden.

Thorne pulled away from her slightly. He bent to pick up his walking stick and, with one arm still about her waist, he steered her into deeper shadows. She followed his lead blindly, fully aware that he was protecting her.

He stopped to turn and look at her. "That should not have happened."

"Are you sorry it did?" She held her breath, waiting.

He was quiet for what seemed a very long moment. "No. I am not sorry, but I should not have taken advantage of you so."

"Well, as to that," she scoffed, "it seemed wholly mutual to me."

"For which I am most appreciative." He gave her a gentle squeeze, kissed her on her temple, and released her. "It will not happen again. Come." He offered his arm. "I believe we are to have supper together now."

She smoothed her dress and tucked in an errant curl. Then she took his arm and they blended with other couples returning to the ballroom and the supper room beyond.

"Oh, there you are," Celia cried as they joined the line at the buffet table. "Letty is saving us seats in that far corner."

Just as she had at the Literary League meeting, Annabelle quietly took charge and unobtrusively aided Thorne in filling his plate and getting it to the table Celia had pointed out. Hovering servants provided drinks for everyone.

Celia and Letty shot her inquisitive looks, but they chatted freely and Annabelle thought she and Thorne both held up their portions of the conversation.

That in itself was a miracle, she thought later—for nothing in her life had ever shaken Annabelle Richardson to the depths of her soul as had Thorne's kiss.

Eight

A few days later Annabelle returned from a drive in the park with young Lord Stimson, who had halfheartedly paid suit to her for two Seasons. Both she and Stimson knew he was not ready to settle down. Their relationship was in the nature of a friendly flirtation that kept them both active participants in Society's matchmaking games—but neither of them was serious about the chase.

Annabelle removed her cloak and bonnet and joined Harriet and Marcus in the library. Marcus had stood at Annabelle's entrance. As she perched on a settee nearby, he reseated himself in a wing-backed chair matching the one his wife occupied. Annabelle noted that both Harriet and Marcus wore serious expressions.

"Is something amiss?" she asked.

Harriet held up a magazine—*The London Review.* "Rolsbury has written an essay of literary criticism. His subject is novels and novelists."

"Yes, I knew he was working on such a piece."

"I thought he usually dealt with social or political issues," Marcus said.

"I think Lord Rolsbury has rather wide-ranging interests," Annabelle responded. "Would you not agree, Harriet?"

"Oh, yes. Very wide-ranging." Harriet's ironic tone confused Annabelle. "They even extend to—how does he put it?" Harriet flipped through the magazine and folded the pages back to read. "Ah, yes, to 'an examination of the sort of sentimental silliness and titillating terrors that appeal largely to the female of the species.' "

"It would appear his lordship is fond of alliteration," Annabelle observed with unconcern.

"Well, he is *not* overly fond of most women writers—and he is particularly critical of the works of Miss Emma Bennet," Harriet said emphatically.

"Wha-at? I must see this for myself." Annabelle reached for the magazine, but Harriet did not release it immediately.

"Annabelle, promise you will read this with an open mind and not be hurt by his treatment of your work."

"Is it *that* awful?" Annabelle felt a sudden sense of trepidation.

Harriet still held the magazine in her own hand. "He presents a relatively fair analysis and he admits his biases, but it is not a very flattering view overall, especially of *your* work."

"But of course he does not know it to be your work, does he?" Marcus asked.

"No. I feel certain he remains ignorant of Emma Bennet's identity," Annabelle said.

"It would appear so from this." Harriet tapped the magazine with a forefinger. "But he also still harbors resentment over that bit of satire—that much is clear here."

"Oh, dear." Caught off guard, Annabelle was uncertain of her own feelings—especially as she had not yet read Thorne's comments. "Well, let me read it," she said with a note of resignation.

Harriet handed her the *Review.* "There is another matter to consider as you read this."

Annabelle waited.

"We accepted Lord Rolsbury's invitation to his house party," Harriet reminded her.

Annabelle nodded. "So we did."

"It would look very strange—particularly to Rolsbury—if we now canceled our acceptance."

"Is it so very bad that we would want to cancel?" Annabelle asked, beginning to feel really anxious now.

"Just read it and see what you think," Marcus advised.

Annabelle took the magazine to her room. She removed the dress she had worn to go driving and sprawled across her bed in a dressing gown to spend the next hour or so imagining the sound of Thorne's voice as she read his words.

He began by saying that, like many other men, he had long held the writings of women in some disregard—and the writings of women for women readers to be usually beneath dignifying. However, his research revealed careful attention to craftsmanship in many instances, making such a blanket view inaccurate at best and mere prejudice at worst.

"Well, that is not such a bad thing to say," Annabelle said to herself.

Rolsbury admitted that Mrs. Radcliffe's characters often deserved the praise they garnered from other critics, but for his taste her stories relied too heavily on the standard clichés of Gothic novels. "After a while," he wrote, "the discerning reader will cease to find secret passages and moldy vaults at all frightening." He went on to note that, in his opinion, Mrs. Radcliffe's readership consisted largely of bored women who "possess too much free time and look for cheap thrills to alleviate their prevailing sense of ennui."

"Oh, my!" Annabelle murmured and read on.

He credited Mrs. Edgeworth with an "admirable ability to depict the social scene in Ireland" and he went on to say it was high time someone created Irish characters who were more than mere caricatures—parodies of their national traits. However, he noted, Mrs. Edgeworth's stories were far too predictable, though they probably appealed to "females who regularly require fairy-tale endings to life's problems."

As for Miss Fanny Burney's stories, those were "fluff for schoolroom misses—stories of star-crossed lovers who overcome incredible odds in ways only the most naive could possibly credit."

"Why, the man has nothing good to say of anyone," Annabelle fumed. "His opening was merely to put one off. What *will* that dreadful man say of Miss Bennet?"

As she read on, however, she discovered that it was not true that he had "nothing good to say of anyone." He praised Miss Austen's work highly. "Unlike Mrs. Radcliffe, whose stories are set in distant, exotic lands with which the author is too often clearly unfamiliar, Miss Austen wisely limits herself to her own milieu of country gentry. Her work has a sense of the familiar about it, though a clever turn of phrase offers fresh insight." He went on to laud Miss Austen's realistic portraits of ordinary people and the subtle irony with which she presented a babbling spinster or a self-important clergyman.

"... Which brings us to the last writer to be considered here, Miss Emma Bennet. Allow me to digress here to point out to *my* readers that mine, as many will have surmised, may be considered a prejudiced view of this particular writer, but I shall try to present an assessment of this lady's work that is as objective as the others."

"Oh, I am sure you will," Annabelle muttered sarcastically, but she read on, dreading what she would

find, yet driven to find it—however negative it might
be.

> "Unlike Miss Austen—whose satire is never
> mean-spirited—Miss Bennet's approach may be lik-
> ened to one wielding a sledgehammer. In addition,
> one may note that, while Miss Austen's portraits are
> meant to depict general *types* of persons, she clev-
> erly creates recognizable individuals in such memo-
> rable characters as Miss Bates or Mr. Collins or
> Fanny Dashwood.
>
> Miss Bennet, on the other hand, has apparently
> attempted to depict real individuals only thinly dis-
> guised as fictional creations. Where the facts of a
> particular person were unknown to her, she simply
> made up characteristics and actions with no regard
> for reality—and certainly with no regard for the con-
> sequences of her error-ridden portrayals."

" 'No regard for—'? 'Error-ridden'?" Annabelle
fairly sputtered her indignation. Did he think so very
little of her sense of integrity? She forced herself to
calm her emotions enough to finish reading the essay.

> "In all fairness, I must point out that her latest
> work, *Innocence Betrayed* is inferior to her earlier
> endeavors. So far as this reviewer could determine,
> she published three novels prior to this (blessedly!)
> shorter piece. The earlier works show a command
> of the craft of writing and understanding of human
> nature that is almost wholly absent in the infamous
> *Innocence Betrayed.*
>
> "In short, were it not so generally known that
> the events to which she so clumsily alludes in *In-
> nocence Betrayed* occurred only a few months ago,
> one might well assume this to be an earlier work—

produced by some overly emotional schoolroom miss. I would say to Miss Bennet—were she not hiding behind a coward's veil of anonymity—'I am sorry, my dear, but this simply does not live up to the promise shown in your earlier works.' "

Annabelle threw the magazine across the room. Now she was sputtering in earnest. " 'Clumsily alludes'? 'Overly emotional schoolroom miss'? 'Hiding'? 'Coward's veil'?" She balled her fists and pounded the bed in frustration.

The kiss that had dominated her conscious thoughts ever since the event had meant nothing to him! All the while he had been planning to attack the most defining aspect of her character—her writing. If this was his opinion of her work, he could not think much of her as a person. The kiss was a lie! She felt excruciating pain at this idea. Then she sat up and wiped at her watery eyes.

"Annabelle, my girl," she muttered at the partial image she caught in the looking glass, "you are not thinking straight. He apparently sees no connection between the woman he kissed and the writer he maligns."

Oh, Lord! How could she face him again?

She arose and rang for Molly to help her dress for dinner. She washed her face and wished fervently that she would never again have to see one Thorne Wainwright.

Harriet was alone in the drawing room when Annabelle went down. "Did you finish reading it?"

"Oh, yes."

"And . . . ?"

"I have not really sorted out my feelings yet. I need to read it again." This was true. Anger and humiliation and despair warred within.

"Will you be all right with this house party at Rolsbury Manor?"

"I think so. I do wish we were not going, but I can hardly develop a life-threatening illness only a week before the event. I will, however, ask you to plead my excuses to Lady Grimsley this evening. Were I to encounter Lord Rolsbury tonight, I think I might be tempted to do him bodily harm."

"I might be inclined to join you, my dear," Harriet said.

"His house party is likely to be very difficult for me." Annabelle was thinking aloud.

"It is to be quite a large affair, I believe." Harriet turned with a smile for her husband, who had just entered the room. "Did you not tell me, Marcus, that Rolsbury had invited several members of Parliament to his place in the country?"

"Yes, he did. In addition to Winters and me, I know of four or five others, Whigs and Tories alike, who have been invited—and their wives, of course."

"Of course," Harriet echoed. "And I have heard some ladies talk of having invitations who have no connections with Parliament."

"It promises to be a sizable group," Marcus said. He gave his wife an inquiring look. "The question is, my love, will you be able to leave our son for that length of time?"

"I own I shall miss him dreadfully, but as we shall be absent for only a week or ten days, I feel sure Nurse will be able to handle anything that comes up. Perhaps the mothers Rolsbury has invited will welcome a short holiday from child care." She sounded more hopeful than positive about this, though.

"A sizable group . . ." Annabelle mused.

"Yes, dear," Harriet said. "So you see? You need not

expend excessive worry. Rolsbury is sure to be quite busy with his duties as host."

Thorne was rather pleased with his first attempt at literary criticism. He felt he had presented a balanced analysis of fiction by and for women. He wanted to discuss the article with Annabelle, but in the days after its publication, he had seen little of her. He had heard she had been unwell for a day or so, but he also knew she had gone riding one morning with Luke.

He told himself he wanted only to discuss writing and books with her. She was Luke's special friend; there could be no other reason for Luke's brother to want to see her. Yes, he had been deeply shaken by that kiss. And for that reason alone it was necessary to put his own friendship with her on a less personal basis.

The upcoming house party would afford him the opportunity to do that—along with giving Luke a chance to further his interests with her. Somehow, that idea did not set too well—especially in view of her uninhibited response to his own kiss. Luke was right, though—the younger brother *was* only a few months short of reaching the age of majority. The lad—no, the young man— had a right to live his own life. It was not as though the girl were unsuitable. And it was apparent now that Annabelle Richardson was no fortune hunter. So why did Thorne have such negative feelings when he thought of her kissing Luke—or anyone else—as she had kissed him?

It made no sense. In any event, all Thorne wanted—in view of their previous discussions of books and writers—was to discuss her reaction to his article in the *Review.* When he thought about it, though, that made little sense either. After all, he had published numerous articles in the past without this urgent need to know another's reaction.

Meanwhile, he had no opportunity to speak with her. He had seen her at the theater one evening and he called at Wyndham House one afternoon along with Luke. They found the Wyndham drawing room full and there was no opportunity for serious discussion in such a scene.

In certain quarters, though his article had not always been well-read, it was received enthusiastically.

"Good job, Rolsbury." A member of White's whom Thorne knew only fleetingly clapped him on the shoulder.

" 'Twas beyond time some saner voice chimed in on that drivel," another member of the gentlemen's club said. "Now—if only someone could stop the females swooning over Byron's moronic moping."

"See you hit back at that Bennet woman," a fellow member of Parliament said. "Good. Women need to know they cannot be allowed to go around besmirching a man's character so."

Thorne thought about this for a moment. He was tempted to ask the man if he thought it acceptable for a man to besmirch a woman's character as was so often done with the infamous betting books in the gentlemen's clubs. He let it go, though, and merely said, "My intent was to show patterns or general trends in certain types of literary works—not attack a particular writer."

The other man gave him a look of "have it your way" and changed the subject.

When he later attended a *conversazione* at the home of Lady Ellerton, a member of the London Literary League, he found a warm reception for himself, but a mixed reaction to his essay.

"Maria Edgeworth is here this evening," his hostess told him with a sly look. Lady Ellerton, Thorne surmised, was one of those women who saw controversy among others as something of a spectator sport.

"Is she? I should like to meet her," he said in an even tone and glanced around the room. He observed another of those London drawing rooms overly decorated in the Egyptian style. What *is* it with rich Englishmen and the craze for all things Egyptian, he wondered silently. Small groups of people stood or sat here and there conversing, some quietly, some more animatedly. Only when he spotted her talking with two scholarly-looking gentlemen, did he realize he had been searching for Annabelle. She caught him looking at her and gave him the barest little smile of recognition.

His request to meet Mrs. Edgeworth was no sooner made than fulfilled, and he found himself taking the hand offered by a woman who reminded him of his Aunt Dorothy. Mrs. Edgeworth was of an age with his aunt and her eyes twinkled with that same gleam of intelligent good humor as his aunt's did.

Seeing that his meeting with Maria Edgeworth was attracting a good deal of attention in the rest of the room, Thorne thought merely to exchange polite formalities with her and move on. However, she detained him.

"You know, Rolsbury, there are those who would have us lady writers ignore you—give you the cut direct, as it were."

"Ah. And are you of such a mind, madam?"

"Not at all. I came here this evening specifically because I thought you might be here."

"Is that so?" He was surprised that this should be so—and that she would own up to it so frankly. He took the empty chair next to her when she gestured to it rather peremptorily. She had been talking previously with another lady on her other side. Two gentlemen who had been passing the time of day with Mrs. Edgeworth and her companion hovered nearby.

"Yes," she answered. "I wanted to meet the young fellow who has set himself up as such an expert on women's writing." Her tone was challenging, but not aggressive.

"I laid no claim to expertise in the piece I wrote," Thorne argued. "I merely made what I thought to be a scientific, though admittedly limited, study and then I wrote up my findings."

Her eyes twinkled. "Oh, is that all?"

"That is all I *intended*." He noticed that several others had drifted over to listen to their discourse. Among these was Annabelle Richardson.

"Well, the truth of the matter, young man, is that you were quite right much of the time. A trifle offensive in the telling, mind you, but on the mark, mostly."

"Thank you, madam. I appreciate your saying as much."

She nodded and went on. "You were right in saying that Mrs. Radcliffe sometimes exaggerates her settings, but we get so caught up in the intrigues of her tales that we overlook her flaws."

"I suppose we do," he agreed.

"Perhaps you should have said as much." It was a reprimand, albeit a gentle one.

"Well . . ." He struggled for a polite response, but she did not wait for it.

"And you were quite right about my work. I freely acknowledge that plotting is the weakest aspect of my work. As you and my friend, Sir Walter Scott, have pointed out—I do concentrate most on presenting my Irish characters in a sympathetic light."

He regained his voice. "How gracious of you to say so, madam."

Others in their little group murmured, "Hear. Hear."

"However," Maria Edgeworth continued, "you were especially harsh on Miss Bennet, were you not?"

He looked up to see an enigmatic expression cross Annabelle's pretty face. Then it was replaced with a bland look of polite interest.

"No. Not really," he answered. "Her earlier works *are* better than her feeble foray into satire."

He thought he heard someone gasp at this.

"Oh, I quite agree with you on that point," Mrs. Edgeworth said. "Again, I think it more a matter of the *tone* you adopted in writing of her work. But, then, I gather you had particular reason to take that tone with her?"

Had he allowed his personal antipathy to so color his own work? "I should like to think I was fair to all the works I reviewed." He knew he sounded a bit stiff.

"I am sure you tried to be," Mrs. Edgeworth responded, her tone kind. She looked up and caught sight of a newcomer. "Oh! Sir Walter, you must meet this young man."

She introduced Thorne to Sir Walter Scott. Dressed adequately, though not in the first stare of fashion, Scott was of an age with Mrs. Edgeworth. It was readily apparent to Thorne that these two were, indeed, friends of long standing. He was somewhat amused at the way Scott focused the conversation on his own works. After awhile, Thorne excused himself and drifted from group to group. Then he saw that Annabelle seemed momentarily alone and he crossed the room to join her.

"Good evening, Annabelle."

"Thorne." She dipped her head to acknowledge his greeting.

She was dressed in a lavender creation with white lace trim. The gown had a wide neckline and elbow-length sleeves.

"You are looking very fetching this evening," he said.

"Why, thank you."

He liked the fact that she was not coy or self-effacing in response to his compliment. If it occurred to him that he often found things to like in Miss Richardson, he quickly thrust that idea aside.

"Did you agree with Mrs. Edgeworth?" he asked.

Annabelle gave him an inquiring look. "On what point? She made several, I think."

"That I was too harsh in my assessment of Miss Bennet's work."

"I . . . uh . . . I am not sure."

"Perhaps you have not read my review. 'Twas rather self-centered of me to assume you had done so."

She gave a short little laugh. "I read it. I think all London has read it."

"Well? What did *you* think?" He was not sure why, but her answer was very important to him.

"I . . . I thought it was well-written." She sounded hesitant. Surely, he thought, she was not afraid to be honest with him?

"But . . . ? You do not sound overly confident in that opinion."

"I am *very* confident of that opinion," she said decisively. "You have a clear, readable writing style."

He snorted. "As do most of the nation's schoolboys. But what of the *content?* What did you think of the substance of the review?"

"Well, as you probably know from our previous discussions, I found your views of Miss Austen's work brilliantly *apropos*. They so precisely paralleled my own, you see." Her smile caused a stirring sensation in his nether regions.

He returned her smile, his gaze holding hers. "Just so. And Miss Bennet's work? You did not answer my question. Do you agree with Mrs. Egeworth that I was too severe with her?"

The smile left her eyes and she seemed to be groping for words. "I . . . I think your motivation may have been more . . . more personal with the Bennet works."

"I *tried* to treat her in the same vein as all the others."

"By referring to her as a *coward?*" There was an undertone of bitterness in her challenge that he did not understand.

"I did not say she was a coward—merely that she behaved in a cowardly fashion in launching invective from behind a barrier of anonymity."

"Now you are splitting hairs, my lord."

"Perhaps I am. I simply find it easier to respect people who are honest and straightforward."

"And perhaps," she replied in a rather caustic tone, a parody of his own tone with the word *perhaps,* "you have never bothered to consider what it demands of one to be known as a 'lady scribbler' as most men would describe women who choose to express themselves that way."

Irritated by her condescending tone, he said, "Why do you defend her? She made you, too, an object of ridicule."

"Only indirectly."

"Still, her failure to own up to her work is not exactly what anyone could call an act of integrity."

"Perhaps she has good reason to remain anonymous. Even your precious Miss Austen was not known as a writer until after her death."

"That was different. She was a shy country woman. Emma Bennet is a sophisticated member of the *ton*. I would stake my life on it."

"Let us hope you will not have to do so," she said. "Now, if you will excuse me, Lord Rolsbury, I see that Harriet and Aunt Gertrude wish to leave."

Thorne fumed all the way home. She had as much

as accused him of insensitivity. He was certain now that she knew the Bennet woman.

And at what point had he suddenly become "Lord Rolsbury" again?

That irritated him, too.

Nine

The encounter with Thorne at the meeting of the Literary League had Annabelle in a dither. His comments about Emma Bennet had unnerved her, unleashing impotent fury.

Rolsbury's questioning Emma Bennet's integrity—or lack of it—was especially galling. That dratted man knew nothing—nothing, mind you—of the struggles women faced as writers. His mere gender made it easier for him, and his title had automatically assured that *his* works would be accepted for publication. She remembered well her own struggle to get someone in the publishing world to *look* at her work. Even then, it had been at least partly through the intervention of Aunt Gertrude that Mr. Murray had agreed to consider it.

She often wondered what would have happened without Aunt Gertrude. But then she would answer that question herself—she would still write. For Annabelle, writing ranked right up there with breathing as a necessity of life. Having her work published and appreciated by others was mere frosting on her literary cake.

"I saw you talking with Lord Rolsbury," Harriet said in the carriage after they had dropped Lady Hermiston at her own residence.

"Yes. He was reading me a lecture on cowardice and integrity."

"He was *what?*" Harriet's voice rose in surprised outrage.

"Not directly, you understand. He was merely explaining to me that Emma Bennet behaved in a very reprehensible manner."

"He is *still* chafing over that story, is he?"

Annabelle answered slowly, thinking as she spoke. "I am not so sure. To some extent—yes. But I think it goes to a deeper aspect of his own character. Something in him deplores deceit and chicanery."

"Is that so unusual? When was the last time you met someone who openly embraced those traits?"

Annabelle chuckled at this. "You have a point. But Th—Lord Rolsbury's sense of integrity is rather rigid, I think."

"He is stiff-necked, you mean."

"Not exactly. He has quite a marvelous sense of humor. And he relates well to the plight of those who have not the advantages chance has bestowed on certain of us."

Harriet sat silent for a moment, then spoke slowly. "Annabelle, my dear, are you developing a *tendre* for Thorne Wainwright?"

Annabelle's response was quick. "No! Of course not. That would be the height of foolishness on my part."

"Why? He seems a perfectly eligible *parti* to me. And quite a number of debutantes and their mamas seemed to agree this Season, for all that he could not literally dance attendance on them."

Annabelle recalled her dance in the garden with him and a kiss that cast everything else into oblivion. No. It would never do. Aloud, she said, "It . . . it would not be feasible. He . . . he despises Emma Bennet. And my work is very important to me."

"I am not sure he does despise Miss Bennet so much," Harriet said.

"What do you mean?"

"I reread the piece in the *Review*."

"And . . . ?"

"He admired your earlier works. Mind you, he did so grudgingly. I think perhaps he *wanted* to hate them."

"Oh, Harriet, you are too generous by half. The man simply cannot get beyond the fact that Emma Bennet held him up to ridicule."

"He might be able to get beyond that—were he not frustrated by the fact that his adversary is such an unknown."

"What are you suggesting? That I reveal myself as the infamous Miss Bennet?"

"I do not know . . . it might clear the air and allow you to start over with him if you were to do so."

"Harriet! *You* were the one who insisted I write under a pseudonym. Remember?"

"Yes, but that was when you were still a schoolgirl. It would not have done to have you labeled a bluestocking—or worse—before you even had your first Season."

Annabelle gave a ladylike snort. "Do you think it will 'do' now?"

"You are very nearly of age now. What would be frowned on in a young miss just making her come-out will be tolerated—it might even be celebrated—in a woman who is of age."

"Perhaps you are right," Annabelle mused. "All this secrecy and dissembling is not very comfortable."

"Because it is not in your nature."

"However," Annabelle went on, "I cannot see Lord Rolsbury welcoming such a revelation."

"Well, think on it, dear. You need do nothing immediately," Harriet said as they arrived at their own doorstep.

Over the next few days, Annabelle did "think on it." She drove herself mad deciding first one way, then the other. She fancied scenes in which Thorne was taking Miss Bennet to task yet again and she dramatically revealed that *she* was Miss Bennet. She longed to put him in his place on that score.

Then her imagination would conjure the disgust and disdain she would see in his eyes, and she could not bring herself to do it. Perhaps he had the right of it after all. Emma Bennet might not be such a coward, but Annabelle Richardson certainly was!

The Wyndham entourage set out for Rolsbury Manor in Lincolnshire during the last week of July. The Season had been prolonged because of the coronation and now the social elite were leaving the city—like the proverbial rats leaving a sinking ship, Annabelle thought. The festivities surrounding the coronation had been spectacular—and exhausting.

As women were not party to the actual coronation, Annabelle and Harriet had merely observed the grand spectacle of the procession going into Westminster Abbey. Later, Annabelle, along with Marcus and Harriet, attended two balls to celebrate the occasion.

"Our new king certainly spared no expense on this ritual," Harriet observed the next morning at a late breakfast.

Marcus looked up from his newspaper. "He has ever been one to enjoy spending the nation's money."

"Careful, dear. You begin to sound like a radical Whig," his wife teased.

"Much as I hate to agree with *some* of those fellows, they do occasionally have the right of it."

"They object to a coronation ceremony?" Annabelle asked.

"No. Only to the exorbitant expense of this one," Marcus said.

Harriet spread honey on a slice of toast. "The king might have been more prudent in the planning, but he seems to be enjoying greater popularity than he did a year ago."

"The people's collective memory is a short one," Marcus said. "But—not all of them have forgiven him for his attempt to be rid of his wife and his denying her all royal privileges."

"There is a certain hypocrisy in a husband charging his wife with adultery even as he publicly enjoys the attentions of a long-time mistress," Harriet said dryly.

"Just so, my dear."

"Still," Annabelle interjected, "there was a certain lack of dignity in the queen's going around to all the Abbey doors, demanding to be let in when he had denied her entrance. I think people were embarrassed for her."

"Well," Harriet said in a note of closing the topic, "he has been in limbo for ten years with the duties of king, but without the title. Now he has the title in a very official way. We must hope for the best."

"And work to divert the worst," her husband added.

"Later, dear," Harriet responded. "For now, we prepare to remove to Lincolnshire and then to Timberly. I will be so very glad to get home to Timberly."

Summer with its heat and stench had invaded London, sending those who could afford to do so in pursuit of cooler, less odiferous sites. The city at this time of year was a breeding ground for pestilence. Many of the children of the *ton,* including the Wyndham heir the day before, had already been sent to the country. Most of the guests attending Rolsbury's house party would go on afterward to their own country estates—or make prolonged visits with friends and relatives elsewhere—anywhere but the city in late summer.

The Wyndham party would journey on to Timberly, the earl's main property, for the remainder of the summer. The Earl of Wyndham annually hosted a grand harvest festival at Timberly. Annabelle knew that Marcus accepted the harvest celebration as a sacred duty. This duty had been curtailed only when the family were mourning the two previous earls, who had died within months of each other.

She also knew that several of Rolsbury's guests had been invited to Timberly's harvest festival and Marcus had invited both of the Wainwright brothers as well. Marcus had explained that he, like Rolsbury, planned to use his entertainment as a means of also furthering certain political measures that both men held dear. However, the Timberly affair was a good two months off. Meanwhile, she must see herself through the Rolsbury party unscathed.

The Wyndham group included Lady Hermiston as well as Marcus, Harriet, and Annabelle. What with personal servants and luggage, they required three coaches and, of course, coachmen and footmen who would provide protection from dangers offered travelers. After a blessedly uneventful journey of three days, they arrived at Rolsbury Manor early one afternoon.

Annabelle had surmised that the Manor house would be fairly large to support the number of guests known to have been invited. However, she was not prepared for the sheer size of the estate and its primary building. A gatehouse guarded the entrance as they turned off the public thoroughfare. They rode for another quarter of an hour on a pleasant, tree-shaded lane before reaching the house itself.

Built of gray stones quarried locally, the house was a full three stories with an attic above. Annabelle thought it probably sported a sizable basement as well. At first she thought the house was built on a giant U-shape with a sweeping driveway leading to the entrance in the deep middle of the U. Massive wings stood guard on either side of the entrance. Later she found this impression was only half right, for the rear of the house mirrored the front, making its design that of a giant H with a charming courtyard between the extended wings in the rear.

Most country houses seemed rather austere when one approached them and one's first impression was likely to be of stone and glass. But this one had a profusion of potted shrubs and flowers as well as a sparkling fountain around which the driveway circled.

" 'This castle hath a pleasant seat. The air Nimbly and sweetly recommends itself Unto our gentle senses.' " Annabelle murmured the quotation as a liveried footman handed her and Harriet from the carriage. Aunt Gertrude's carriage was just behind; Marcus had chosen to ride beside their carriages most of this day.

Harriet laughed aloud but spoke softly so the servants would not hear as she and Annabelle stood on a wide expanse of stone steps, waiting for Aunt Gertrude and Marcus to join them. "I hope your quoting the ill-fated King Duncan on his visit to Macbeth's castle is not a portent of some sort."

"No. Duncan found his surroundings most pleasant. And so do I." She thought a moment. "Though I suppose it is possible our host will want to be rid of me before our visit is over."

Just then, even as Aunt Gertrude and Marcus joined them, their host appeared in the doorway to bid them welcome. He was dressed casually in buff-colored pantaloons, a forest green jacket, and shiny black Hessians. Unlike many dandies of the day, Lord Rolsbury, Annabelle thought, probably needed little padding in his coats. His appearance quite took her breath away. She knew her reaction was not merely surprise at his apparent eagerness to welcome them to his home.

"You have a lovely property here," Harriet said. "I am quite anxious to see more of it."

"Thank you, my lady. It shows to great advantage in this season."

"I would venture a guess that that tree-lined drive is fairly spectacular in autumn," Annabelle said.

He gave her an appreciative smile. "Yes, it is. Mind you, it is lovely in spring, too, when the leaves are just turning from gold to green. And there is a kind of stark beauty to them in winter. I shall be ever grateful to my great-grandfather for planting those trees!"

He ushered them into a generous entrance hall. Rather than the cold marble one found in so many entranceways, this one welcomed arrivals warmly with carved wood paneling and a slate floor. As they were shown to their rooms, Annabelle noted—and thoroughly approved—a generous use of wood throughout.

"His lordship chose this chamber for you, miss." The housekeeper, a Mrs. Petry, gave Annabelle a speculative look as she opened the door.

"How very nice," Annabelle murmured, dismissing the woman's comment as polite chitchat. He had to assign each guest *some* room, after all.

Hers was a charming bedchamber on the second floor, decorated in blues, greens, and a soft yellow. She was delighted to find a dressing room that connected to a very modern bath. A bouquet of yellow roses sat on a table near the window.

When she had freshened up, she found a maid posted in the hall to show her down to the main drawing room on the floor below. There she found Celia and Letty and their husbands as well as two other couples. Annabelle recognized the gentlemen as members of Parliament.

Luke approached. "Welcome to Rolsbury Manor, Annabelle. May I get you something to eat or drink?" He gestured to a table laden with what appeared to be an elaborate tea. "We shall have a proper supper later, but we did not want our guests starving on their arrival."

"I see little danger of that." She looked around, but no, Thorne was not in attendance. She surmised that he might be receiving other guests.

Celia and Letty gave her quick hugs in greeting. "Had you any idea this would be so very grand?" Celia bubbled.

"I knew," Letty said airily. "I was here once as a child. Rolsbury's father was one of my father's friends."

"Is it as you remembered?" Celia asked.

"Not really. Everything seems refurbished. But tastefully so."

"Have you noticed?" Celia asked. "There are flowers everywhere! I love it."

"I certainly did not remember those under the previous earl," Letty said, "though I think the rose gardens here have always claimed a marked degree of fame."

"Maybe the Manor has a new housekeeper," Annabelle said.

"Hmm. I do not *think* that to be the case," Letty said absently.

"Well. We *know* it has a new earl," Celia declared.

Just then their host entered, accompanied by Charles and Helen Rhys. They were obviously not brand-new arrivals. Helen looked quite at home hanging on Thorne's arm, Annabelle noted with what could only be a twinge of sheer jealousy.

"Helen and Charles arrived yesterday." Celia confirmed Annabelle's observation. "They all knew each other in Belgium, you know."

"Yes," Letty said softly. "I think she had a schoolgirl's infatuation for Major Wainwright."

"Well, it appears to have blossomed into a genuine *tendre* for his lordship," Celia quipped, again confirming Annabelle's thoughts.

Annabelle recalled seeing the Rhys brother and sister at *ton* affairs. Now that she thought of it, yes, Thorne had seemed especially friendly with them on occasion. Was he paying suit to the sister? And if he were, of what concern could that possibly be to Annabelle Richardson? Immediately, she wondered if he had kissed Helen Rhys with the same fervor he had shown in the garden at the Finchley ball.

By early evening all the guests had arrived and it was a lively group that collected in the music room after a hearty supper. Several ladies showed off their skills and the company was generally pleased. This was not an area in which Annabelle excelled. She loved music, but had always felt all thumbs at any instrument. Tonight she felt her inadequacy acutely.

Helen Rhys enlisted Thorne's aid in turning her pages, but from the way she kept casting him coy glances, Annabelle surmised she knew the piece by heart and needed no aid at all. Then she mentally shook herself for her pettiness.

"She plays so beautifully," one of the matrons sitting with Aunt Gertrude gushed as Miss Rhys performed.

"The two of them make a very attractive picture there," observed Lady Conwick, who had been introduced as Thorne's aunt and his hostess.

Annabelle had to agree sourly that they did. His dark good looks provided startling contrast to Helen's fragile silvery-blond beauty.

Later in the evening, Thorne announced that he had made mounts available for those of his guests who would care to ride but had not brought their own cattle.

As a small child, Annabelle had been given a pony by her doting papa. When both her parents were lost at sea, Annabelle's riding days had abruptly ended. She spent the next six years confined to a girls' boarding school with very few riding opportunities. Only when she came under the guardianship of Marcus and Harriet had she taken up riding again. She had done so with gusto. Even in the city she rode in the early mornings three or four times a week. Thus, she welcomed Thorne's offer.

She arose early the next morning, donned her riding habit, and made her way to the stables. A groom welcomed her at the stable door with some surprise.

"We didn't expect any o' his lordship's guests quite so early, miss."

"Oh? Well, I *should* like to go riding, but I do not wish to inconvenience anyone. If you'd rather I came back later . . ."

"No. No. 'Tain't no inconvenience. We'll get ye a mount right quick-like. Luckily, they've been fed already and we was just groomin' them."

Annabelle smiled at the man. "As I am the first, have I a choice?"

"Well, I s'pose ye do at that. Never ye fret, miss. We'll get ye a fine mount."

She waited patiently despite her eagerness to be off. In a few minutes the groom returned, leading a small, roan-colored mare who appeared to be quite docile. The animal stood quietly at the mounting steps.

"Is this the horse you have for *me?*" she asked.

"Yes, miss. Penney's a sweet thing. No trouble at all."

"I am quite sure she would be a most proper mount for a child. But I had in mind something taller and with more spirit," she said firmly. She thought she heard a chuckle from beyond the stable door.

The groom gave her a doubtful look that clearly measured her petite stature. "Be ye sure now, miss? Penney's easy ta handle . . ."

"I am *quite* sure."

The groom led Penney back into the stable and returned shortly with another mare, a taller dappled gray whose pricked ears and alert eyes exhibited more interest in her surroundings.

"This'n we calls Jessie." The groom's voice held a note of warning. "I have ta tell ye, though, that's short for Jezebel—an' with reason!"

Annabelle approached the horse, who seemed wary. She extended her hand to the horse's muzzle to allow the animal to smell her, then patted the mare's neck. "Oh, I think Jessie and I will be able to come to terms with each other."

"Yes, miss. Well, if you will hold on for a few more minutes, I'll jus' saddle another mount for meself. His lordship don't want no ladies goin' off by theirselves."

"Well, if he insists . . ." Annabelle was prepared to honor the rules of the house.

"He does," called a voice from within the stable. "That's all right, Tom. I shall accompany Miss Richardson this morning." Thorne Wainwright led a magnificent black gelding from the stable.

"Have you been in there the whole time?" she asked, indignant.

He grinned at her. "That I have. Interesting exchange, that was."

"Well! You might have said something earlier."

"I *might* have," he agreed calmly, holding both horses as she climbed the mounting steps and settled herself in the sidesaddle. Then he swung himself onto the black and they were off.

Annabelle was busy for a few minutes in a struggle of wills with Jessie, but eventually the mare seemed to recognize that she had met her match and settled into an even gait. Annabelle was very conscious of Thorne watching from behind, ready to come to her rescue if necessary. She felt mildly triumphant when it clearly was not necessary.

"Well done, Annabelle."

"Thank you, my lord."

"Hmm." He made a mockery of pretending to think. "Correct me if I am mistaken, but I seem to recall that we agreed on 'Thorne' and 'Annabelle' as forms of address. Have I done something to lose that privilege?"

Annabelle swallowed and tried to think. She could not very well scream Yes! you insensitive dolt, you attacked me in my most vulnerable spot! Instead, she said as casually as she could, "Why, so we did, Thorne." She met his gaze only briefly, then said, "What say we see what these splendid animals can do?"

"What have you in mind?"

"A race."

"I never race without a wager," he said.

She laughed. "For what stakes? Shall I offer you my firstborn son if I lose?"

"Hmm. That would be tempting." She felt herself blush at his wicked grin. "No. Nothing so drastic. The winner will determine the forfeit."

"Jessie and I will need a head start."

"Fair enough. We shall race to the edge of that copse of trees on the hill there." He pointed some distance away. "There is a marvelous view from up there. And you may have a lead as far as that old elm in the middle of the field." He pointed again.

The mare was game, but even with a lead, she was no match for the black. Thorne turned in the saddle to await Annabelle's arrival. He dismounted somewhat awkwardly and reached to help her dismount. She slid into his arms cautiously, afraid of unbalancing him.

"I promise not to fall," he said.

"Oh, well—if you promise . . ." She laughed nervously.

He set her on her feet and released her. Did he do so reluctantly? she wondered. She stepped back and put her hands on her hips.

"Well? You won. What is the forfeit to be?"

He grinned and gazed at her mouth. She felt herself holding her breath.

"I am sorely tempted to demand a kiss," he said. "But that would be far too dangerous. So I will settle for a smile and your promise to ride out with me again."

She smiled broadly, masking her disappointment at his not opting for the kiss. "Done!"

He took her elbow. "Now, come. I want to show you the most spectacular view for miles around."

They walked only a short distance until Annabelle found herself standing on the edge of a cliff. Below, a blue ribbon of water wound its way through gloriously changing shades of green as fields and forests blended.

"Oh! It *is* spectacular," she breathed, trying to take it all in at once. She spotted a structure of some sort across the way, a mass of gray stone demanding the eye of the viewer. " 'I have felt A presence that disturbs me with the joy Of elevated thought . . .' " she murmured as she gazed out at this scene.

He looked at her in amazement. "My sentiments exactly. This scene always puts me in mind of Wordworth's lines, too—for, as he said, 'Nature never did betray The heart that loved her.' "

Shaken by their shared emotions, she held his gaze for a long moment, then looked away. "Well," she said brightly, "I know that is *not* Tintern Abbey, but what is it?"

"It *is* what remains of *an* abbey, though. Destroyed by Henry VIII, who then gave over these lands to the first Earl of Rolsbury."

"How interesting. May we visit it during our stay?"

"We have planned just such an outing—complete

with a picnic. That was Luke's idea. Luke's plans for any outing nearly always involve food somehow." He ended with a chuckle. They turned back to the horses, but Annabelle was not quite ready to give up the mood of the moment. When he had handed her up into her saddle, she looked down at him, holding his gaze.

"Thank you, Thorne, for sharing this special place with me."

He merely nodded and turned to his own mount.

Ten

Thorne cursed himself as they returned to the stable and he escorted her back to the house. He had no business welcoming time alone with the woman his brother wished to court. And he intended to repeat his transgression! By now more of his guests were stirring and he was sidetracked into telling other riders about likely trails they could take. For some reason, he told none of them of the view from the cliff.

By the time he had changed from his riding clothes and reported to the dining room for breakfast, Annabelle was already there—after all, *she* had not been detained in giving directions to others.

His Aunt Dorothy announced a planned outing for the ladies—a visit to Lincoln and its splendid cathedral which was but an hour away by coach. The cathedral, accounted one of England's most spectacular—along with shopping opportunities offered by the town itself—would keep the ladies of the party occupied for the day.

Luke had taken the gentlemen off to a pugilistic contest down near the town of Stamford. Thorne planned to use the absence of guests for a few hours as an opportunity to catch up on estate business. In the afternoon, he had already spent over an hour wrestling with

We'd Like to Invite You to Subscribe to Zebra's Regency Romance Book Club and Give You a Gift of 4 Free Books as Your Introduction! (Worth $19.96!)

If you're a Regency lover, imagine the joy of getting **4 FREE Zebra Regency Romances** and then the chance to have these lovely stories delivered to your home each month at the lowest price available! Well, that's our offer to you and here's how you benefit by becoming a Regency Romance subscriber:

- **4 FREE** Introductory Regency Romances are delivered to your doorstep

- 4 BRAND NEW Regencies are then delivered each month (usually before they're available in bookstores)

- Subscribers save almost $4.00 every month

- You also receive a **FREE** monthly newsletter, which features author profiles, discounts, subscriber benefits, book previews and more

- No risks or obligations...in other words, you can cancel whenever you wish with no questions asked

Join the thousands of readers who enjoy the savings and convenience offered to Regency Romance subscribers. After your initial introductory shipment, you receive 4 brand-new Zebra Regency Romances each month to examine for 10 days. Then, if you decide to keep the books, you'll pay the preferred subscriber's price.

It's a no-lose proposition, so return the FREE BOOK CERTIFICATE today!

Say Yes to 4 Free Books!
Complete and return the order card to receive this $19.96 value, ABSOLUTELY FREE!

If the certificate is missing below, write to:
Regency Romance Book Club
P.O. Box 5214, Clifton, New Jersey 07015-5214
or call TOLL-FREE 1-888-345-BOOK

Visit our website at www.kensingtonbooks.com.

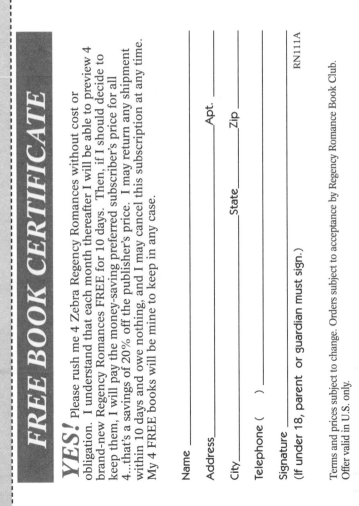

FREE BOOK CERTIFICATE

YES! Please rush me 4 Zebra Regency Romances without cost or obligation. I understand that each month thereafter I will be able to preview 4 brand-new Regency Romances FREE for 10 days. Then, if I should decide to keep them, I will pay the money-saving preferred subscriber's price for all 4...that's a savings of 20% off the publisher's price. I may return any shipment within 10 days and owe nothing, and I may cancel this subscription at any time. My 4 FREE books will be mine to keep in any case.

Name _____

Address _____ Apt. _____

City _____ State _____ Zip _____

Telephone ( ) _____

Signature _____ RN111A
(If under 18, parent or guardian must sign.)

Terms and prices subject to change. Orders subject to acceptance by Regency Romance Book Club.
Offer valid in U.S. only.

a pile of paperwork and was congratulating himself on his progress when there was a knock on the library door.

"Come," he called, expecting a footman or his butler.

To his surprise, Helen Rhys entered the room. He rose to greet her, but stood behind the desk.

"I hope I am not disturbing you," she said, closing the door behind her.

"Not at all," he lied. "You did not care to accompany the other ladies?"

"No. I was suffering a beastly headache earlier. Besides, I have seen quite enough moldy old churches in Belgium and elsewhere to last me a lifetime."

"I see. I understand there was to be some shopping— and a luncheon was bespoke at a hotel there."

"Oh, I would have enjoyed that, I am sure. But my head, you know." She put the back of her hand to her forehead in a dramatic motion. "I thought a book might help me pass the time."

He gestured to the book-lined room. "Help yourself. Our collection boasts quite a variety. Or did you have something specific in mind?"

"Oh, no. Just something to entertain me until the others return."

Thorne thought this was a subtle hint that, as host, *he* should entertain her. Perhaps she would select a book and be on her way. He came from behind the desk and casually opened the door she had closed. He nodded approvingly at a footman in the hallway.

Noticing a frown flit across her pretty face as he left the door open, he smiled inwardly. I was born sometime prior to yesterday, my dear, he thought. Aloud, he said, "May I help you find something?"

"Oh, would you, please?"

"What would you find most entertaining?"

She gave him an arch look and laughed softly. "That is a leading question, is it not?"

"To read," he said firmly.

"Oh, I am not sure. Allow me to browse for a moment."

He watched silently for several minutes as she pulled first one book and then another from the shelves. It struck him that the books she chose all seemed to require great stretching and turning that showed her considerable charms to great advantage.

"Oh, Thorne," she said prettily, "could you get that one for me?" She pointed to a shelf above her head.

"This one?" He started to remove a book bound in green leather.

"No. No." She moved closer to him and he caught a strong whiff of an exotic perfume. "That red one." She turned so her breast touched his arm and gazed at him invitingly.

Do not even think of it, Rolsbury, he told himself. He quickly put the book between them. "Here you go." He looked at the title. *"Songs of Innocence?"*

"I thought the title looked intriguing."

"I think you will find Mr. Blake somewhat deceptive. The poems are far more serious than their titles suggest."

"Well, I shall just sit here and read a bit of his work to see if I want this. You will not mind, will you?"

"No, of course not," he lied again. He returned to his desk and attempted to get back into estate business. However, he was very aware of her. Not only did her perfume now permeate the entire room, but she kept shifting noisily on the settee. Occasionally she sighed loudly or murmured incoherently. He tried to ignore her presence.

"Oh, listen to this, Thorne!" She read him a passage dealing with mercy, pity, peace, and love. "Is that not a perfect statement about love?"

"Well, yes . . . but the poem is really about God's image being in all mankind."

"It is?" She looked at the poem again. "Yes, I can see that now. How very clever of you to see that on only the lines I read."

"I am quite familiar with Blake's work."

"Of course. Silly me."

She went back to her fidgety perusal of the book.

Thorne sat wondering if Annabelle were familiar with Blake. Would she be able to bandy quotes from Blake, too? Then he gave himself a mental shake.

He was glad when a few minutes later he heard the carriages return with the other ladies. As the women were enjoying refreshments of tea or lemonade, the gentlemen, too, returned and Thorne felt relieved. He marveled at how much easier it sometimes was to entertain many than to entertain one.

Annabelle had noticed the absence of Miss Rhys on their outing to Lincoln. Miss Rhys's friend, a Mrs. Sawyer, had explained that "poor Helen had a dreadful headache." However, on the ladies' return to Rolsbury Manor, there was Miss Rhys looking very chipper on the arm of their host. Later, Helen Rhys had let fall the information that she and Rolsbury had spent the afternoon reading poetry.

"Oh, how very romantic," gushed Mrs. Sawyer.

"Wordsworth, no doubt," Annabelle muttered sourly to herself. But she smiled blandly and answered coherently when someone directed a specific question to her.

Luke approached and Annabelle gave him a broad smile of welcome and bade him sit with her in the windowseat.

"Thought you looked a bit out of sorts," he said.

"What? Me? Never," she said. "Besides, has no one

bothered to inform you that that is not exactly a conversational ploy to use with a lady?"

"I thought that sort of nonsense applied only to ladies
on whom one had designs."

"Are you telling me you no longer have designs on
me?" she teased.

"I think you cured me of that," Luke said. "I like
you better as a friend anyway."

She impulsively squeezed his arm. "Oh, Luke, I am
so glad. I have much more need of a friend than a
suitor."

He looked into her eyes with the sincere devotion of
friendship. He patted her hand on his arm and they went
on to talk animatedly of other matters.

She looked up to catch Rolsbury looking at them.
She could not read his expression, but she thought it
might be disapproving.

Very late in the evening, when they had already bade
their guests good night, Thorne sought out his younger
brother and offered him a nightcap of brandy.

"You must have something on your mind," Luke said
and Thorne thought he detected a hint of trepidation in
his tone.

Thorne finished pouring and handed his brother a
glass. "I have. I have been thinking of what you said
several weeks ago."

"About what?"

"About your being nearly of age and your capability
of deciding certain matters for yourself."

"Is that so?" Luke sounded confused.

"I merely wanted you to know that I shall put no
obstacles in your way should you wish to pay your addresses to . . . well, to any young lady."

"I . . . I do not quite understand."

"What I am trying to say is that, should you decide to marry, I will not stand in your way. Nor will I deny you access to your fortune in that event."

"Oh. Well . . . that is nice to know—gives me a deal more freedom, does it not? Annabelle will be surprised. I told her you were a great gun!"

This comment confirmed Thorne's view of the relationship between his brother and Miss Richardson.

The next morning Annabelle arose to discover it had rained during the night; in fact, there was still a fine drizzle coming down.

"The weather has effectively postponed our picnic outing," their hostess announced with regret at breakfast.

"Never mind, Lady Conwick," Aunt Gertrude said. "I feel certain we can all busy ourselves indoors."

And so they did.

Annabelle knew the gentlemen gathered in the billiards room located on the ground floor. It opened onto a covered terrace, thus allowing them opportunity to go out and smoke occasionally. The ladies all gathered in the drawing room where Helen Rhys played the pianoforte softly as others sat around reading, doing needlework, or playing cards. Annabelle sat at a small writing table which had a pull-down leaf with a blotting pad. Behind the leaf were concealed quills, ink, and other paraphernalia for writing. A drawer beneath contained fine vellum paper with the Rolsbury crest. She had been intending for some weeks to write Mr. Murray. Only lately had the idea for a new book jelled in her mind and now she burned to get it down for his approval.

She wrote quickly, dipping the quill pen repeatedly as her fingers fought to keep up with the words forming in her mind.

"Oh, dear!" she murmured softly as the quill slipped

from her fingers at one point, sending scattered splatters of ink across the page. She sighed and began to recopy the page, finally slipping the damaged page to the bottom of the stack of paper. When she was finished, she folded her letter carefully, sealed it with wax, and slipped the missive into her pocket. She would ask Marcus to frank it for her later.

She then wandered over to the card table where Celia and Letty were at play with Mrs. Sawyer.

"Will you join us, Annabelle?" Letty asked. " 'Tis more fun if we have partners."

"Oh, yes! Isn't it just?" Celia gave a naughty giggle.

"Celia, dear, do behave," Letty admonished as the others laughed.

Annabelle joined them and they passed the time until luncheon was announced.

By noon the rain had stopped and most of the guests welcomed the chance to be outdoors in the clean-smelling air. A number of the gentlemen went off for the afternoon to hunt pheasants. Other men stayed behind to accompany their ladies on ambling walks along the graveled paths in the Manor's extensive gardens. In the evening, when the gentlemen rejoined the ladies after dinner, there were more card games and a lively game of charades.

As she climbed into bed, Annabelle thought that, all in all, it had been a very pleasant day. Not once, so far in the visit, had anyone even mentioned Emma Bennet or her work.

The next day dawned sunny and bright and the picnic was back on the day's schedule. The abbey ruins—remains of a once-magnificent achievement of man—were enhanced by the magnificent achievements of nature that surrounded them—woods and a lake.

The Rolsbury guests reached the site of the picnic after a carriage ride of a quarter of an hour. Several of the gentlemen, including their host, chose to arrive on horseback. The Rolsbury servants had already set up a table with covered dishes of food. And there were a number of blankets spread upon the ground.

Off to one side, Annabelle noted that the hoops and pegs for a game of Pall Mall had been set into the ground and there was a basket with the colored balls and wooden mallets needed for the game. A net for lawn tennis had also been set up with the "court" marked out on the grass with powdered chalk.

"Goodness! Rolsbury's staff must have been out here at dawn," Harriet commented as the vehicle carrying her, Celia, Letty, and Annabelle arrived at the picnic spot.

"I would venture to say that the reclusive Earl of Rolsbury has outdone himself these last few days," Letty said. "Oh, thank you, dear." The marquis, the first of the riders to dismount, extended his hand to assist his wife and the other ladies from their carriage.

Annabelle noticed that Thorne performed the same service for the ladies in the next carriage, including Helen Rhys. She immediately took herself to task for her recurring twinges of jealousy. She had never before resented others' happiness or friendships. Why should he not seek out the blond beauty? They would probably be a good match. But this idea sent her spirits plummeting.

"Annabelle!" Luke's voice distracted her from that pointless train of thought. "Would you care to go on the lake?"

"On the lake?" she asked blankly, looking toward the water.

He laughed. "There are rowboats. I am not asking

you to walk on water—though I daresay an angel such as you might manage such."

She grinned as he came to take her arm. "If you continue with such taradiddles, the *devil* will be after you!"

Luke led her toward the lake. Sure enough, there were several rowboats that had been previously hidden by a small rise in the ground. He held a boat steady as she got in and sat down, then clambered in himself and used an oar to push the vessel away from the bank.

Both were silent until they were some distance out. Annabelle looked back to the bank where the ladies' colorful dresses and parasols stood out like bright flowers against the more staid greens and grays of their natural surroundings. She trailed her hand lazily in the water.

"What a glorious day," she said.

"Thought you seemed a bit blue-deviled earlier."

"You, sir, are too perceptive by half."

"Do you want to talk about whatever is bothering you?"

"Maybe—sometime. But not now. This day is too perfect to be marred with petty problems."

He gave her a penetrating look. "As you wish, fair lady. But if you need a friend's ear, you know where to find one."

"Thank you, Luke. I am so glad we have come to that."

"To what?"

"Being friends. I like you so much better as a friend . . ." Her voice trailed off as she worried that she might be embarrassing him.

"Better than a suitor, you mean," he said frankly.

"Well . . . yes."

She saw color flood his face briefly. "I suppose I was pretty obnoxious," he admitted glumly.

"Well . . . yes." She deliberately repeated her words and smiled to take the sting out of them. "But I must own that such attentions were flattering, too. Mind you," she warned, "I need no more such flattery."

"Never fear, my friend. I learned my lesson. If Thorne had not impressed it upon me, that Bennet woman's ridiculous story would have done it!"

"Did that story hurt you so very badly then?"

"Truthfully?"

"Yes, truthfully."

"At first I was mad as hops about it. People kept giving me these sly looks, you know. But then, after a while, I reread the thing. It really is pretty funny."

"Do you truly think so?"

He chuckled. "Yes. Especially the part where the older brother was giving 'Lester' advice how to butter up a young lady with flummery."

Annabelle said nothing, but she squirmed inwardly.

Luke went on. " 'Course, Thorne didn't think it was so funny—at least not then."

"And he does now?" She wondered if Lord Rolsbury would be able to forgive and forget.

"I don't rightly know. He hasn't said anything lately. I imagine he's still peeved about it, though. Thorne usually just blows up about things—and then it's over. He has not been able to vent his anger at the unknown Miss Bennet, you see."

"Oh, I would not say that," Annabelle argued.

"You refer to that article he wrote?"

"Yes, he was quite specific in his criticism there."

"I suppose he was." Luke's tone was rather vague. "Don't tell Thorne, will you? . . . But I didn't read all of that article. Not my cup of tea, you see."

"Oh, yes. I do see." She was silent for a few minutes, then a movement near the boat caught her attention. "Look, Luke! Look! There's a fish. It's hu-uge!"

He laughed. "Not that huge at all. But this lake is full of carp and they can get quite large."

"Well, it looks big to me," she said defensively.

A number of others had joined them on the lake and there was some banter about the fish and competition among the rowers. Annabelle was glad to leave the subject of Emma Bennet.

Thorne was very conscious of Annabelle's going off with Luke. Was Luke even now attempting to advance his suit with her? Well, so be it, if that were so. And if he were to be successful? Well . . . Thorne had no idea *how,* but he would learn to live with such a possibility.

Thorne had included on his guest list other young, single people in addition to his brother and Miss Richardson. There were the Rhyses, of course, as well as Clara Wentworth, a red-headed sprite who had made her come-out this Season. She had arrived accompanied by her parents. Thorne was well aware that the mama in that quarter harbored some hope of her daughter becoming a countess.

He was therefore pleased but puzzled by Luke's behavior. Having returned from rowing on the lake with Annabelle, that infernal boy joined a party including Miss Wentworth to go off hunting wildflowers. Later, Luke joined Miss Wentworth when the luncheon was served.

The meal was an *al fresco* affair with the food arranged attractively on a table brought for that purpose. A server stood behind the table ready to offer assistance and replenish dishes as needed. Guests filled their plates and then found convenient spots at any of a number of rustic tables with benches that seemed permanent fixtures at this site. When they were settled, footmen offered them a choice of drinks.

Seeing Annabelle momentarily alone, Thorne thought to join her, but he was waylaid by Helen Rhys.

"Will you join my brother and me?" she asked brightly. "Oh, and do allow me to assist you, Thorne. I am sure that infernal stick of yours is most inconvenient."

He found himself rather resenting her ostentatious kindness. After all, had he not planned this affair carefully so that he would not *need* such assistance? Immediately, he also wondered why he felt resentful toward Helen. Had he not on previous occasions happily accepted such aid from Annabelle?

Nevertheless, he joined the Rhys brother and sister and the Sawyers. The meal over, a number of guests, fully sated, stretched out on the blankets. Others took leisurely strolls around the abbey ruins. Certain couples chose this time to go rowing, and Thorne saw that Luke had taken Miss Wentworth out this time. Helen hinted strongly about going out on the lake, but Thorne managed to escape this by pleading duties as host. He made a small show of conferring with his aunt to cover what might otherwise appear to be rudeness.

Lady Conwick chuckled softly. "That gel's got to you, has she?"

"I . . . uh . . . which one?"

She laughed even harder, though discreetly, and leaned closer. "I wondered how long you would welcome those clinging ways. Miss Rhys has her eye on you—or I miss my guess."

"Aunt Dorothy! Do you never cease seeing possible matches in unmarried persons?"

"No. Never." There was not a shred of embarrassment in her tone. "I have never understood why anyone would go to a menagerie to watch animals cavort. Watching people is far more entertaining." They sat in silence for a few moments, then she added, "You know, I have been forced to alter my opinion of Miss Richardson."

"Oh? In what manner?" He tried to sound casual.

"Well, I doubt she is a fortune hunter." This time her laugh had a touch of irony.

"No. She is not."

"And—now that I have seen her in action, so to speak, I doubt she is one of those misses who measure their own worth by the number of broken hearts they leave in their wake."

"Is that so?" He made no effort to hide his amusement at his aunt's change of heart.

Lady Conwick's tone became more serious. "But I fear that young lady is in for real disappointment in life."

"Why would you think that? She has looks, wealth, charm—all the attributes that sell well on the marriage mart. And," he added softly, "she is intelligent, well-read . . . and . . . and, well, interesting."

He knew he had said too much when his aunt cocked her head to the side and gave him a questioning look.

"Well—they do. Sell well. Do they not?" He sounded lame even to himself.

She apparently decided to let him off the hook. "Oh, yes. Those are worthy traits. But Miss Richardson is an all-or-nothing kind of person. She holds out for a love match."

"How do you know that?"

"I heard her talking with her friends, Mrs. Hart and Lady Winters. They were teasing her rather unmercifully about Lord Stimson."

"And . . . ?" he prompted, again striving for a casual tone to cover inward tension.

"And she did not hesitate to put them in their places. Told them very precisely that she would never marry for any reason but love."

"Did she now?" He felt a heavy packet of lead lying in his gut. "Well, Luke—"

"Luke!" Aunt Dorothy issued a decidedly unladylike snort. "No, the wind does not lie in that direction—any more than with Stimson. In three Seasons, that little gel has not found a direction. I wonder if she ever will."

Thorne did not respond. Was his aunt right? Was poor Luke doomed to disappointment after all? Why did that notion fill Luke's brother with relief?

He looked around and spotted Annabelle in the center of a small group. He saw her lean forward and pat Frederick Hart's arm, then she threw back her head and laughed, her hair catching the sunlight.

In that instant, he knew. He was himself in love with Annabelle Richardson.

Eleven

So—the stalwart Earl of Rolsbury was not immune to Cupid's capricious arrows. This discovery rocked Thorne mightily. He tried to hide it away, even from himself. However, for the rest of the afternoon, his eyes strayed to wherever Annabelle was and he noticed—jealously—whoever it was she talked or laughed with.

When the day waned and chill threatened, the party returned to the Manor house. Throughout the evening he found himself looking first for Annabelle whenever he stepped into a room. Much, much later as he lay abed, he tried to examine this strange behavior. Then it hit him. He had, in fact, been doing these things for weeks. He fell asleep wearing a silly grin. The next morning he would ride with Annabelle again.

Morning brought a wake-up of another sort. Here he was—looking forward to a meeting with Annabelle, but he truly had no idea of her feelings—or Luke's. Years of looking out for Luke's welfare and the more recent ones of watching and guiding as his younger brother bridged the gap between boyhood and manhood would not be forsworn. If Luke's feelings were truly engaged . . .

He shook himself. That was not likely. Had Luke not spent most of the previous afternoon with Miss

Wentworth? Yes, he had—but he had also been Annabelle's partner at a card table most of that evening. What was more—or what was worse from Thorne's perspective—Annabelle always had a ready smile for Luke and the two of them seemed to enjoy a special camaraderie.

Again, he shook himself. His whole world was turned topsy-turvy. Never before had he been in the untenable position of envying his younger brother!

He reached the stables only moments before Annabelle arrived. He hesitated briefly before deciding *not* to ask a groom to accompany them. He might never again have time alone with her and he was in no mood to share her company. So what if they continued to bend the rules of propriety a bit?

Annabelle's blue riding habit set off the honey-brown color of her hair. Designed on the popular pseudo-military style, it was trimmed with black epaulettes and black frogging. Her black silk hat was also a feminine version of masculine headgear, the light blue veiling on it adding a softness to the whole look. Thorne thought she looked very fetching—even before she flashed him that glorious smile.

When she was mounted, she gathered up her reins and waited for him to mount, then shook an admonitory finger at him. "No wagers today, Thorne. I am inclined to think you and that black beast there took unfair advantage of poor Jessie and me the other day."

"Unfair advantage—? May I remind you, my dear, that her *real* name is Jezebel?"

She patted the mare's neck. "Do not pay him any mind, will you, Jessie?"

They rode aimlessly and in comfortable silence for a few moments.

"Have you a preference on where you would like to go?" he asked.

"Yes," she answered without hesitation. "I reread Mr.

Wordsworth's lines on Tintern Abbey last night. I should like to see that view again."

"By all means. We shall come upon it from a slightly different direction, though." Her wanting to repeat an experience they had shared pleased him.

As they rode through a wooded area, the sounds of birds and the mild wind soughing through the trees mingled with occasional creaks of leather and the horses' hooves on rocky trails.

Annabelle took a deep breath. "The country has its very own perfume, does it not?"

"Wood and pine and dead leaves—that is your idea of perfume?" He gave her a teasing smile.

"I smell violets as well—and . . . perhaps honeysuckle?"

"Perhaps."

"I freely admit I am not much of an English country girl. My earliest memories are of Jamaica and the plantation. Then I came to England and that first—truly horrid—school."

"I think most boarding school experiences—male or female—can be pretty awful at times," he said sympathetically.

"Mine was better than some. The best thing to come out of it, though, was my friendship with Letty."

"Interesting. Winters and I were good friends at school, too."

"Yes, I know."

"You do?" He was mildly surprised.

"Letty told me." She pulled on the reins to stop her mount and pointed at the side of the path. "See? Violets."

"Yes. Now—if we find honeysuckle as well, you will be fully vindicated, my dear."

They rode on at a leisurely pace.

"Well," she said, returning to their topic, "school was

tolerable, but I really learned more useful lessons from Marcus and Harriet. She was my principal instructor for nearly a year."

"Was she?"

"Then Letty and I both changed to a school Celia attended. That was great fun. However," she added in a firm tone, "should I ever have children, they will be educated at home until they are about . . . oh, thirty, I think."

He gave a bark of laughter at this absurdity.

"Well, maybe a little earlier," she conceded. "But, believe me, *my* children will not be sent off to a boarding school to be rid of them."

"Will your husband not have some say in the matter?"

"Oh, yes. But if he intends any degree of domestic felicity, I believe he will cooperate on this small matter."

"Small matter." He laughed again. "I can see you will be a wife to be reckoned with!"

She blushed furiously and laughed. "However did we get off to such a topic?" They broke out of the shade of the trees and there was relief in her voice as she said, "Ah, we are here, I see."

He dismounted, then reached to help her dismount. He grabbed his walking stick, which he had thrust into a special loop on his saddle. It was still early and the sun shone on the scene below at an oblique angle, casting strange and interesting shadows. They stood very close and in utter silence, taking it all in. He caught a whiff of the lilac scent of her hair and leaned closer to breathe more deeply of it. Just then, she turned and their heads bumped.

"I'm sorry," she said.

"My fault." He was embarrassed, but not uneasy. "You are wearing a lilac scent, I believe."

She gazed into his eyes and said, "Yes, they are my

favorite flowers." However, the words were lost in the message of her eyes.

"I like them, too," he said meaninglessly.

He pulled her close and lowered his mouth to hers. He dropped the stick and tightened his arms around her, conscious of her arms around his neck. She was neither shy nor coy. Her response was open, honest, and enthusiastic. When he pulled back, she seemed dazed.

"Thorne?" It was a question.

"I . . . Annabelle . . ." He could not help himself. He took her lips again in a kiss that was at once firm yet gentle, demanding and seeking. And—wonder of wonders—what he demanded she gave. What he sought, she supplied.

He finally gripped her shoulders and put her from him slightly. "My God!" he breathed. "I never . . ."

"Nor did I," she said, almost as though she read his mind. She wrenched her gaze from his and turned in his arms to look out on the increasingly sunny scene below them. He wondered fleetingly how much of it either of them actually saw. He clasped his hands around her waist and pressed his face against her neck. He drank in her scent, lilac mixed with some special essence of her, and touched his lips against the soft flesh beneath her ear.

"Annabelle? You felt it, too. I know you did."

"Yes, Thorne, I did." Instead of gladness, there was remorse in her tone. "But it cannot be."

He released her. "I see." He stared silently out on the scenery before them. But he did not see—not at all.

He bent to pick up the abandoned walking stick and it crossed his mind that perhaps *that* was the cause of her hesitation. Well, he thought bitterly, why *would* a young, vibrant woman such as Annabelle Richardson—a woman who could have practically any man of her choosing—why would such a woman welcome the addresses of a cripple?

He helped her remount and they turned the horses toward the stables. They engaged in polite conversation, but later he remembered not one word either had said—and he would have wagered she did not remember either.

That kiss had unnerved Annabelle as nothing else in her life ever had. The previous kiss, in the garden at the Finchley ball, had been but a prelude to what this one had done to her. She had noted his casual use of endearments. It probably meant little, but she hugged it to her. She had been on the verge of telling him about Emma Bennet, but she could not stand the thought of seeing his warm regard for her turn to disgust. She had foolishly compounded the initial problem by not owning up to writing that infernal story. Of course, she had had no notion of falling in love with the man—

Falling in love?

Had she indeed fallen in love with the one man in all of Britain who had the strongest of reasons to dislike her?

Surely not.

But she had.

And her own foolishness, her own cowardice had doomed that love before it had even blossomed.

Thank goodness she and the Wyndhams were leaving Rolsbury Manor on the morrow, she thought miserably.

Thorne returned to the house in despair. But he was also angry. He could not believe Annabelle would reject him only because he walked with a limp. Not after that "dance" at the Finchley ball. Yet she offered no other reason. And she had certainly not been repulsed by his kiss. However, he was damned if he would go crawling to her, begging for an explanation. That really would be the mark of a weak cripple!

He tried—none too successfully—to put the matter from his mind. She had not yet come back down when he went to the breakfast room. He hurried through the meal, chafing at the necessity to keep up with the inane chatter around him. He finally escaped briefly to the library.

He was sitting, staring unseeing at papers on his desk, when his housekeeper asked for a word with him.

"What is it, Mrs. Petry?" He noticed she had a sheet of paper in her hand.

"My lord, while your company was away for the day at the picnic, the staff took the opportunity to do a thorough cleaning."

"Very good," he responded absently.

"One of the maids found this paper in the desk in the drawing room. It appears to be waste, but she wasn't sure and neither was I. There is no name of a guest on it." She laid the paper on his desk.

He glanced at it. It was a letter—or the beginning of one. To a Mr. Murray. Now why was that name familiar? He examined the thing more closely. The tone was quite formal. A proposal for a book? Then he remembered. Of course. Murray was a publisher. Emma Bennet's publisher, among others! He looked more closely at the script.

With a sinking feeling, he opened a desk drawer and retrieved the sample of Emma Bennet's handwriting he had obtained from the printer. It was a perfect match.

Good God! The woman had been a guest in his home for the past week! But who was she?

"Mrs. Petry, will you please find Lady Conwick and ask her to wait upon me here?"

"Certainly, my lord."

A few minutes later, his aunt came in with a puzzled look on her face. "What is it, Thorne?"

He held out the paper. "This was found in the drawing room yesterday. It must have been written the previous day."

She took the paper and sat down in a chair opposite him to peruse it. She turned it over. "There is no name on it. You think one of our guests . . . ?"

"Must be one of them that wrote it. It was found in the writing desk in the west drawing room."

"Would you like me to ask the ladies who might have written it?"

"I doubt any of them would own up to it. Did you notice anyone writing at that desk?"

"Not really. I think several letters have been written in the last few days. Have you not franked some of them?"

"Yes. But none from this hand."

"What is so particular about this? It appears to be waste paper with all these ink splatters."

His voice was grim. *"This* was written by Emma Bennet."

"Emma—? Ohhh. . . . Are you sure?"

"Very sure."

"Right here in your own home?"

He gave a bitter laugh. "That's right. A viper has been in our midst."

"Oh, dear. What will you do?"

"I am not sure. I need to think on it. At least this narrows the hunt down considerably."

"How is that?"

"Instead of all the women in London, it has to be one of the twelve or fifteen who have been guests here the past week."

"But which one?"

He ran his hand distractedly through his hair. "I cannot call them all together and ask for handwriting samples. I am sorely tempted to do so, mind you, but I am no Bow Street Runner."

"You had best act quickly, dear boy. The Meltons are leaving after luncheon today and most of the others depart tomorrow morning."

"I am aware of that," he said glumly.

"Wait! I know!" She leaned forward eagerly.

"You know who wrote this?"

"No. But I know how you may find out who did."

He raised a quizzical brow and waited.

"Thank-you notes!"

"Thank-you notes?" He wondered if his aunt spent too much time talking only with her dogs.

"Yes. Do you not see? Each of the women will undoubtedly pen you a thank-you note. It is the polite thing to do. And then you will have your answer."

Thorne was dubious about this solution. If it produced no results, he *would,* by God!, hire Bow Street Runners to track down every woman who had been here in the last week!

The house party wound down and he bade his guests farewell. Mrs. Wentworth seemed disappointed and Helen sighed heavily, but finally they, too, were gone. Annabelle and the Wyndhams were among the earlier departures.

Luke seemed at loose ends for a few days and finally took himself off to join a friend's yachting party. There was no mention of his calling on Annabelle. Thorne buried himself once again in estate business, often going out to join laborers in hard physical work. However, Annabelle's passion and rejection and Emma Bennet's deceit were never far from his mind. He mentally ticked off the female guests. Who among them would have the intelligence and talent to produce Miss Bennet's work?

There was Lady Wyndham, of course. Reclusive as he had been in recent years, even he had heard the stories—never openly confirmed—of her being the political writer known as "Gadfly" some years before. Fiction seemed rather a far cry from political tracts, though.

Lady Hermiston? Wyndham's aunt was a possibility. He remembered suspecting her before. Celia and Letty were intelligent enough, but he wondered if Celia had such powers of concentration. Letty was a better possibility, for the marchioness certainly moved in the most exalted circles.

Helen Rhys seemed most unlikely—she had never indicated any interest in literary matters—except as a means to an end, he thought ruefully. He frankly doubted Helen's friend, Mrs. Sawyer, was bright enough to have created the characters and flow of prose that delighted so in Miss Bennet's early work.

Annabelle? He finally let himself come to her. Please, God, not her. But he had to admit that many things clicked with her. Her ready wit, her knowledge of the literary scene—she was no mere bystander at the meetings of the Literary League. Even the name *Emma Bennet,* now that he considered it closely, would appeal to Annabelle and her love of Miss Austen's work. Had the inimitable Jane Austen not used those very names with key characters? Against his will, he concluded that Annabelle was, indeed, a likely prospect.

The next day, he knew for sure.

His aunt had been right.

Annabelle Richardson's thank-you note was written in the same script as that printer's sample of Emma Bennet's handwriting.

Twelve

Thorne sat for some minutes, stunned. It was one thing to suspect, quite another to be hit on the head by the truth of one's suspicions. Soon enough his shock became fury and the fury intensified to a white-hot level.

It was not enough that she had written that ridiculous piece—she had compounded her treachery with this elaborate hoax. She had been laughing at him for weeks! While he was falling in love with her, she was enjoying a great joke at his expense. That must have amused her mightily!

How *could* he have been so wrong about her? He had thought her so honest—and possessed of a generosity of spirit that was entirely natural. Instead, deceit and mean-spirited shallowness marked her character. . . .

He congratulated himself on having learned the truth before he had made a *complete* fool of himself. Why, he had virtually given Luke permission to bring her into the family! Good God! Face it, Rolsbury, he sneered at himself, you came within a hair's breadth of offering for her yourself. In his mind he again heard her say, "It cannot be." Had she been laughing inwardly even then?

Hamlet was wrong. It was not *frailty* whose name was *woman,* but *deceit.*

How *could* he have been so damned wrong about her? How *could* he have misinterpreted her response to his kisses so? She had not *appeared* to be an accomplished flirt. She seemed to be open, honest, and giving. Yet, there it was—Annabelle Richardson was Emma Bennet.

He gave the bellpull a harsh jerk. When Larkins, the butler, answered, he said, "Bring me a bottle of brandy."

"Very good, my lord." Larkins was obviously surprised at such a request at this hour of the day, but was too well trained to betray his emotion.

"And I am not to be disturbed—for anything!"

A few minutes later, Larkins returned with the bottle and a single glass on a tray.

For three days, the Earl of Rolsbury remained shrouded in an alcoholic fog, trying to shield himself from pain. However, Annabelle's image kept intruding. Her golden brown hair, laughing brown eyes, and that delicate lilac scent—all assailed him when he least expected them.

He was vaguely aware that members of his staff were perplexed by his behavior. He even ignored important decisions on estate matters, refusing to see his steward. On the third day he sat in disheveled splendor in a chair in front of the fireplace in the library. He had spent the better part of each of the last two days in this same spot—brandy bottle at hand.

There was a knock on the door.

"Go away!" he shouted.

But the door opened and his aunt entered, carrying one of her dogs. "I have come to bid you farewell. I am returning to town."

"Deserting a sinking ship, are you? Well, I cannot say I blame you."

He struggled to rise, but it was obviously such an effort for him that she waved him back to his seat and quickly took the opposite chair.

"If I thought for even a moment that I could be of help to you, I would, of course, stay. But there are things in town I could be doing."

"Have a good journey."

She did not move. Her eyes expressed puzzlement and sympathy. "Thorne, I have never seen you like this. Can you not tell me—someone—what has put you in such a state?"

He knew she worried about him, but how could he possibly explain the degree of his humiliation? "Suffice it to say, I have suffered g-great disappointment," he said in a mockingly dramatic tone, his words slurred only slightly by drink.

"I can see *that* much," she said in mild disgust. "I strongly suspect this has something to do with Emma Bennet. Have you discovered who she is?"

"Oh, yes."

"And . . . ? Are you—or are you not—going to share this information?"

He did not answer for a long while. Finally, with that same studied precision of one far gone in drink, he said, "Not just yet, I think. Need to c-contemplate the matter and decide on a course of action."

"I see . . . Well, your powers of concentration would be greatly improved if you stopped muddying them with *that*." She pointed to the bottle.

"Perhaps. But . . ." His voice trailed off. He could not bring himself to explain—even to Aunt Dorothy—that the amber fluid helped dull his pain, if only temporarily.

She rose and put a hand on his shoulder, pressing him back into his own chair. "I should like to help, my dear, but I have an idea this is a matter of the heart—and one you must resolve for yourself."

He covered her hand with one of his own. "I shall

survive. You must not fret about me. I always come about—eventually."

She squeezed his shoulder and kissed his brow. "Right, dear. Boney did not keep you down, so some slip of a girl is unlikely to do so. Come, Sir Lancelot," she called to the dog, which jumped down from the chair she had vacated.

Ridiculous name for a dog, Thorne thought. Only later did his aunt's parting words sink in. What did *she* know of "some slip of a girl?"

Annabelle welcomed the return to Timberly, the primary seat of the Earl of Wyndham. Timberly had once been a glorious medieval castle complete with moat and crenelated wall and towers. The moat had long since been drained and the wall quarried for building stones for tenant cottages. However, the main house was still a marvelous structure that never failed to fascinate. The surrounding countryside afforded scenic riding trails.

She spent long hours in the saddle. Her rides served two purposes. She not only tried to sort out her feelings about Thorne, she also tried to resolve difficulties in the writing she was doing—difficulties that arose when images of the Earl of Rolsbury intruded too heavily for her to continue. After yet another hard ride one morning, she returned to the house, changed out of her habit into a muslin day dress, and made her appearance in the breakfast room. Harriet was alone there.

"The others have already finished?" Annabelle asked.

"Yes. Marcus had some business to attend to and Aunt Gertrude has gone into the village."

Neither said anything as Annabelle made her selection from the sideboard and poured herself a cup of coffee from a china pot on the table. Harriet set her own cup back on its saucer.

"Are you ready yet to talk about whatever it is that is bothering you?"

Annabelle smiled ruefully. "I thought I had covered myself so well, too."

"Not well enough to fool those who love you. What is it, Annabelle? Can I help?"

"Probably not. I have fairly done it, this time."

"Are we discussing Emma Bennet again?" Harriet asked.

"And Thorne Wainwright."

"What happened? Did you tell him . . . ?"

"No. And that is the whole problem. How *can* I tell him at this point?" It was a cry of pure anguish.

"Oh, my dear girl." Harriet rose and took the chair next to Annabelle. She put her arm around the younger woman's shoulder. "You care for him so very much, do you?"

Annabelle sucked in a deep breath, stifling a sob. "Yes. Yes, I do. And it is so . . . so . . . impossible!"

"Are you quite sure of that?"

Annabelle nodded. "Perhaps if I had told him immediately . . . but it did not seem important then. And now . . . it is far too late."

"Maybe. Maybe not." Harriet sounded encouraging. "What if you wrote him a note explaining it all to him—"

"No! I cannot *write* it. I have behaved the coward enough. This is something I must tell him face-to-face."

"You should have the opportunity to do so at the harvest festival in a few weeks. Rolsbury accepted our invitation, you know."

A few days later, however, Harriet came into the drawing room waving a note. Annabelle caught a glimpse of the Rolsbury crest.

"Rolsbury is not coming to our harvest celebration," Harriet announced.

A lead ingot settled in Annabelle's innards. "Does he say why?"

"No, not really."

"What about Luke?"

Harriet glanced at the note. "This says nothing of Luke, so I assume he, at least, will join us. Rolsbury writes that estate business requires his presence in Lincolnshire. This is addressed to Marcus and he ends by saying he looks forward to working with Marcus on parliamentary matters at a later date."

"May I see it?"

Harriet handed her the note. She read it slowly. Then she reread it. Finally, she handed it back. "The tone is very formal."

"Yes. I noticed that, too. He does ask that Marcus convey 'regards to your family.' "

Annabelle could not hide her hurt at his not mentioning her or sending *her* a note of his intent to forego the hospitality at Timberly. She had looked forward to the prospect of seeing him, even knowing that telling him of Emma Bennet would be extremely difficult.

Now he was not coming. And he had offered the flimsiest of excuses. But *why?*

Timberly's harvest celebration continued as planned, including a house party, a three-day market fair, and a grand ball. It was an annual affair that dated back to the Middle Ages. Annabelle had always loved this most important of holidays, for it brought the entire Jeffries family together. The Earl of Wyndham's younger brother and sister customarily returned to Timberly then, along with their ever-growing families.

This gathering always made Annabelle feel that she really belonged—that she was very much a treasured member of the clan. For a young girl devoid of family, this acceptance had been an important turning point in her life. Now, she had a distinct feeling that she was on the threshold of another such turning point, but she knew she could not pass through that portal quite yet.

Luke arrived and his cheerful enthusiasm did much to lift Annabelle's spirits. He conveyed his brother's regrets again, and expressed his own happiness at being at Timberly.

He joined Annabelle on her morning rides. One day they had paused to rest at a scenic spot. They dismounted and sat on a huge flat boulder. The groom who satisfied Society's dictates of propriety watched over the horses as they cropped grass nearby.

"I see why you love this place so," he told her. "It has vistas rivaling those at Rolsbury."

"Yes. I suppose it does." She recalled the abbey there as seen from the cliff and the man who had shared that special view with her. "Th-Thorne is well, I assume?"

"Oh, yes. Working very hard, though. Wouldn't even take a break to go fishing in Scotland with me—and he loves to fish. Taught me himself."

"I did not know that about him." She said this casually, making conversation, but in truth she hoarded every scrap of information about Thorne that Luke gave out.

"Come to think of it," Luke went on, "he's been out of sorts."

"Do you know why?"

"No, I don't. I went off yachting—mostly in the Channel—and when I came back, he was like a bear with a sore paw. Almost like he was after Waterloo."

"But he has come around, has he not?" she asked.

"Some. He is involved in so many projects, though, it quite makes a sane person's head spin."

"What sorts of projects?"

"Well, let me see." He ticked them off on his fingers. "There's an irrigation project—if it works on Rolsbury, he will expand it to other properties. Then there's the one involving breeding sheep for better wool. He is building two schools that I know of."

"Schools?"

"Yes. Day schools. One in the village for villagers' and farmers' children. And another over near Holston-Weir—that's where the Rolsbury Knitting Mills are located."

"I see." Once again she realized how very wrong she had once been about the Earl of Rolsbury. "Schools for workers' children? That is not likely to go over well in certain circles."

"No. It doesn't. I believe Thorne has had some strong letters. Lord Teasdale called personally—very irate, he was—to complain about it. He told Thorne that he and other mill owners see such things as schools and improved housing and medical care for workers to be merely a foolish waste of money."

"How does Thorne react to such criticism?"

Luke shrugged. "He just says it is the right thing to do."

"Hmm." She sat quietly for a time, thinking of the attitudes of other landowners and mill owners. "Luke, I have long meant to ask you about something . . ."

He looked at her, swishing his riding crop back and forth against the toes of his boots. "Ask away."

"Thorne told me once there was—an 'unpleasant history,' I think he said—between him and Lord Beelson."

"He told you *that?*" Luke was clearly surprised.

She nodded. "And I wondered about it—but I would not intrude on his—or your—privacy. . . ."

Luke scratched his head. "He told me something similar, but I have no idea what it is. Must be something that happened when I first went away to school."

"Oh. Well . . . I was merely curious."

As they prepared to return to the stables, Luke added, "Thorne is not usually one to carry a grudge, though."

Annabelle found this heartening. Maybe after she told him the truth of Emma Bennet, he would at least continue to be courteous.

Annabelle threw herself into her writing during the waning months of the year. She had long since received Mr. Murray's enthusiastic approval of her project. It was by far her most ambitious undertaking to date.

Her heroine, Portia, was a talented artist from a prominent family. Portia's pencil drawings were as important and as expressive as the paintings later made from them. Because Society not only frowned on women bringing attention to themselves, but also had a general tendency to denigrate the works of women, the artist hid her identity. She was further motivated to work in a cloak of anonymity to protect her family from public censure that might carry over to them. The hero was Nathan, a proud man whom the artist admired. However, one of her drawings, intended as a working sketch for a painting and which seemed to depict him in an unfavorable light, was inadvertently published in a newspaper and misunderstood by both Society and the gentleman himself.

"How is the new book coming along?" Harriet asked of Annabelle one day in late autumn.

The two of them had met for tea, both having been preoccupied elsewhere the whole day. Harriet announced that she had spent most of her time in the nursery and now welcomed adult company. Annabelle's ink-stained fingers bore testimony to how she had spent the day. Aunt Gertrude had returned to London right after the harvest festival. Marcus had gone hunting with some local men.

Annabelle had brought the first chapters with her to the drawing room, hoping to get Harriet's reaction. "See for yourself." She handed the pages over and sat quietly sipping her tea and nibbling biscuits as Harriet read.

"Good heavens! You are writing about yourself," Harriet said at last.

"Well, yes . . . and no. This is not merely Portia and Nathan's story. I am trying to convey also an overview of Society—blemishes as well as beauty. The heroine draws portraits of all sorts of people, you see. I have tried to make her *work* the focus of the story."

Harriet smiled and reached for her tea cup. "And only incidentally prove women capable of such creative work, is that it?"

"That *is* one of the underlying ideas, but I want the portraits of different *types* of people to come through."

"So far, it does—and without the strident tone of *Innocence Betrayed.*"

"I do hope so," Annabelle replied. "Actually, I *hope* this story is peopled with believable human beings. I want to present them sympathetically—even those who are basically silly and shallow have *reasons* for behaving as they do."

"I think you are doing that very well. This is far finer than any of your earlier work, Annabelle."

Annabelle basked in her mentor's praise for a few minutes.

Harriet spoke again. "There *is* this parallel between your heroine and yourself, though."

"Do you not think all writers put something of themselves into their characters? Maybe show their made-up heroes and heroines as the kind of people they would *like* to be?"

"Hmm. Probably. But this may cause yet more speculation about who Emma Bennet is."

"Well——" Annabelle drew a deep breath. "I think this book will signify Emma Bennet's come-out."

Harriet's eyebrows rose. "You will publish under your own name?"

"I plan to. I am truly tired of the subterfuge."

"Well, at least *you* are not likely to be accused of sedition."

Harriet's voice was laced with irony and Annabelle laughed sympathetically, for she knew Harriet referred to her own essays written under the pseudonym of "Gadfly." Certain reactionary members of the government had attempted to arrest the Gadfly for sedition.

"No, I will not," Annabelle said. "But my work may not prove any more acceptable in some quarters than Gadfly's did."

"We shall see. This is going to be quite good." Harriet handed the sheets back to Annabelle.

Portia and Nathan continued to occupy Annabelle's waking moments right through the Christmas and the seasonal festivities. Thorne Wainwright occupied her unwaking moments—against her will and in spite of her efforts to banish him. She would awake suddenly, still feeling his arms about her, his lips pressed to hers.

"This is ridiculous!" she muttered on more than one occasion. "You would hate me if you knew the truth. So—please—leave me alone."

She drove herself beyond the point of exhaustion every day. She spent long hours at her desk. She rode every day. And she played with the children every day so long as the nursery was full of visitors. "Auntie Belle" was a favorite playmate of the little ones.

When the Christmas and New Year celebrations were ended, Annabelle returned to London with Aunt Gertrude, who had come to Timberly for the holidays. The book was finished and Annabelle wanted to be there when Mr. Murray dealt with it. He had already seen and approved the first chapters, so she did not worry that he would not like it. Still—this was her baby. She wanted to be there. She admitted privately to caring more about this book than any of her previous work.

Accompanied by her maid and driven by Aunt Gertrude's coachman, Annabelle visited Mr. Murray in his own offices. Located in an area that was probably downright dangerous after darkness fell, Murray's working quarters consisted of a large room where several clerks sat copying. A low partition separated visitors from these scribes. Murray's office was in the rear. As soon as she was announced, he came running out.

"What are you doing here?" he asked, ushering her and Molly into his office and quickly closing the door. "Surely you know I cannot quell the speculation of my employees."

She took the comfortable seat he offered her across from his large mahogany desk and motioned Molly to a chair next to the wall. "We can talk about that later, sir. I want to discuss some minor details about the book."

"This is your best effort so far," he said, extracting her manuscript from a pile on his desk.

"I think so, too." She made no pretense of false modesty.

"This will be your break-out book."

"My what?"

"This one will break you out of the mold—the niche—into which your previous work has fallen. *This* one will be well received by the critics. Even Lord Rolsbury will be praising it in *The London Review.* Just you wait and see." Murray's enthusiasm was contagious.

She winced inwardly at his mention of Thorne's name,

but she smiled and said, "I hope the reading public will like it, too."

"They will."

They proceeded to cover the matters of text, over which Annabelle fretted. Murray pointed to some minor changes he wanted. Finally, they were finished and Murray returned to his initial concern.

"I am happy to see you, Miss Richardson, but really, I do wonder about the wisdom of your coming here. You should have sent me a message."

"It matters not. You see, I wish this one to be published under my own name."

"Are you quite sure of that?" There was dawning wonder in his voice, then Annabelle could see the businessman's calculation going on behind his affable smile.

"Yes," she said. "I have discussed this at length with Lord and Lady Wyndham. They agree that the protection of anonymity is no longer necessary. I shall be of age in only a few weeks, you see."

He seemed hesitant. "Hmm. You must know the name Emma Bennet would alone account for some of our initial sales. Takes time for a new name to catch on."

"I had not really thought about that," she said. "I am simply tired of hiding behind a pseudonym."

"We could put both names on the book." He seemed to weigh her response to this idea.

"Both?"

"Yes. Say, 'Miss Emma Bennet, also known as Miss Annabelle Richardson' or perhaps 'Miss Annabelle Richardson, who is Miss Emma Bennet' or '—who formerly wrote as—' or whatever phrasing you wish."

"I think I should like my own name first. Yes. I want to be frank and open about the authorship of this work."

"This comes as very good news to me, Miss Richardson." He rubbed his hands together. "It will sell a good many books—especially with your standing in Society."

"Perhaps . . ." She was doubtful.

"No 'perhaps' about it! It will mean increased sales."

"But that is not why I am doing this."

"I understand, Miss Richardson. You are the sort who would write whether you sold or no."

She laughed self-consciously. "You know me too well, I think."

"I know a good many *writers,* miss."

She felt the interested gazes of his staff as she and Molly left the office.

"Well, the die is cast," she muttered as she and Molly climbed into the waiting carriage.

"I beg your pardon, miss?"

"Never mind. 'Tis not important."

She wondered how Thorne Wainwright would react when he learned that Annabelle Richardson was Emma Bennet—or vice versa. Well, the book would not be out for another six weeks or so.

In the event, however, she did not have to wait that long to learn his reaction to such news.

Thirteen

Thorne returned to London early in the New Year, for he wanted to be in the city as the nation's political power brokers drifted back into the capital for the opening of Parliament and the social season. He hoped to begin building early—and strong—support for some of his reformist measures.

He knew the very word *reform* struck fear in many a breast. England still had vivid memories of the cataclysmic changes France had endured in the last thirty to forty years. Such fear in recent years had manifested itself in restrictions that appalled much of England's free-thinking citizenry. A number of basic freedoms had been severely curtailed.

Many, not necessarily motivated by fear, nevertheless advocated harsh restrictive measures because doing so achieved some self-serving end. Thus, Thorne saw many of his fellow mill owners instituting ever harsher measures against workers. Among the most vocal of these unfeeling fellows who fought tooth and nail to keep labor costs down was Viscount Beelson. The labor of women and children was vastly cheaper than that of men. Therefore, unscrupulous mill owners were especially vehement in their opposition to reforms that would curb exploitation of weak workers.

Specifically, they opposed any measures approving workers' rights to organize. Meetings of more than fifty people were banned. Education of poor children was simply a waste of public money. For some jobs—notably, cleaning chimneys or gaining access to veins of coal in narrow crevices—the smaller bodies of children were essential to the task. To oppose the use of children for such work was a threat to the natural order of things.

For the Thorne Wainwrights of the nation, it was beyond time for change. His days of military campaigns were over, but there were other battles to be fought and other strategies to employ. For the Beelsons of Britain, the status quo was just fine. So the battle lines were drawn and the battle*field* was Parliament.

Knowing that Lord Wyndham—despite his being a member of the opposite party—shared many of his views, Thorne visited their club on his first night back in town. He was disappointed to learn that the Wyndhams had not yet returned to the city. There *was* a positive side to the delay, he told himself. At least it would postpone the probably inevitable meeting with Annabelle.

The days had become weeks and the weeks blended into months, but he still thought of her often—the recurring positive images mixed inextricably with the pain of her deception. On the one hand, he dreaded seeing her again; on the other, he would dearly love to wring her pretty little neck!

The next night he attended a meeting of the London Literary League—and there she was.

Annabelle was surprised to see him. Celia had said nothing of his return to town when the two women had called on Letty in the afternoon. However, even had Letty or Celia known, there would be no special reason to inform their friend, would there? How could they know how nervous she was about seeing him again?

Annabelle wished now she had dressed more fashionably. She was wearing a simple gown of soft wool. Midnight blue and trimmed with light gray lace, it was one of her favorite outfits—but it was also a holdover from last year.

Their parting at Rolsbury Manor had been cordial, but reserved. She remembered thinking as they said their goodbyes that both of them seemed to be mindful of that kiss above the abbey ruins. Nevertheless, both had been formally polite as she and the Wyndhams took their leave. Would that cool formality prevail now at their first meeting since then?

As soon as he entered the room, he was taken up by first one small group and then another. Given the size and informality of these gatherings, he might avoid her all evening if he were so inclined. After all, he had chosen to ignore her for months now—proof positive, if she needed such, that their friendship—let alone those kisses—meant nothing to him. She tried, with little success, to concentrate on the conversations swirling around her. She wished she could leave, but Aunt Gertrude had especially desired to hear tonight's featured presentation on modern poetry.

In the way of these affairs, the persons she had been talking with drifted away and she stood momentarily alone. She turned abruptly on hearing his voice just behind and to the side of her. He was dressed in gray Cossack trousers and a dark green jacket that reflected the color of his eyes. He was simply the most attractive man in the room and all her senses leapt to attention at his nearness.

"Good evening, Miss Richardson."

"Good evening, Th—uh, Lord Rolsbury," she said,

"You are saying," she said, her voice at last clear, "that I, too, must show some family loyalty in protecting Marcus—and his goals."

Aunt Gertrude smiled. "Precisely. Can you do it?"

"I—I think so. In a few days."

"Do not hesitate too long. Marcus and Harriet will return to town soon."

Annabelle took another sip from the glass, then set it aside and squared her shoulders. "I shall pull through this. I know I will."

She bade Aunt Gertrude good night and at last escaped to her own chamber, where she allowed herself one last bout of tears, grieving for what might have been.

Thorne watched her leave the Melbourne drawing room, annoyed that he could not control his own conflicting emotions. He should be feeling triumphant, vindicated. Instead, he felt deflated. Those unshed tears shimmering in her eyes had nearly undone him. Part of him wanted to run after her—walking stick be damned—and take her in his arms to comfort her. Another part scorned that idea as foolish weakness.

He observed a footman approach Lady Hermiston and speak softly to her. She hurried from the room, but neither she nor Annabelle returned. When it dawned on him that he was responding to others with polite nothingness and not really listening to what they were saying to him, he took his own leave.

That night, for the first time in several weeks, he sought forgetfulness in a brandy bottle.

Over the next several days, more and more of the *ton* returned to the city and the social whirl picked up its pace to a fevered level. Thorne spent the days making calls, usually at the home of this or that Member of

Parliament who might lend him a sympathetic ear. His evenings were filled with routs, soirees, and an occasional dinner party. He did not accept invitations to balls. Not anymore. His acceptance of other invitations was entirely dependent on assessing the political advantage of attending an event.

"I swear, Thorne, you are becoming a real bore, always prosing on about some reform or another." Luke, who had returned to town two days after Thorne's encounter with Annabelle, grinned at his brother at the end of a rather unproductive day, in Thorne's view.

"Hmmph!" Thorne sniffed in derision. "One social flutterby in the family is quite enough."

Luke ignored this and said, "And what is wrong between you and Annabelle?"

Thorne was guarded in his response, for he had as yet said nothing to Luke—or anyone else—about Annabelle being Miss Bennet. "Why do you ask? What has she said?"

"She has said nothing—and that in itself is strange. Whenever *I* mention either of you to the other, you both change the subject."

"Well, then—leave it alone." Thorne hid his own confusion behind his blunt tone.

"As you wish, big brother." Luke changed the subject.

Thorne had no idea why he did not reveal the whole story to Luke. Was he actually protecting the woman who had held the Wainwrights up to ridicule? Or was he protecting Luke from hurt and disappointment if he knew the truth about his friend? Thorne preferred to think it was the latter, but was honest enough—at least with himself—to acknowledge a desire—nay, a need—to protect her as well. *This* fact brought more confusion and disgust aimed at himself. The whole sorry mess was over, for God's sake! Why could he not let it go?

Annabelle frequently appeared at the same large social affairs to which he was invited. When they met, each was studiously civil and each sought to avoid any prolonged contact. One evening he was invited to the Winters House for a dinner party. He knew this was to be Letty's first stint as hostess since presenting the Winters heir in November. Knowing how inseparable Letty, Celia, and Annabelle were, he steeled himself for Annabelle being there.

She had not yet arrived when he was announced. Nor did she come later. His pride would not allow him to ask about her, but he listened intently when Celia did so.

"Where is Annabelle?" she demanded of Letty. "I should have thought she would be here for the new mama's first outing."

Letty laughed. "This is not my first outing. It is merely the first I have hosted. But—to answer your question—she sent round a note saying she had a headache."

"Annabelle? A headache?" Celia's disbelief was clear.

"That is what her note said. She quite threw my numbers off."

"And when did *you* care overmuch about odds and evens at your table? Something is wrong," Celia said. "Did you have words with her over some trifle?"

"No, of course not. *Nor* about anything important."

"I shall call on her tomorrow and have the truth from her if I have to thrash her to do so."

"Do stop for me," Letty said. "I shall accompany you."

Thorne grinned at the image of Celia "thrashing" Annabelle with Letty in the midst. He found the evening pleasant, the conversation interesting, and the company charming. But something was missing. She rarely dominated everyone's attention, but Annabelle always added something warm and cheerful to a gathering.

* * *

Annabelle knew she really *was* acting the coward in not attending Letty's party. Letty had let slip the fact that Thorne would be there—*and* that it was to be a very small group. Annabelle felt sure she could not bear a whole evening of his chill in such a close atmosphere.

His attack at the League meeting had come as a shock. Yes, she wanted him to know the truth, but had feared his reaction to it. She had wanted to tell him herself—but now he had found out some other way. And he had certainly proved her fears well founded!

Having expended her store of tears that evening, she awoke the next morning to the ravages of her pain—swollen, puffy eyelids and a general redness that could not even be disguised with a veil. She fumed at Thorne Wainwright anew for forcing her to give up her morning ride. But that infernal man was getting no more tears from *her*.

She rang for Molly to order up cold cucumber slices for her eyelids. Molly returned with cucumbers, toast, and chocolate. Annabelle knew she could cure the effects of the tears. She could even will away additional tears. But she seemed to have precious little control over where her mind drifted.

That stubborn organ kept drifting back to him. So— he knew the truth. How long before he spread it around? Or would he? How long had he known? And how did he find out? He apparently had not shared the information with his cronies. Winters would have told Letty and Letty would have challenged Annabelle again with a triumphant "I told you so." Nor had Luke said anything when she saw him.

What did it matter? She intended to tell Celia and Letty anyway, but Mr. Murray had persuaded her not to make the information known until closer to the publication date. That little advertising coup would probably sink before it was launched. She smiled at the mixed metaphor.

The next evening she attended a musicale given by the wife of the Baron Lenwood. Annabelle thought there must be eighty or a hundred people there—not a huge crowd by any means, but a large enough group to ensure that one could avoid undue attention to oneself.

She and Aunt Gertrude had just stepped into the Lenwood drawing room when Lady Hermiston was approached by Mrs. Lenwood, who detained her in conversation. Annabelle stood slightly aside, politely waiting. She tried to be discreet in surveying the room at large. Yes. Drat it. There he was. Thorne Wainwright stood in conversation with a number of others, including Helen Rhys. Well, Miss Rhys was welcome to him!

"May I have a private word with you, Miss Richardson?"

Annabelle turned at the unwelcome voice just behind her. "Lord Beelson. I cannot imagine that you would have ought to say of interest to me."

He showed his teeth in what might have passed for a smile were there any warmth in his eyes. He gripped her elbow. "You may be surprised, my dear."

To jerk away would cause a scene, so she merely said through clenched teeth, "Take your hand off me!"

He tightened his grip. "I *will* speak with you. Lenwood has kindly offered his library just across the hall. Five minutes will not compromise you."

She weighed her choices. "Very well. Five minutes."

He relaxed his grip, but only slightly, as he steered her out the door and into the room across the hall. She jerked away from him, but noted with some small relief that the door remained open.

"Now—what is it that you want?"

"A little ordinary courtesy might be in order. Especially as I am in a way of offering you a service."

"A service? I want nothing—nothing—of you."

"I think you will want my silence, *Miss Bennet.* I think you might even be so very appreciative of my silence as to be willing to pay for it."His voice was smooth, oily, smug.

She looked at him in surprise. "You are out of your mind."

He laughed, a dry, mirthless sound. "Oh, I think not. You *are* Emma Bennet. I paid one of Murray's idiot clerks dearly for that handy bit of information."

"And now you expect me to reimburse that expense?"

"And then some. Just recompense for the embarrassment I suffered at your hands. I figure a monkey will do nicely."

"Five hundred pounds? Five *hundred* pounds?" Her voice rose in astonishment. "You want five hundred pounds—from *me?*"

He seemed taken aback by her vehemence. He glanced at the open door. "Keep your voice down," he said sharply. Then he added in a falsely conciliatory manner, "If you would find that sum difficult all at once, I would settle for half in—say—two days and you can pay me the rest in a week."

"Or—you could settle for nothing at all. For that is what you will have from me—*nothing.*"

"You had best think very carefully about that, my dear. How will the exalted members of the *ton* react to this news? Your friend Rolsbury will likely find it quite interesting."

"You despicable cur!" She had heard of people being so angry as to "see red," but it was a new phenomenon for her.

"Tut! Tut! Save the name-calling. It could only cost

you more, you know." He still sounded insufferably smug.

"Now you listen to *me*." She pointed a finger at him, her hand shaking in her fury. She clipped each word precisely. "I shall not pay five pounds—let alone five hundred—not even a farthing!"

"Brave talk for a girl who has avoided public censure before. How will you like this news in every drawing room in the city tomorrow?"

It will be in every drawing room in a week anyway, when the book comes out, she thought irrelevantly. Aloud, she said, "And how will *you* react to having the doors of those same drawing rooms closed to you? Just which hostesses would still receive you if our little talk here became general knowledge?"

She could see that he was totally surprised by her counterattack. He had undoubtedly expected her to dissolve into a flood of tears, begging his mercy or some such thing. Six months ago, his threats might have been effective. But now? She gave him a contemptuous look and strode toward the door.

"You had best reconsider my offer," he said, nearly snarling, but he did not touch her again. Which was just as well, she thought, for she would have screamed like a mad woman, scandal or no.

She returned to the drawing room, still shaking with rage. Looking for Aunt Gertrude, she found her gaze locked momentarily with Thorne's. He simply raised an expressive brow and turned away. Oh, Lord! He had seen her leave the room with Beelson. She gave a mental shrug. So? Let him make of it what he would. She resented his apparent dismissal of her.

Fourteen

Thorne had watched her leave the room with Beelson and he could tell she was upset on her return. Had that cad done something to hurt her? By God, if he had—he caught himself up short. If he had—what? It was no concern to Thorne Wainwright. Two days later, she did not appear at her friend Letty's party and he worried now that Beelson had threatened her in some way.

Thorne knew very well that Beelson lived on the fringes, so to speak. The man managed to continue to be accepted in Society, but only barely. He was known to be a high-stakes gambler, and rumor had it that his scruples in certain gaming hells were none too nice. However, he cleverly did not practice those arts at *ton* gatherings.

Beelson had a reputation for—and took pride in—being a ladies' man. But Thorne would have staked his life that what transpired between Beelson and Annabelle at the Lenwood affair was *not* a romantic assignation. Had Beelson perhaps found out about Emma Bennet, too? After all, *Innocence Betrayed* had leveled its harshest invective against Beelson and Ferris. And Thorne knew Beelson well enough to know the viscount would be seeking revenge.

"Luke." Thorne addressed his brother when that young man finally showed for breakfast one morning.

"Hmm?" Luke grunted in response.

Thorne chuckled. "I know you to be of little use before you have been fed and watered—so do drink deeply of your coffee. I want to ask you something."

Luke took a big swallow and nearly choked. "Dang it, Thorne, I do believe you must have developed cast-iron innards in the army."

"Put some water or milk in it if you are not quite up to *real* coffee."

"If you can stomach this, so, by golly, can I!"

"That's the spirit, little brother!"

Luke took another swig and swallowed with greater ease. "So, what did you want to ask me?"

"Have you seen much of Beelson lately?"

"You aren't going to ring another peal over my head about associating with Ralph, are you?" Luke sounded defensive, his guard up.

"No. I warned you about him. You know how I feel. The man is a blackguard, but if you want to associate with him anyway, so be it. However—"

"I know. You want nothing to do with him." Luke seemed less defensive now. "As a matter of fact, I've not seen him much of late. I hear he has money problems, though."

"Up the river Tick, is he?"

"Well, standing on its banks anyway. Jessup said something about a ship he and Beelson invested in— went down in the Indian Ocean."

"But Beelson owns a good deal of property—as well as knitting mills in Manchester."

Luke took another sip of coffee and began to plow into the plate of food set before him. "All mortgaged," he said around a mouthful of eggs and bacon. He swallowed. "Mortgaged to the hilt, Jessup says."

"Hmm."

"Why are you interested? Thought you hated him."

"Hate? Maybe. I do not like him. That's certain. I was just wondering, that's all."

"Cut line, Thorne. This is me—Luke—you are talking to. You never 'just wonder' about such things."

Thorne gave his brother an assessing look. "Very well. I saw him the other night with Miss Richardson at the Lenwood affair."

"Annabelle? With Beelson? I don't believe that!"

"Not *with* him, exactly—"

"I wouldn't think so. I don't think she likes him."

"Why do you say that?"

"Hell, Thorne. You read that Bennet woman's piece. Most of that stuff was true." Luke blushed at this admission.

"That so?" Thorne gave him a teasing grin. "Ah, well, some lessons come that way."

"I suppose so." Luke found his food of particular interest at this moment.

"Given his character, Beelson would hold a grudge against Miss Bennet."

"Yes, he probably would," Luke agreed. "That is, he would if he knew who she was. But I doubt he knows any more than the rest of us."

Thorne made no reply to this. Luke excused himself and Thorne was left to muse alone. He wondered why he had not told Luke—or Aunt Dorothy—of his own discovery of Emma Bennet's identity. Then it dawned on him that he had heard no whispers in that regard. He had encountered Wyndham at the club and at a committee meeting and there had been no change in the man's attitude. Apparently, then, Annabelle had said nothing, either. He wondered why she would keep silent, but at the same time he was grateful.

You might have thought that through more thoroughly

before lashing out at her, he told himself in some disgust. After all, it was not as though he had not enough time to consider all the angles. He needed to start thinking less like a hot-headed soldier storming the ramparts and more like a politician plotting careful strategies.

He picked up the stack of mail Perkins had placed near his plate. He recognized the handwriting on two of the missives. The first came as a distinct shock. It was Emma Bennet's—that is, Annabelle's. He started to put it away to be dealt with later. "Maybe in the next decade," he muttered. But something stopped him. He quickly broke the seal and scanned the contents.

Dear Sir,

While you probably do not welcome a missive from me, I feel circumstances dictate some communication about the matter you brought up at the League meeting last week. Therefore, for the sake of a good many others beyond ourselves, I would ask you to meet with me.

I ride in the park every morning between the hours of 8 and 9. If that would be inconvenient for you, please apprise me of a time and place more to your liking.

Yrs.

A. Richardson

"Hmm." Thorne sat thinking about this, reading and rereading. It was certainly formal and to the point. She was right. The consequences of the situation could go far beyond themselves. Picking up the rest of the mail, he went to the library, where he quickly penned a one-line response.

Tomorrow morning at 8 will be fine.

R.

He dispatched the note with a footman, then turned with more warmth to the other letter—also in a feminine hand. His sister Catherine wrote that at last she was accepting his standing invitation to visit in town. She would, of course, be accompanied by her husband and the children—all four of them, ranging in age from seven years to five months.

Thorne was delighted at the prospect of her visit. He had always been close to Catherine, who was a mere two years younger than he. Her first Season had ended disastrously. Thorne had fretted when he was en route to the Peninsula by the time of her second Season. But she had met and married a fine man in the Baron David Brideaux, whose family dated back to the Norman invasion. By the time Thorne finally met the man, the couple had been married over three years and already had two children.

Catherine had written him faithfully while he was in the army, keeping him informed of her happiness, and her growing family. She also supplied him detailed news of his father and brother—beyond his father's cryptic "status reports" of the earldom and Luke's labored schoolboy notes.

Thorne had repeatedly urged Catherine and David to come to London for the Season—even in those years when he could not or would not visit the city himself. Now they were coming.

He rang for Perkins and Mrs. Ewart, the housekeeper, to inform them of the impending visit.

"Oh, my," Mrs. Ewart said. "The nursery rooms have not seen service since Master Luke was a boy. They will need a thorough cleaning and airing."

"I am sure you are up to that task," Thorne said.

"Yes, my lord. And it will be very nice to see Miss Catherine again—that is, Lady Brideaux—and her wee ones."

ficial levels. Confession was supposed to be good for the soul, but why did it have to hurt so much?

He looked after her and the groom following, but did not try to catch up with them. Their horses were going at a comfortable gait, though not hurried, past a thick copse of elms. Suddenly, he saw her horse rear and twist. Annabelle slid off the saddle and fell to the right of the panicked animal onto the soft grass beside the riding lane. Thorne kicked his own mount into a gallop, arriving at Annabelle's prostrate form just as the groom did.

"You get the horse. I'll see to her," he shouted at the groom, who promptly responded to the orders of a man long used to having hurried orders obeyed.

Thorne quickly dismounted and knelt awkwardly at Annabelle's side, only vaguely aware of the pain in his bad leg.

"Annabelle! Can you hear me?" He was afraid to move her lest he injure her further than the fall might have. "Please, love, speak to me."

She groaned and opened her eyes. "Wh-what happened?"

"Something frightened your mount. Are you all right?"

"I—I think so." She levered herself to a partial sitting position and moved her legs. "Nothing . . . seems . . . to be broken. Just need . . . to catch my breath."

"Thank God!" he said fervently. He put his arm around her shoulder to support her as she struggled to breathe normally. He noted the lilac scent he would always associate with Annabelle. He resisted the urge to enfold her in his arms tightly.

"I—I think I am fine now," she said, "if you could just give me a hand up."

He rose and extended his hand to her. Standing close, he held her hand firmly until he determined that she *seemed* steady enough on her feet.

She disengaged her hand from his. "The fall merely knocked my breath away for a moment."

"You were lucky then. You might have been seriously injured."

"But I was not," she said brightly. "However, I cannot conceive what might have got into Princess. She is usually a very steady, even-tempered animal."

"Something startled her," Thorne said. He looked toward the dense cluster of trees, but saw nothing out of the ordinary. The groom returned, leading the sweating and now somewhat skittish mare. "Did you see anything that might have caused her to panic?" Thorne asked the servant.

"No, sir. She acted like she was hit sudden-like. She ain't usually so edgy."

"Do you think she is safe for Miss Richardson to ride now?" he asked the groom. Then addressed Annabelle, "Or should I take you up with me?"

"She be settlin' down now," the groom said.

"She will be fine, I am sure," Annabelle answered quickly. "Jamie will ride more closely and we shall be fine. Really. Thank you for your concern."

With that formal dismissal, he knew she had regained full control of the situation. The groom held the mare still as Thorne gave her a lift into her saddle. He turned to his own horse and remounted. "Good morning again, then."

Once more, he watched them ride off and kept them in sight until they left the park. Then he set his own mount to a hard ride, fully aware that he did so to postpone thinking about this meeting with Annabelle.

Fifteen

The fall had shaken Annabelle more than she cared to admit to Rolsbury. She found riding an immensely enjoyable activity, but readily acknowledged that she was not a "bruising rider." "A *bruised* rider at the moment," she observed on removing her habit and discovering a blackening mark on her thigh. Still, it was embarrassing to have lost her seat like that—in front of Thorne and just as she had made a dramatic exit. She wondered again what could have set Princess off like that.

She thought over the conversation with Thorne. He had not actually agreed to anything she had said. On the other hand, there had been no outright rejection, either. And he had, however grudgingly, accepted her apology. Perhaps the whole situation had been smoothed over enough to prevent any wide-ranging damage.

Now she faced another tough interview, this one with Celia and Letty. The ladies had called briefly the day after Letty's small gathering, but Annabelle knew she had satisfied neither friend with her evasive answers. They left just as worried about her as they had been on arriving. Annabelle felt guilty over their worry.

She arrived at the Winters town house just as Celia was removing her cloak and bonnet in the entrance hall. The two were shown together to Letty's charming private sitting room. They found the mother playing with her baby, a nursery maid standing by. Celia and Annabelle made proper cooing noises over the Winters heir as Letty bragged about his latest achievements.

"He smiles and tries to talk and he will stand in my lap when I hold him under his arms. And he loves to play peek-a-boo."

"He tries to talk?" Annabelle laughed, unable to keep the skepticism from her voice as she held out her arms to take her turn at cuddling the babe.

"Very well, Miss Perfectionist. He babbles. But *he* knows what he is saying."

They all laughed at this and soon the maid took the babe to return him to the nursery. Letty rang for tea.

They sat at a small table, talking of everyday, superficial matters—babies, fashions, the latest *on dits*—until the tea tray arrived and Letty finished serving.

Annabelle took a last fortifying drink of tea and set her cup down. "I have something to tell you."

"Oh!" Letty gave a little squeal. "You accepted Lord Stimson's offer. Well, I knew it was coming after watching you waltzing with him at Almack's last week. When is the wedding?"

Annabelle laughed. "No. Lord Stimson and me? No."

"Who, then? You have not paid anyone else any mind. Of course, it could be Hamilton. I have heard he is quite smitten with you. . . . Oh! Never say it is Rolsbury! Though, now that I think on it, you did go riding with him in the summer."

"Letty!" Celia called through her laughter. "Allow the poor girl to explain."

"Very well." Letty returned her teacup carefully to its saucer and sat forward on her chair, waiting expectantly.

Annabelle looked from one to the other of her friends.

"It is nothing of that sort at all." She paused. This was far more difficult than she had anticipated.

"Oh," Letty whimpered in disappointment.

"What is it, Annabelle?" Celia touched her hand in a reassuring gesture.

"Promise you will not hate me."

Celia and Letty chanted in unison, "I promise not to hate Annabelle." Each of them made a cross over her breast in a ritual that had developed in a "secret society" at school.

"Now, do tell us," Celia said, her voice serious and gentle.

"Well . . ." Annabelle took a deep breath. "You were right, Letty. And I am sure you suspected, Celia. I *am* Emma Bennet."

There was utter silence in the room. Annabelle wondered if any of them was breathing.

"You *do* hate me," she said.

"No. Of course we do nothing of the sort," Celia said. " 'Tis such a surprise is all."

"I knew it! I knew it!" Letty cried gleefully. "Why did you not tell us before—and why are you doing so now?"

Annabelle explained the reason behind protecting a young girl's name early on.

"That makes perfect sense to me," Celia said. "You would surely have been an oddity that first Season."

"So why now?" Letty demanded.

"Because I have a new book—it will be in the shops in a few days. It is being published under my own name and I wanted you to be among the first to know of it."

"It . . . it is not . . . uh, like the last one, is it?" Celia asked with marked hesitation.

Annabelle laughed ruefully. "Not at all. This one is serious. My best work so far."

"What is the title?" Celia asked.

"Heroism Rewarded."

Letty had been quiet for a moment. "Wait until Lord Rolsbury finds out about *this*."

"He knows," Annabelle said.

Again both the others spoke at once. "He knows?"

"He knows."

"And how did he react?" Letty asked.

"As one might expect," Annabelle said. "He is not happy about it, but I think he will have moved beyond his extreme reaction to *Innocence Betrayed*." At least I hope so, she prayed silently.

"What is this new one about?" Celia asked, clearly changing the subject—for which Annabelle was grateful.

"Heroism," she answered smugly. Her friends rolled their eyes. She grinned and went on, "It is about types of heroism, from the swashbuckling heroics of a soldier in battle to the quiet kind of one who stands up for a principle." She gave them a brief summary of the story of Portia and Nathan.

"It sounds *good*," Letty said.

"It seems to have a serious theme running through it," Celia observed. "I shall look forward to reading it."

"I shall bring you copies as soon as I receive those promised me in advance," Annabelle promised. "And . . . thank you, both."

"For *what?*" Letty asked in surprise.

"For not being angry at my deceiving you—even lying to you on occasion."

"Oh. Well. As to *that*—" Letty laughed. "Celia and I will work out a proper revenge. But for now you will have made us the most sought-after of dinner guests—after all, *we* are best friends of the famous Emma Bennet."

"Or infamous Emma Bennet." Annabelle sounded dubious. "In any event, I feel better that you finally know.

* * *

The Baron Brideaux and his lovely wife arrived at Rolsbury House late one afternoon. On hand to greet them were both the Wainwright brothers. Luke picked up his eldest nephew, Samuel, and swung him around in a great circle and then was faced with a chorus of "Me! Me!" from five-year-old Katie and Benjamin, who was three. The children were shyer around their uncle Rolsbury, whom they knew less well.

Rather than dispatch the children immediately to the nursery, Thorne invited them, along with their parents, into the smaller and less formal of the two drawing rooms. Luke carried the babe and Thorne was surprised at the ease with which his care-for-nothing younger brother handled the children.

"Luke, you will be a wonderful father one day," Catherine voiced aloud Thorne's thoughts. She had the same dark hair and gray-green eyes as her brothers. Thorne thought her prettier now than she had been in the first bloom of youth.

"Not anytime soon, I hope," Luke said, turning the babe over to its mother, who kissed it and gave it up to a hovering nursery maid. As soon as Luke sat down, little Benjamin climbed onto his lap.

Thorne rang for refreshments and then sat close to Catherine on a settee. The boy Samuel stood by his father's chair and Katie clung to her mother's knee, eyeing Thorne with curiosity. He winked at her very deliberately. She giggled and hid her face, but moments later she was happily seated on his knee.

"Hmm." Catherine looked from her daughter to her older brother. "It looks as though you have conquered yet another female heart, big brother."

Thorne hugged the child to him. "Katie and I are going to become great friends, are we not, Katie?"

Katie's answer was another shy giggle.

Mrs. Ewart accompanied the footman bringing in the tea tray and there was a flurry of greetings and "oohs" and "aahs" over how much the children had grown.

Thorne was struck by how ordinary it all seemed to him, despite his having had little to do with children and real family life in the course of his own growing up. He thought suddenly of Annabelle and the picture she had painted of her own childhood. He shook himself mentally for allowing his mind to drift in that direction.

That evening their Aunt Dorothy joined the Wainwright siblings and Brideaux for a family dinner. Lady Conwick also spent a fair amount of time in the nursery marveling over the next generation.

After dinner, all but Luke, who had excused himself early, sat in the drawing room talking idly. Despite her usual antipathy to stirring from her own house, Lady Conwick invited Catherine to go shopping the next day.

"That will be wonderful," Catherine responded. "Just like old times. I remember fondly our shopping for my come-out. Oh! And I should like to visit Hatchard's. I have a long list of books I am dying to have."

"My wife, the bluestocking," Brideaux said teasingly.

Catherine grinned at her husband. "I am not sure, my love, what the male equivalent of 'bluestocking' is. There *must* be such a term—for you, dear heart, would certainly fit the description."

"Pay her no mind, David," Thorne said. "She always did have a sharp tongue, that one."

Catherine turned on him. "And you, brother dear, also fit that description to a T. I suppose one day you will find some long-faced, dry-witted lump among your literary friends and bring her home to reign as the Countess of Rolsbury."

"Oh-ho. You get the brunt of it now," David said.

Aunt Dorothy cleared her throat meaningfully. "Actually, Catherine, my sources tell *me* that the Earl of Rolsbury is considered quite a catch among the so-called diamonds of the Season."

"And why would he not be so regarded?" Catherine said loyally. "He has title, riches, looks—"

"And could present a prospective bride with a charming sister-in-law," her husband interrupted.

"Well, yes. That, too."

They all laughed at this sally.

Later, Thorne marveled at how much simple pleasure he had had this day.

Annabelle was nervous and had been for two days—ever since *Heroism Rewarded* had arrived in bookstores. She had distributed her advance copies and already received accolades from Aunt Gertrude, Harriet and Marcus, Letty and Celia—but she expected nothing less from these, her faithful champions.

She thought of sending a copy over to Rolsbury House, but recalling Thorne's attitude, she thought better of that idea.

Now, she was to attend a theater performance, her first public outing since the book began selling. Annabelle chose a gown of pale green silk for this event when a good many eyes would be focused on the Bennet-Richardson woman. The simple elegance of the gown was complimented perfectly by a beautiful paisley shawl of the lightest wool and her emeralds—the grandest pieces of her own family jewelry that had not been on the ship with her mother.

Just as she had expected and as Harriet had warned, her entrance made a stir in the theater. There were six chairs in the Wyndham box. Marcus had invited Aunt Gertrude and her friend, Lord Marchand, and Annabelle's friend, Lord Stimson, to make up their party.

Annabelle would have taken a less conspicuous seat in the second row of chairs, but Harriet said, "Oh, no, no, no. We are not hiding you in the back as though we were ashamed of you!" The ladies sat in the front. Stimson had the chair placed at an angle behind Annabelle's. He leaned over her to observe the rest of the theater.

"Good crowd tonight for your debut," he observed.

"Thank you, Robert, for lending your presence to this little drama," Annabelle said softly. His arm lay across the back of her chair. He gave her shoulder a brief pat. "I would not have missed it for the world, my dear."

Annabelle loved the theater. She loved the opulence of the auditorium as well as the splendor of stage sets and the magic of another world created by dramatists and actors. She lifted her glasses to survey her surroundings—and looked squarely into the eyes of Thorne Wainwright.

He was sitting in a box across the way with several others. She recognized Captain Rhys and his sister, and Lady Conwick. The couple with them were strangers to Annabelle. Then the woman leaned toward Thorne and a vague similarity in their hair color and the way they held their heads clicked—she was surely Thorne's sister.

Annabelle quickly lowered her glasses and focused her eyes on the stage. Her mind, however, stayed on that box across the way. Helen Rhys. He had brought Miss Rhys to the theater—with his sister. Surely that fact carried great significance. She tried to concentrate on the play once it started.

In the Rolsbury box Thorne was pleased that Catherine was enjoying herself so. She and Brideaux were quite content in their country living and it was entirely by choice that they so seldom came to town.

"At home, I always forget how much I enjoy things like shopping on Bond Street and going to the theater." Her eyes were bright with eagerness. "Thorne, who *is* that lovely girl who seems to have attracted so much attention?"

Thorne looked up just as the "lovely girl" trained her sweeping glasses on his box. Annabelle. She quickly lowered her glasses and turned her head.

Before Thorne could reply, Helen Rhys answered, "Oh, that is Annabelle Richardson." When it became apparent to Helen that the name meant nothing to Catherine, Helen added, "It has only recently come out that *she* wrote the books attributed to an Emma Bennet."

"Ah, yes. Of course. I just bought the newest one—her fourth or fifth work, I think. I have read all the others, but not the latest yet." Catherine quickly looked again at the subject of their discussion.

Brideaux's gaze followed his wife's. "Pretty girl," he said. "Looks too young to have written that much."

"Looks can be deceiving," Helen said. "And so can Miss Richardson, I am afraid."

Thorne was aware of the look Helen slanted at him, but he refused to respond to it.

"Do you refer to that story she wrote, 'Innocence something-or-other'?" Catherine asked.

"Innocence Betrayed. Yes. It was quite clearly a *betrayal*—of her friendship with your brothers."

"In all fairness," Thorne said, "I must point out that she and I had not yet even met when that was written."

"Which makes her caricatures even more unfair," Helen said.

Thorne merely shrugged, unwilling to defend that particular work, but also strangely unwilling to enter into criticism of Annabelle. He racked his brain for a change in topic that might divert both Catherine and Helen.

"As I say, I have read her work," Catherine said. "Even in the country, popular fare eventually comes to us."

"Do you not agree that that piece was unfair to the people she so cruelly depicted?" Helen persisted.

"As a matter of fact, except for the portrait said to be Thorne—whom the author clearly did not know—I felt the characterizations were amazingly on target."

"Are you serious?" Helen sounded appalled.

"Not gentle, mind you," Catherine said. "Perhaps not even kind. But she apparently had ample motivation for what she wrote."

"Well, she has apparently had second thoughts," Helen said. "She dedicated this new book to R."

"R?" Catherine asked.

"It has to be R for *Ralph*. Ralph Nettle is the Viscount Beelson," Helen said knowingly. "He was the most severely maligned in the earlier work."

Thorne noted a sharp intake of breath on Catherine's part and quickly pointed out, "Miss Richardson is accompanied tonight by Lord Stimson. *His* given name is Robert."

"So it is," Helen said.

Thorne was glad when the curtain finally went up—and equally glad that he, Catherine, and David were provincial enough to find what happened on stage fascinating.

But he found it difficult to concentrate on the play. Who was the R of Annabelle's dedication? Of course it was within the realm of possibility that it referred to himself, but given the strained relations between them of late, that was highly unlikely.

"The *Post* has a nice review of your book, Annabelle," Harriet said as Annabelle entered the breakfast room the next morning.

"Oh? Read me the pertinent parts, please," Annabelle said as she began making her selections from the breakfast buffet.

" 'Miss Bennet—or should we say Miss Richardson?—has written a readable, well-paced story. Beyond the particulars of action and character, she attempts to explore one of mankind's more admirable traits. We refer, of course, to the heroism of the title. A weaker writer might have dealt only with physical courage of, say, a battlefield. Miss Richardson recognizes and presents other kinds of heroism as well.' " Harriet folded the paper back to the review and laid it beside Annabelle's plate. "There is much more, and almost all of it praises your achievement."

"As it should do," Marcus said matter-of-factly.

Annabelle flashed him an appreciative smile and delved simultaneously into her breakfast and the review. When she had finished reading, she looked up to see Harriet watching her expectantly.

"Quite nice, is it not?" Harriet asked.

"Yes, it is, but I do wish the reviewer had not alluded to *Innocence Betrayed* as he did. This is the third reviewer who felt he had to mention that infernal earlier story."

"I suppose it is only natural to compare a new book with an author's earlier work." Harriet poured herself another cup of coffee and lifted the pot to offer more to Marcus and Annabelle, who both declined.

"They *do* usually say something to the effect that 'Innocence' was not typical of your work," Marcus noted.

"I know. And I am an ungrateful wretch to object so," Annabelle said, "but they keep it alive when I should like to forget about it!"

"Give it time." Marcus rose. "I must be off."

When he had gone, Harriet put her cup down and

said, "You *are* pleased about the responses to the book, are you not?"

"Oh, yes. Of course I am."

"I sense a certain degree of hesitation. Do you regret publishing under your own name?"

"No. However, my own name has raised a few eyebrows. Not everyone approves a woman putting herself forward so."

"Never mind the tabbies," Harriet comforted. "Some people—and a surprising number of them are female—would have a woman of intelligence and talent hide her abilities. And they are particularly judgmental if such a woman has youth and beauty besides."

Annabelle smiled. "You always manage to make me feel better."

"Good! Now, while you finish your breakfast, I shall just run up to the nursery for a few moments. Then, I should like your assistance in the library." Harriet rose and placed her serviette on the table beside her plate.

"Of course. With what?"

"Writing out invitations to a ball."

"A ball? You are planning a ball—here?"

"That I am. And I need your help with the guest list."

"Is there some occasion for such a grand undertaking?" Annabelle asked.

Harriet assumed a mockingly formal tone. "The Earl and Countess of Wyndham, my dear, are giving a lavish birthday ball for their one-time ward to mark the occasion of her coming of age."

"For me? You are planning a ball for me?"

Harriet laughed and hugged her. "Unless you know of another ward we might have had."

Sixteen

Thorne had scarcely seen the adult members of his family for three days. During the day he had been busy with business matters or with issues before Parliament. As usual, Luke had an engagement of some sort every night. One night Thorne attended a dinner for the officers of his regiment, hosted by Wellington at Apsley House. Another night the Brideauxs were invited out by friends.

He had, however, spent some time with the nursery set, and found himself growing increasingly fond of these small persons. Samuel had recently acquired a set of toy soldiers and had endless questions about how they should be arranged for battles. Thorne had no idea, really, of how one dealt with children, so he merely treated them as adults, albeit on their terms. To his surprise, the three older ones responded amazingly well to such treatment. Late one afternoon, Catherine discovered him seated in a big overstuffed chair, Katie on one knee, Benjamin on the other, and Samuel on an ottoman in front. Thorne was reading them a story with appropriate sound effects for the animal characters of the tale.

"Well! I see my offspring have found a new champion," she said.

He grinned. "We are getting along quite nicely, thank you."

"Do not allow them to plague you to death, now will you, Thorne?"

"I assure you, dear sister, I am here voluntarily."

"Oh, well, in that case, I shall cease worrying."

He finished the story, then joined David and Catherine in the drawing room, where they shared a settee.

"I must say, you looked quite natural in the guise of doting uncle," Catherine observed.

"I enjoy your children," he said simply, taking a chair across from them.

"They *are* a joy—most of the time. But believe me, rearing children—at least doing so properly—is a full-time job. Even when one has capable help as we do, you worry about them all the time—and hope you are not doing some abominable thing that will mar them for life. Right, darling?" She patted her husband's knee.

"Right," he grunted.

"So? What have you been doing with yourselves?" Thorne asked.

"David spent most of the day with bankers and at his club. And I finished Miss Richardson's book. Have you read it yet, Thorne?"

"No. Nor do I intend to do so."

She looked surprised. "Whyever not? It is quite good. And the reviews have been positive. Do not say you are developing one of those too-nice sensibilities that despise fiction."

"No. I merely have little interest in reading any more of this writer's work." He did not add that he would find that a painful task.

"Well, I really think you should read this one. I think you, in particular, would find it most . . . interesting."

"How so?"

"Well, it is about a soldier, for one thing. You always used to devour such tales."

"Having been to war, I doubt any woman could write very tellingly of what it is like." Thorne looked at his brother-in-law. "Would you not agree, David?"

"In general, yes . . ."

Catherine was not giving up. "Apparently Miss Richardson agrees with you, for she carefully skirts the details of battles."

"And she still writes about 'heroism rewarded'?"

"She does, indeed, for she deals with many types of courage."

"Such as . . . ?"

"The courage to overcome personal obstacles or some trait in oneself, the courage to persevere in the face of great opposition, the courage to place oneself in a precarious situation for the sake of others—and 'precarious situation' may or may not be physical danger."

"Well, I can see she certainly got to *you*," Thorne said, wondering at this unusual degree of enthusiasm.

"Yes, and I think she will get to you, too. I think she will get to *you* on a very special level."

He threw up his hands in defense. "Very well. I shall read it—someday."

"Read it now."

"Why? Is there some urgency involved?" he asked disbelievingly.

"Sooner is better." Her voice was firm.

"Give it up, Thorne," David said. "When she gets that tone, a mere man is lost. You must at least *pretend* to agree with her."

"What do you mean—'pretend'?" she asked, her twinkling eyes belying the attempt at shock in her tone. "Of course you agree with me."

"Yes, dear." David's tone was a parody of a submissive husband's. He pulled his wife close and kissed her on the cheek.

It was an innocent and casual display of affection, and so utterly natural that Thorne found himself—again—in the position of envying one of his siblings.

"Read it *now*," she repeated through her laughter.

Thorne made a great pretense of giving in with a heavy sigh. "Very well, now."

She pointed behind him. " 'Tis on that table by the door."

A few minutes later, as he left to dress for dinner, he picked up the book and took it to his chamber. He tossed it on the bed and set about dressing for dinner and a ball he had agreed to attend only to lend his support and his presence to Catherine and David.

Annabelle had not wanted to attend the Carstairs' ball. She suspected she was on the guest list because of her association with the Wyndham title and because of the recent stir caused by *Heroism Rewarded*. However, Harriet had insisted, so here she was.

Early in the evening, she was sitting out an energetic country dance when she was approached by none other than the Viscount Beelson.

"May I have this dance, Miss Richardson?"

She did not bother to hide her aversion to the very idea of dancing with him. "I just this instant refused Lord Torrance—I could hardly stand up with you."

"Well, then—I shall just sit this one out with you." He plopped himself in the empty chair next to hers.

"You might have waited for an invitation." She knew she sounded testy. Mentally, she was even testier as she added to herself, And you would have waited and waited and . . .

"Yes, I might have done," he said cheerily, "but I

did not think such formality necessary between us any-more."

"Whyever would you come to such a presumptuous conclusion? I do hope you do not intend pressing me for funds again."

"Not at all, my dear. That was merely in the way of a joke—"

"A joke? You have a very curious sense of humor, Lord Beelson."

He ignored her and went on, "And now that I know your real feelings, I am prepared to forgive you and renew my suit. I must say, love, you have pushed coy reluctance to a new level."

Annabelle felt her jaw drop in surprise at this. The man was mad. Totally addled. "My real feelings? Forgive me? What *are* you talking about?"

"I saw the dedication of your book. 'To R—with apologies.' " He grasped her hand. "And I *do* accept your apology, my dear."

She discreetly jerked her hand away and stood, afraid there were spots of color on her cheeks that would display her agitation to dowagers and wallflowers nearby. "You, sir, are completely mad." She turned abruptly and walked away, even as he rose from his chair, and she had a fleeting glimpse of astonished rage on his face.

Harriet was just coming from the dance floor. "Anna-belle? Is something wrong?"

"You will never credit the conversation I just had!" She drew Harriet aside so the two of them were nearly hidden by some large potted plants. Then she described her encounter with Beelson.

"Good heavens!" Harriet exclaimed. "The man is delusional."

"My thoughts precisely. That—or very desperate."

"Be careful, my dear."

They came from the semiseclusion of the potted

plants to see Marcus coming toward them, accompanied by the Earl of Rolsbury and the guests who had been in his theater box a few nights before.

"Lady Wyndham, Miss Richardson, may I present my sister Lady Catherine Brideaux and her husband Baron David Brideaux?" Thorne spoke formally, his tone neutral.

They exchanged appropriate greetings, then Catherine said, "I am very glad to meet *you,* especially, Miss Richardson, for I've only today finished reading your book."

"I hope you liked it," Annabelle said politely.

"Oh, I did. Very much. I am now persuading the rest of my family to read it."

Why is she telling me Thorne has not read it? Annabelle wondered. She gave Lady Brideaux a penetrating look, but it was returned with only a bland smile. Annabelle shifted her gaze to Thorne, but could not read his expression.

"I understand the book is doing well," Lord Brideaux said. "The reviews I have seen have been positive."

"Yes. I am gratified that the reviewers have been so kind," Annabelle replied.

"She is far too modest," Harriet said fondly, linking her arm with Annabelle's.

"I agree," Lady Brideaux said. "I quite liked the book and I wonder—that is, if you would not consider it too presumptuous of me—I wonder if I might call upon you, Miss Richardson, to discuss it? I have some questions I should very much like to ask you."

Surprised, Annabelle looked from Lady Brideaux to Thorne. He seemed taken aback by his sister's request, too.

"Why, I . . . of course you may," Annabelle said. "Tomorrow, perhaps?"

It was agreed upon and Rolsbury drifted away, his guests in tow.

"What do you suppose she has in mind?" Harriet asked.

"To discuss the book?" Marcus offered, sounding practical.

"I wondered, too," Annabelle said.

"That lady is not an overly impressed, undereducated enthusiast dabbling in literature," Harriet asserted. "She has a purpose."

"A method in her madness?" Marcus teased.

"We shall know tomorrow," Annabelle said.

Thorne was surprised at Catherine's wanting to meet Miss Richardson and then at her wanting to call on her. It was out of character for Catherine. Nor was he sure if he wanted the two women to know each other. Then he shrugged. What difference should it be to him? He just hoped they would not become bosom friends, for if they *did,* it would make forgetting Annabelle that much more difficult.

As he climbed into bed, he had to move Annabelle's book. Well, he would just look it over—scan a few pages—before he went to sleep.

The first thing to catch his eye was, as he expected, the dedication. "To R—with apologies." *With apologies?* She was apologizing to Beelson? Perhaps. He had seen her sitting with him briefly earlier in the evening, though he had thought then she did not appear to be in charity with the man.

Still, R could also refer to Stimson. *Or* to yourself, he thought in a fit of self-disgust. Face it—that is what you *want* it to be. Just read the damned book!

And so he did.

For the rest of the night and into the morning.

He found himself absorbed in the struggles of the heroine, Portia, as she worked to perfect her artistic technique and develop a style of her own—and then had to face Society's censure in getting her work accepted. He sympathized with Portia's longing to have her work recognized even as she sought to protect an aristocratic family name. Portia also faced censure and contempt within her own family, for her father was violently opposed to her daubing paint on canvas and always smelling of turpentine instead of roses.

Except for this last, Thorne recognized the parallel between Portia and Annabelle. Annabelle, after all, enjoyed the wholehearted support—and unswerving loyalty—of her "family." But she must have faced—be facing—similar slights in certain other quarters. Yet, she had chosen to publish this book under her own name. The addition of a disapproving family added poignancy and drama to Portia's story.

Then Annabelle began to intertwine Portia's story with Nathan's. The two clashed because Portia was headstrong and Nathan was stubborn. Nathan was a much-acclaimed war hero whose feats on the battlefield were famous far and wide. Home on leave, he was feted by royalty and cheered by commoners.

"Overdoing it a bit there," Thorne muttered to himself, but read on.

On his return to the wars, Nathan was terribly wounded and would have died but for the ministrations of his batman. Thorne was struck by the accuracy of Annabelle's descriptions of the return of wounded on overcrowded troop ships and hospital conditions once they arrived in England. She had apparently talked with men who really knew.

Then she launched into what she obviously felt was Nathan's greater heroism—his struggle to walk. And now Thorne knew for sure he was reading about himself.

"I shall kill that errant brother of mine," he grumbled. But, again, he read on.

The details did not always coincide with his own situation, but the essence of the tale did. He was especially moved by the faithful servant patiently aiding Nathan, keeping up appearances with his short-tempered employer, and then dissolving in "unmanly" tears belowstairs.

"I'll be damned. I had no idea," he said quietly, humbled. He knew it was true, though. This was not merely a detail she made up to add emotion to her story. "Hinton deserves a raise."

The author was not finished with her at times irascible hero and his courage. Now, as Nathan worked not only to cope with matters of his estate, he also took up social issues that had long been overlooked. And now, Thorne observed, Annabelle had created a composite figure, drawing on not only the Earl of Rolsbury, but also the Earl of Wyndham.

The sun was well and truly up when he closed the book. Knowing sleep would be impossible now, he arose and donned riding clothes. A hard ride would clear his mind, he was sure.

Annabelle and Harriet welcomed Thorne's sister cordially as she was shown into the drawing room. Harriet rang for refreshments and the three of them talked of mundane matters for a while. Then, Harriet excused herself, murmuring something about seeing to her son in the nursery.

"You . . . uh . . . wanted to discuss my book, Lady Brideaux?" Annabelle asked.

"In a manner of speaking—yes. But please—may we dispense with the formalities and be just 'Catherine' and 'Annabelle'? I do feel you and I could be friends."

Perhaps. Under different circumstances, Annabelle thought. She smiled and said, "Of course. I should like that."

"I read your book with a great deal of interest."

"Yes, you have said as much."

"It is about Thorne, is it not? Thorne and you."

Annabelle was nonplused. Was she really so transparent? "I . . . I beg your pardon?"

"I live in the country, Annabelle, but not under a rock. I do have friends here in town. Moreover, I am quite close to my aunt, Lady Conwick, and even closer to my brothers, especially Luke. Luke told me everything— about that . . . that worm, Beelson, about Ferris—*and* about his own lovesick histrionics and the scene he created."

"I . . . see."

"Your retaliation was clever, pointed, and understandable."

That dratted story again, Annabelle thought. "But it was unfair to Thorne." She saw Catherine raise her brows slightly at her casual use of Thorne's given name. "I am sorely afraid his pride suffered dreadfully."

"I doubt Thorne's reaction was motivated by pride," his sister said.

"What then?"

"He probably wanted retribution for Luke's humiliation."

"Retribution?"

Catherine drew in a breath and stared off into the distance for a few moments. "Yes. I think that is why he attacked Emma Bennet as he did. From the time of our mother's death, Thorne has always been inordinately protective of Luke and me. Our father was rather old when his second wife—our mother—finally gave him his heir. He was also an undemonstrative man. He was like a cold and distant grandfather. Any love we had came from Thorne—and Aunt Dorothy."

Annabelle was moved by these disclosures, but also somewhat embarrassed—and puzzled.

"But why—"

"Why am I telling you this? Because I know of the rift between you and Thorne. Because I know of the devastation he felt when he discovered it was you who had written that earlier story."

"He told you?"

"No. Aunt Dorothy did. She put two and two together some time ago."

Annabelle felt herself blushing at this. She twisted her hands in her lap.

"Please. Do not be embarrassed." Catherine lifted her teacup and took a swallow of what must have been cold tea, but Annabelle doubted a sudden thirst had hit her visitor. "Now, I want to tell you a story. And I should prefer that it went no further—but I think it will help you understand Thorne better."

"Very well."

Catherine took another deep breath. "When I made my come-out, I was truly a green girl. I had a very handsome dowry, of course, and was much sought after. I was certain all that attention was for my marvelous self." Bitter regret sounded in her voice. "I was besotted by one man in particular. Unfortunately, he rushed his fences and tried to seduce me."

"Oh, my goodness."

"He would have succeeded, too, had Thorne not intervened. Well, Thorne could not challenge him to a duel. Not only would that ruin my reputation, it would also have ruined his military career. Wellington did not approve of his officers dueling." Catherine paused.

"What happened?"

"The man thought himself quite a boxer. Thorne met

him in the boxing ring and quite literally beat him sense-
less. I am not supposed to know of that, of course. But
I do."

"I think the scoundrel got what he deserved."

Catherine smiled. "So do I. That scoundrel was Ralph
Nettle. He was not yet the Viscount Beelson then."

Annabelle gasped. "Beelson?"

Catherine nodded.

Annabelle considered the woman before her. "Catherine, I . . . I find your story interesting and moving,
but what has it to do with—?"

"With you and your book?"

Annabelle nodded.

"That book is nothing less than a declaration of love.
You are in love with Thorne and it shows on every
page."

Annabelle felt intense heat rush to her face. "Now,
really . . ."

Catherine reached to touch Annabelle's hand. "Please.
Do not be embarrassed. I doubt anyone else will see as
much as I and Aunt Dorothy saw in it. Aunt Dorothy
quite likes you and, from the little I have seen, I shall,
too."

"Thank you." Annabelle regained some of her poise.

"More to he point, *Thorne* does, too."

"Now, *that* I have reason to doubt. You came here
today to tell me this?"

Catherine smiled. "And to tell you to stand firm.
Eventually his own common sense will win out over
his pride."

Seventeen

The ride did not clear his mind. He returned to join his family at breakfast with his mind and emotions as jumbled as ever.

What was he to make of Annabelle's "Nathan"? There was not a syllable of satire in this story. There *were* touches of humor to lend contrast and balance to an emotionally charged drama, but no ridicule of real people. In fact, the characters were so subtly drawn, he thought, that few readers would identify him at all. Only his own household and Hank Watson knew the telling details.

He had no doubt whatsoever that the "R" referred to *Rolsbury*. But what did the word *apologies* mean? Was she apologizing for this book? For the earlier story? Or for deceiving him all those months? Obviously, what was needed here was a simple, uninterrupted conversation with Annabelle. But that was easier to arrange in his mind than in reality, given his schedule in the next few days. He knew this was merely an excuse. What he really wanted was more time to examine this turn of events—and his own emotions.

He had never doubted the physical attraction between him and Annabelle—nor that it was a *shared* phenomenon. Now, this book showed a deeper level of caring—

and here, too, she seemed to share his own feelings. Could he really put aside the fact that she had held him up to embarrassment? That she had deliberately deceived him for months? Perhaps, in time . . .

That evening, he attended a meeting of the Literary League, fully expecting Annabelle to be there. She was not. At least not physically. However, the members were abuzz with talk of *Heroism Rewarded*.

"Well! Thorne!" Henry Watson greeted him. "Have you changed your mind about Emma Bennet's writing?"

"No. I do think, however, that this book fulfills the promise shown in her earlier work."

"Yours wouldn't be a prejudiced view, now would it?"

Thorne was discomfited by this comment. "Hank, I would appreciate it if—"

Hank clapped a hand on his friend's shoulder. "I know. I know. You want your privacy protected. And I shall respect that."

"Thank you. Actually, the privacy issue *is* important to me—but even more I should like Annabelle's—Miss Richardson's—book to stand on its own merits."

Watson gave him a penetrating look. "Hmm. Like that, is it?"

"Well . . . yes. I suppose it is, but that is not the point."

"And the point is . . . ?"

"Her book should be judged for itself—not become the focus of irrelevant gossip. You are one of only a few people who know the details of my convalescence—and most of those are my own people and in the country."

"You are doing it again, aren't you?" Watson asked.

"Doing what?"

"Charging in on that white horse, shining sword raised, to protect someone you care about."

Startled by this idea, Thorne just looked at Watson for a moment. "I had not thought of it in those terms—"

"You never do. Well, never fear. Your secret is safe with me. Now—let us hear what others are saying of the book."

Others were, in general, praising the book. Some objected to the pacing of certain plot elements and others mentioned variations on heroism that *they* wanted to see included. Overall, Thorne noted, this group of rather demanding readers liked what they had read.

"I wish Miss Richardson were here tonight to answer our questions," one matron complained in a querulous tone. "She comes to every meeting—and misses this one!"

"She had a previous engagement. I know she wanted to be with us tonight."

Thorne recognized that voice and he turned to see Lady Wyndham, who nodded to him in greeting.

Suddenly a particularly strident voice—this one male—said, "Lord Rolsbury, I am sure we would all like to know what *you* think of this new offering from Miss Bennet's pen. You had a good deal to say of the last one."

Thorne looked around and found all eyes on him. "I believe I have acknowledged before that Miss Bennet possesses an abundance of talent. It showed to advantage in her earliest works. Now, Miss Richardson's book shows realization of that talent—and points the way to even better things to come."

"Hear. Hear," someone said.

Later, Thorne had a moment of relative privacy with Lady Wyndham and Lady Hermiston. They chatted of inconsequential matters and as he took his leave of the ladies, Thorne said, "Please give Miss Richardson my regards. I am sorry to have missed her."

Harriet said, "I shall be glad to. Do you attend the

Lord Mayor's ball tomorrow night? We shall, of course, be there."

"My sister is looking forward to it quite eagerly."

That was encouraging, Thorne thought later. Lady Wyndham had made a point of telling him when he might encounter Annabelle on a casual basis.

The next morning, Harriet supplied a thorough accounting of the meeting for Annabelle.

"I should like to have been there, but I promised Letty—"

"I know, dear. But you were sorely missed. And even in your absence, almost all the discussion of the book was positive."

"Which is gratifying, but not especially helpful."

Harriet paused in the act of buttering her toast. "Hmm?"

"One learns little from praise. The craft is honed when one corrects faults or weaknesses. I want to know how I can be *better.*"

Harriet laughed. "That is *precisely* something your Portia would have said! If ever I had any doubt about your source of inspiration for that character, you just removed it!"

"Well!" Annabelle pretended to be affronted. "I have had a very good example these last several years—there is a great deal of one Harriet Knightly, later my Lady Wyndham, in the character of Portia."

"How flattering."

Annabelle's voice took on a more serious tone. "Do you think others will . . . uh . . . see real people in my characters?"

"I doubt they will. I heard nothing to that effect last night—and the League probably has your most observant readers. And believe me, if a newspaper writer knew—or even suspected—it would be all over town already."

Annabelle breathed a sigh of relief.

"Speaking of which," Harriet added, "Rolsbury was very particular in sending his regards. And he was very generous in his comments about your work."

Annabelle smiled at this news. "Was he now?"

She had told Harriet a great deal of the inspiration for Nathan and that Thorne's sister had recognized her brother in the portrait of the fictional hero. She had *not* admitted to either Harriet or Catherine the extent of her regard for Lord Rolsbury. Good heavens! She scarcely dared admit it to herself yet.

The Lord Mayor's ball was an annual event at which the Lord Mayor of London entertained political and social leaders in order to advance the interests of the city with Members of Parliament. It was a grand affair, full of pomp and ceremony, but also usually great fun. Unlike the Lord Mayor's parade and banquet in November, when the Prime Minister made a symbolic report to the city's chief administrator, this ball emphasized the social prestige of city leaders. It was not held in the Guildhall, seat of city government, but in the Lord Mayor's mansion.

Arriving with Aunt Gertrude and Marcus and Harriet, Annabelle was struck by the nobility of the mansion itself, though it was crowded by surrounding buildings. The guests were shown up a large stone staircase, covered in deep carpet, to the elegant Egyptian Hall, a gargantuan room where dinner would be served. From there, guests would, Annabelle knew, ascend to the second-floor ballroom.

She had no idea of the exact number of people at this grand affair, but she estimated it to be several hundred. Trying not to be overly bold, she kept looking around, searching for but one face. When she finally spotted Thorne, she was dismayed to see him in company with Helen Rhys. So—there *was* something in that quarter. She tried to shrug it off, but was unable to quell a stab of pain.

There were other familiar faces in this crowd, and she hoped to get around to talking later with Celia and Letty and their spouses. She also saw Catherine and her husband. And then she spotted two faces she would happily *not* have seen—those of Viscount Beelson and George Ferris. Beelson glared at her. Ferris merely nodded, his expression bland. If she were lucky, there would be no need, in this crowd, to talk with either of them.

When the dinner, with its speeches and toasts and chamber music, was over, the guests made their way—slowly, because of the sheer numbers—to the ballroom. Here, too, the interior designer had favored classical styles with pillars and pediments and classical motifs. The Lord Mayor and his wife led the first set. Herself not engaged for the first dance, Annabelle sat on the sidelines with Aunt Gertrude. Suddenly she giggled softly.

"And just what is it that you find so amusing, missy?" Lady Hermiston asked.

"Do the gentlemen in their formal attire not put you in mind of penguins? All that profusion of black and white?"

Aunt Gertrude smiled, sharing the joke. "Yes. I suppose they do. And I also suppose we may compare the ladies to exotic jungle birds."

"Perhaps," Annabelle agreed. Then a thought struck her and she giggled again.

"Now what?"

"Have you ever wondered why it is that in the world of birds, the *male* of the species usually has the more beautiful plumage?"

Aunt Gertrude's eyes twinkled merrily. "No, I cannot say that earth-shaking observation ever occurred to me."

"Well, think on it—the peacock, not the peahen, has those gorgeous eye-like feathers; the male pheasant is far more spectacular than his mate; and even a barnyard rooster has more show than the hen. Quite the opposite of their human counterparts."

Marcus, with Harriet on his arm, strolled over to them. "May we know what it is that so amuses you two?"

There was still laughter in Aunt Gertrude's voice. "Annabelle was just explaining the nature of birds to me."

He raised an eyebrow. "Birds?"

"This is hardly the time or place for a discussion of the birds and the bees," Harriet said, grinning.

"No bees—just birds," Annabelle quipped. Then she explained the source of their amusement.

Marcus and Harriet laughed and then Marcus nodded toward some new arrivals, a group of young men in the colorful garb of bright coats and even brighter waistcoats. "That lot seems bent on disproving your theory about the difference between the bird world and ours."

Annabelle had a quick comeback. "Maybe they are just the exception that proves the rule."

She laughed along with the others, but her eyes were drawn to a group standing not far from the dandies. Or, rather, to one member of the group—Thorne. She wondered where Miss Rhys was, but then she saw her on the dance floor with a certain Lord Hardwick. The dance was just ending and Annabelle watched with interest as Lord Hardwick escorted his partner off the floor and returned her—to the care of Lord Rolsbury. Helen clasped Thorne's arm just as though she were entitled to do so.

Suddenly, all Annabelle's enjoyment was gone from

the evening. Oh, do get hold of yourself, she thought. You have no right to take exception to what those two do. You came here to enjoy yourself. Now, enjoy!

And so she did. For the next two sets, she was determined to be vivacious and cheerful. She gave Lord Stimson a brilliant smile as he came to claim the dance he had bespoken earlier. *"Such* a smile. A shame to waste it on a mere friend," he teased.

"I do not consider a friend *mere* anything, sir!"

He gave her a mocking little bow and swung her onto the floor as the orchestra launched into a waltz.

When the dance was over, Stimson returned her to where she had been sitting, but Aunt Gertrude was not there. Marcus and Harriet were engaged in conversation some distance away.

"Shall I sit with you, then?" Stimson asked.

"Oh, no. That will not be necessary." She patted his arm and sat down. "I am sure you are engaged for the next dance."

"Well, I am, but—"

"Miss Richardson?" A liveried footman addressed her.

"Yes?"

"You are wanted in the ladies' withdrawing room."

"Oh. Thank you. See, Robert? You need not worry at all. I am off on a mission of mercy—Lady Hermiston probably has a problem with a hem, or some pins."

She left the ballroom and stepped into the hallway, which was much darker, being lit with a few gas lamps along the wall. It took a moment for her eyes to adjust. The hall was wide with large, classical statues. There were several small rooms across from the ballroom. One of these at the far end had been set aside for the ladies.

As she hurried past one of the giant figures, she glimpsed a doorway and it crossed her mind fleetingly that the door seemed ajar. However, it was not the ladies' room, so she hurried past it.

Too late, she sensed movement. Suddenly, she felt a blow to her head and everything went dark.

Thorne had attended this affair with the same purpose the Lord Mayor had in mind—politics. He also thought he might get a moment with Annabelle. He had not been surprised to see Helen Rhys and her brother here, but he *was* rather surprised when she turned out to be his dinner partner.

"What a happy coincidence this is," she said brightly.

"Yes, it is." He kept his voice politely neutral, but he wondered how much of a "coincidence" it truly was. A word and a coin to a footman could easily change place cards for all but the most exalted guests.

He knew Helen would welcome the idea of becoming the Countess of Rolsbury. He was not sure how much of her desire lay in the idea of becoming a *countess* and how much in her attraction to *him*. He made a point of not pursuing her. He did not single her out for attention, nor had he called at the Rhys residence.

Nevertheless, he usually found her pleasant enough company when he met her at affairs such as this—and her brother was a special friend. Thorne was, however, a little uncomfortable when she so readily possessed herself of his arm as the company made its way to the ballroom. She also hovered near him once they reached the ballroom, giving the general impression that their being together was planned—and a thoroughly natural turn of events. He recalled Aunt Dorothy's comments about Miss Rhys's "clinging" habits. Thorne was frankly glad when her partner came to claim her for the second dance. He quickly joined a political discussion with a group of men and then moved from one such group to another through the next two sets.

He was intensely aware of Annabelle's presence. He seemed unconsciously to know where she was at all times. When she waltzed with Stimson, he recalled how it felt to have her in his own arms, and he envied Stimson. Still, he himself could not be thumping around a dance floor with a walking stick, he thought bitterly.

He saw the footman speak to her. She then hurried from the room as though she had been sent for. But he knew that all the people who might make a hurried demand on her were still in the ballroom. Lady Hermiston stood chatting with Lord and Lady Winters, the Wyndhams had just taken the dance floor, and the Harts were standing right beside him. Celia was talking idly of the choice of music.

The hair on the back of his neck prickled in intuitive warning. Such unexplained hunches had seen him through many a tricky situation on the battlefield. Something was wrong.

"Mrs. Hart—Celia—I am sorry to interrupt—but would you come with me, please?"

She looked startled, but to her credit, Celia did not bat an eye. "Certainly."

As they left the room, he said, "I think Annabelle may need your help."

Had they been a moment later, he would have missed the slash of white going into one of the rooms across the hall. Had she been lured into some sort of clandestine meeting? He knocked on the door, then turned the handle and pushed into the room. A door on the right clicked shut.

Annabelle lay slumped on the floor beside a long settee.

"See to her," he ordered Celia as he quickly went to the other door.

It opened into another small room like this one. Both were relatively bare of furniture—containing tables and chairs that suggested these rooms usually functioned as small meeting rooms. The second room was empty.

"Damn!" he muttered, cursing the leg that kept him from the instant response he might once have managed. He returned to the two women.

"How is she?" he asked.

"Unconscious. There is a lump on her head. I think she was struck," Celia said in amazement.

Frederick Hart came in just then. "What happened?"

"Annabelle has been injured—someone apparently struck her," Celia said, still bending over the slumped form of her friend.

"I'll get help," Hart said.

"Discreetly," Thorne cautioned.

"Of course."

A few minutes later, Thorne and Celia had managed to get Annabelle on the settee, where she lay unmoving. A footman came in bearing a basin of water and a cloth. He was closely followed by Lady Hermiston, Lord and Lady Wyndham, and Frederick.

"What on earth happened?" Harriet asked, fear evident in her voice.

Thorne explained as much as he knew as Celia pressed a damp cloth to Annabelle's head.

"Someone deliberately lured her in here?" Marcus asked.

"No, I think not. I think she was lured into the hall, struck, and dragged in here," Thorne said.

"But—why?" Aunt Gertrude asked, digging in her reticule. "There! I *knew* I had a vial of smelling salts in here." She handed the vial to Harriet, who now bent over Annabelle, too.

"Probably to compromise her," Hart said.

"If that was the plan, it would surely have succeeded but for Lord Rolsbury's quick thinking," Celia said.

"Not quick enough." Thorne shook his head in disgust. "Whoever did this got away."

"Still—your instincts are as sharp as ever, Major," Frederick said. "Annabelle has as much reason to be grateful to you as I do."

The smelling salts and damp cloth were doing the trick. Annabelle moaned and tried to turn her face away from the vial Harriet held under her nose. "Please. Take it away," she said. She tried to sit up.

"Just lie still for a few minutes," Harriet said.

"What happened?" Annabelle asked.

"You were struck," Celia explained. "Did you see the person who did it?"

"N-no. Just a flash of movement. I thought Aunt Gertrude needed me."

"But I was in the ballroom," Lady Hermiston said.

"Would you recognize the footman who brought you the message?" Thorne asked.

"I—I doubt it. He had brown hair. I remember that much."

"That describes only about three-quarters of the staff," Hart said.

"I'm sorry," Annabelle said softly.

"Never mind, dear," Harriet soothed, brushing a hand over Annabelle's hair. "You are all right. That is all that matters."

"Wyndham, may I have a word with you?" Thorne asked, motioning Lord Wyndham toward the hall.

Thorne closed the door behind them. "I did not want to alarm the ladies, but this is the second time Miss Richardson has been endangered."

He explained about Annabelle's horse being frightened in the park.

"And you said nothing before this?" Marcus asked.

"At the time, it seemed merely an accident. There was absolutely no reason to suspect foul play."

"But now you do."

"After this—it seems likely."

"I shall assign a servant to act as bodyguard whenever she goes out," Marcus said.

Thorne was grateful that Wyndham did not ask what he had been doing out riding with Annabelle so early in the morning. Marcus merely gave him a penetrating look, which Thorne managed to return without flinching.

Eighteen

The lump on her head hurt the next day if she touched it, but otherwise, Annabelle suffered no ill effects from her experience. She had wanted to speak with Thorne—merely to thank him, of course—but as soon as he saw her into capable hands, he was gone.

She thought he might call the next day and, indeed, he did—along with Catherine and her husband and Luke, but by then the Wyndham drawing room was filled with well-wishers; the Wainwright party stayed only the requisite few minutes for a morning call and left. That evening, Annabelle did not feel much like going out.

Luke had arranged to go riding with her the second day after the Mayor's ball—"if she were up to it." She and a groom set out for the park at her usual time. Luke met her at the entrance and the groom dropped back a discreet distance.

"Were you just being friendly when you asked me to ride with you—or have you something on your mind?" she asked.

"A bit of both." He grinned at her. " 'Tis a good thing we became 'just friends.' You read me far too well. A husband will find it difficult to keep secrets from *you*."

She sniffed. "In *my* opinion, he should not want to."

They rode in silence for a while. Finally her impatience won the inner war. "Well? Out with it."

"I think I am in love."

"Again? Or is it still Miss Wentworth?"

The color in his face intensified as he admitted, "No. Do you know Miss Brinkley?"

"Susan Brinkley? Only slightly. *She* is your new light of love?"

"Well . . . I think so. Oh, Annabelle, she is so lovely—"

"Believe me, Luke," Annabelle said with a certain degree of sadness, "if you really loved her, you would not merely 'think' so."

"You know this for a certainty?"

"Yes."

Luke gave her a hard look, but she refused to elaborate, so he merely shrugged and began to sing the praises of Miss Brinkley—which mostly dealt with an alabaster complexion, golden curls, sky-blue eyes, and the voice of an angel.

Annabelle laughed.

"What? What is so funny?" he demanded.

"You."

"Well!" His umbrage was all pretense. "I am glad you find my love life so amusing."

"I think you love the *idea* of being in love. But do not, please, go offering for her until the praises you sing include something deeper than golden hair and blue eyes."

"You sound just like Thorne."

"Do I?" She wanted him to go on and speak more of his brother.

They were nearing the part of the narrow roadway where her horse had panicked before. The mare seemed nervous. Annabelle glanced behind them, looking for the groom. He was not there, but perhaps he was lagging behind a curve in the lane. There was a closed carriage approaching, however.

"A closed carriage here?" Luke said. "That's strange. People usually want to be *seen* in the park."

Luke and Annabelle moved their mounts off to the side to allow the carriage to pass. It did not pass. It stopped and three rough-looking men jumped out. Before she knew what was happening, one of them had jerked her off her horse and was trying to stuff her into the carriage. She screamed and swiped at him with her riding crop. He jerked it out of her hand and pushed her into the vehicle.

She fell, scraping her arm and knocking her hat off. She could see that Luke was no match for the other two ruffians, one of whom carried a thick piece of wood with which he hit Luke on the head. Luke went limp and the larger of the two shoved him into the carriage along with Annabelle, and then climbed up to join the driver as the one who had jerked Annabelle off her horse got into the coach itself.

The third man was left with the horses. The coachman whipped his team to a pace far too fast for the park, but at this hour of the morning, that was of little consequence.

The man with Annabelle and Luke showed her an ugly-looking knife. "If'n ye care any fer this fella, missy, ye'll jest sit there real quiet like."

He took a piece of thin rope from a pocket on the door and bound Luke's hands behind his back. Then he pulled the curtains over all the windows. The light in the interior of the coach was what filtered in from slits of space around the curtains and from several small tears in them. Still, once her eyes adjusted, Annabelle could see her companions quite clearly.

"I demand to know where you are taking us," she said.

"Oh, ye 'demand,' do ye?" he sneered.

"You cannot just go around kidnapping people in broad daylight."

" 'Pears like we done it, though," he said smugly.

Luke groaned and the man shoved him onto the seat with Annabelle. "There. I can see ye both better this way."

Luke shook his head and winced. Annabelle tried to make him a bit more comfortable, but knew it was an impossible task with his hands tied behind him.

"Look," Annabelle said. "Whatever you have been paid, we will pay more. Just let us go."

"Talk don't cost nothin'," the man said. "Unless ye got the ready on ye, don't guess I be over-innerested in yer offer."

Annabelle sat back in dismay, eyeing the man. He appeared to be in his late thirties. His hair was probably dark brown, but it was incredibly dirty. He was missing two front teeth; he sported a scraggly beard; and he had an ugly scar that ran from his left temple to his chin. His clothing, also caked with grime, was that seen on dock workers.

"Tell me—please—who hired you and where we are going." She kept her voice as calm as she could, though she was as frightened as she had ever been in her life.

"I reckon him that wanted ye will tell ye hisself. Now, jus' settle yourselfs down. 'Tis a longish ride."

"I cannot *believe* this is happening to me again," Annabelle said in angry despair.

"Again?" Luke asked.

"Yes. Five years ago a penniless bounder tried to carry me off to Gretna Green. I was only fifteen!"

Luke's eyes widened in surprise. "What happened?"

She raised her voice for the benefit of their traveling companion. "The Earl of Wyndham rescued me. I doubt not he will come after me again."

"And the kidnapper?" Luke asked.

"He ended by shooting himself. However, he *would* have been transported to a penal colony in New South Wales." She eyed the man to see how he reacted to this, but he merely gave her a toothless grin.

Annabelle hoped the movement of the carriage would make their captor drowsy and careless. At one point she thought his attention had wandered and she surreptitiously moved one of her hands behind Luke to try to untie his hands. However, the knots were very tight and when she glanced at the man opposite, his beady black eyes were alert and he turned the knife over and over in his hands.

"The minute he is loose, he dies, missy."

Annabelle jerked her hand back to her lap.

"Not to worry, Annabelle. Thorne will find us somehow." There was a hollowness to Luke's attempt at confidence.

The carriage stopped once to change horses. The change was a hurried affair, and they were on the road again immediately. She thought they had been traveling for about two hours when the vehicle turned onto the bumpier route of a less traveled road.

When the coach finally stopped, one of the men jumped down from the driver's seat. He opened the door and reached for Annabelle.

"I'll take her, you see to pretty boy there," he said to the knife-wielder.

"Watch 'er, Jake. She's sneaky."

Annabelle sank into the cushions, but the one called Jake was a huge man. He merely reached in, grabbed her hand, and jerked her toward the door. She fell against him and was close enough to smell rank body odor.

"Ah, well . . ." Jake said appreciatively as his hands lingered in setting her on her feet. "I begins ta see what the swell in there wants."

In there proved to be a three-story cottage that might once have been the home of a fairly prosperous tenant farmer. It did not look like a farm home now. A hunting box, perhaps? Whatever its current use, it apparently was mostly neglected.

By now, Jake had pushed her up the steps and into a small entrance hall. Luke and the knife were right behind them. Jake rapped on a door and did not bother to await a summons. He turned the handle and shoved Annabelle before him into what was a rather shabby drawing room.

"Ah, welcome, my dear. You are here at last."

At first she saw only buckskin-clad legs, an arm encased in brown wool, and the top of a blond head. The rest of the speaker was obscured by the contours of the chair in which he sat. Then he rose.

Annabelle gasped. "You!" She looked into the mocking face of Viscount Beelson. "How dare you? How *dare* you?" Her voice rose an octave at least.

"For *you,* my own love, I would dare a great deal." He looked up at the commotion in the doorway as the knife-wielder shoved Luke into the room. "Bloody hell! What is *he* doing here?"

"He was with her. Couldn't very well leave him to run for help."

"Well, it was patently stupid—stupid!—to bring him here." Beelson paced the room, enraged, and apparently trying to incorporate this turn of events into his previous plans. "Hmm. I need time to think. Put them both in that back bedroom on the second floor. And lock the damned door! Then the two of you take turns standing guard."

Annabelle racked her brain for some means of stalling to postpone their being locked up. She stamped her foot and said, "This truly is the outside of enough! We have been shoved around and mistreated. We have been in that dark, smelly carriage for hours and I am hungry and my clothes are a mess and . . . and . . . I must use the necessary!" She managed to work a few tears into this diatribe.

Beelson just looked at her. "Cut the drama. It won't work. Chet here will bring you some food. There's a chamber pot in the room. Now get on with it!" he ordered the two men.

Within minutes, Annabelle and Luke were placed in a sparsely furnished chamber. She worked at Luke's bonds and finally freed his hands. He rubbed his wrists and his shoulders trying to restore normal circulation. Then he simply opened his arms and they clung to each other for a few minutes.

"I am so sorry, Luke."

"For what? This is not your doing. And don't worry. We shall get out of this. You shall see. Thorne will—"

"Shh." She put her fingers on his lips to stop the flow of words. "It will be a long while before Thorne— or Marcus—even knows we are missing. Meanwhile, we must try to help ourselves."

They explored the room, but found little beyond what they had seen on first entering. There was a bed with rumpled bedclothes on it, an empty armoire, two threadbare upholstered chairs, a table with a lamp, and—behind a screen in the corner—a washstand with a chamber pot in the cupboard beneath it. When Annabelle drew the drapery aside, she found that the only window had narrowly spaced bars on it.

"I daresay this room has served this purpose before," she noted, sinking into one of the chairs.

Luke stretched out on the bed. "You are probably right. I wonder if anyone ever escaped from it?"

There was a sound at the door. Luke jumped up and stood near it. The door opened just enough so that Chet could hand in a tray. "Here, take this," he said curtly to Luke, then closed the door and they heard the lock fall firmly into place again.

Luke set the tray on the table with a flourish. "Your luncheon is served, my lady. We have here the finest English cheese, a very tasty-looking country bread, some apples, and—marvel of marvels—tea! When *was* the last time you had such an elegant meal?"

Annabelle laughed. "Do stop . . . I think I last enjoyed just such fare when I was being punished at school."

"We shall enjoy our repast first and then put our heads together to try to figure a way out of this mess."

Annabelle nodded regally.

It was midmorning and Thorne sat at his desk in the library going over a report on "The Lives of Children of the Streets." The report dealt with abandoned children and the so-called "flash houses" in which they frequently spent their days. Supposedly compassionately run havens for Society's least fortunate, these institutions were very often little more than schools for thievery and every other debauchery known to mankind. Thorne intended to lend his support to legislation regulating such places.

Perkins interrupted him with news of a visitor. It was Marcus Jeffries, Earl of Wyndham.

Thorne greeted his guest cordially. "To what do I owe the pleasure of this visit?"

"I am not sure it will be a pleasure." Wyndham sounded grim. "Annabelle is missing. She went riding this morning as she usually does. She told Harriet last night she would be meeting Luke. It has been almost four hours now. So, I've come to see if Luke has any idea where she might be. Neither the groom nor their horses have returned. After that business at the Mayor's ball—"

With Wyndham's first words, Thorne felt a very cold, very strong fist clutch at his heart. He jerked open the library door and sent a footman in the hall to look for Luke. He invited Wyndham to sit. The footman came back to say Luke had not returned from his morning ride and his manservant did not know of his plans. Thorne sent him to the stable and he came back shortly with news that Luke's favorite mount was missing, too.

"Something is very, very wrong," Thorne said. "Luke is shatterbrained at times, but not to this extent."

"I doubt Annabelle would go off like this of her own free will," Marcus said.

"Well, the place to start, I suppose, is the park. We could use some help. I will take two of my fellows and send word to Hart as well." Thorne had begun thinking immediately in terms of military strategy and logistics.

"I was hoping it would be a simpler matter," Marcus said.

Thorne knew instantly what the other man's worry was. "My fellows will keep their mouths shut and Hart is the soul of discretion. Her reputation will be protected."

"Very well."

Twenty minutes later, the two earls and three other men were in the park, tracing the route Annabelle and Luke would most likely have taken. Unfortunately, their search was hampered by two factors. They hardly knew *what* to look for, and the park at this hour was filling up with fashionable fribbles out to see and be seen.

After a few minutes, Thorne said, "It was here that Annabelle's horse panicked that day."

"A fellow with a slingshot could have easily hidden in that copse," Marcus pointed out.

"Yes. You two," Thorne said to his servants, "go in there and look around."

Hart had dismounted to examine the grassy verge of the riding lane. "Major—uh, sorry, Thorne. *Something* happened here. Look at the way this turf is scuffed up."

"Hart often served as a scout in the army," Thorne explained to Marcus even as his eyes swept over the area. He spotted something dark lying in the grass. "What is that?"

Marcus, moving more quickly than Thorne, rushed over to pick it up. "Annabelle's hat," he called.

One of the men Thorne had sent into the copse came riding out in a hurry. "My lord, there's something you should see."

The three of them followed the man into the dense thicket of trees and undergrowth.

"Annabelle's mare," Marcus said.

"And Luke's mount," Thorne said.

The two horses were tied to a bush, along with another that Marcus also identified as being from his stable.

"These animals did not arrive here on their own," Hart observed dryly. "Let's have a look around."

Moments later, one of the Rolsbury men called, "Over here."

They found the Wyndham groom who had accompanied Annabelle bound and gagged, leaning against a tree. He looked at them with obvious relief; Thorne noticed that his hands and wrists were raw and bleeding from his having rubbed them against the bark of the tree in an effort to free himself.

They soon had as much information as the groom, Jamie, could supply. There had been four ruffians and a coachman in a nondescript black carriage. They had eliminated Jamie first. Then two of them stayed behind to hide the horses and Jamie.

"Don't know what they was gonna do with *me*," Jamie said, his fear readily apparent, "but they was comin' back tonight for the horses. Couldn't take 'em earlier 'cause someone might reco'nize the horses."

"That makes sense," Thorne mused aloud. "Horse-flesh like this would sell very well."

He conferred with Marcus and Hart beneath the canopy of trees. The two Rolsbury servants would be joined by two others to await the return of the miscreants, for these two were, at the moment, the only known tie to whoever was behind all this.

"Though I have a fairly good idea who it is," Marcus said in bitter disgust. "Beelson."

"His aim must be to compromise or ransom Annabelle—but why would he take Luke, too?" Hart asked.

"It was probably a case of Luke's being in the wrong place at the wrong time," Thorne said. "However, Beelson would not be averse to using Luke for revenge."

"Revenge?" Marcus and Hart spoke together.

Thorne explained briefly, being careful not to mention that the woman Beelson had sought to ruin was Catherine.

"The question now is where would he take them?" Hart asked.

Marcus answered, "He probably wants to take *her* to Gretna Green—or to Paris. Many eloping couples go there now."

" 'Tis my guess," Thorne said, "that he will hide them away for at least this day to throw off pursuit."

"But where?" Hart asked. "We three cannot search the whole of southern England."

"Perhaps we can narrow it down," Thorne answered. "Surely some of those ne'er-do-wells that Beelson hangs out with would have an idea where he would take a ladybird."

Marcus kicked at the leaves beneath his feet. "Even

if we find her before morning, I fear the damage to Annabelle's reputation will be irreparable."

"Maybe not," Thorne said. Again, he took charge. "I have something I want to check out, but you two could go and ask around the clubs for the information we seek. Enlist the aid of Winters. He is trustworthy."

"So is Stimson," Marcus said and Hart nodded.

Thorne accepted their judgment. "Meet me at my house no later than three. That will give us a good five or six hours of daylight for the search if we get a good lead."

Thorne went directly to the heart of the city—to the Court of Arches in Doctors Commons near St. Paul's Cathedral. His business there took him slightly longer than he had anticipated. He stopped in at Lady Conwick's town house to ask for the direction of George Ferris whose mother was one of Aunt Dorothy's friends.

"George Ferris? What would *you* be wanting with him?" his forthright aunt asked.

"I have no time to explain now, Aunt Dorothy. Suffice it to say, it is a matter of some urgency."

She quickly supplied the information. Soon he was being ushered into the Ferris drawing room. Mrs. Ferris replied in a tone of apprehension and suspicion.

"What do you want with my son?"

"Merely some information, madam. I believe he can help me resolve a difficult problem."

"That fellow Stimson said the same thing. Well, I shall tell you what I told him. Georgie rarely tells me where he is going, but I think he usually spends his day at one of those gentlemen's clubs."

"Which one?"

She shrugged. "Whites? Boodles? Maybe Watier's.

No—wait. I think it is Brooks. Oh, dear. I told that nice Stimson lad it was Boodles."

It was neither. It was Watier's where Thorne found that Stimson had already tracked down their quarry. Stimson had Ferris closeted in a small room provided by the club for truly private discussions.

Ferris looked up as Thorne entered the room, his eyes widening in surprise, then apprehension.

"Have you found anything of interest?" Thorne asked Stimson.

"Not yet. But neither have I yet put any of Gentleman Jackson's effective lessons to the test."

Ferris's nervousness increased even more at mention of the famous boxer. "N-now—look—I want no t-trouble."

"Nor do we." Thorne's voice was cold and hard. "But I shall guarantee you extreme discomfort on every level if you do not supply the information we seek."

Ferris shifted, in obvious discomfort already, and whined, "I don't know how I could be of any help to you."

"Ferris, I swear—you will not be able to step into a respectable club in this town," Thorne threatened.

"So answer the question I put to you earlier." Stimson waved his clenched fist under Ferris's nose.

"I—I don't know anything about Beelson's current ladybirds. He has talked a lot of late about renewing his suit with Miss Richardson—said she would welcome him when he was through." Ferris looked crafty. "I say, does this have anything to do with Miss Richardson? I have not seen her around lately. Or did Ralph make the mistake of poaching in *your* territory?" He looked from one to the other of his interrogators.

Stimson drew back his fist. Ferris threw up his hands in front of his face. "Hold on. It makes no difference to me. He has a place beyond Windsor. A hunting box of sorts."

"You will give us the exact location," Thorne said. "And do not consider even for an instant misleading us. For if you do—"

"If you do," Stimson interrupted, "I shall personally beat you to within an inch of your miserable life."

However reluctantly, Ferris parted with the detailed information they wanted.

With the addition of Winters and Stimson to their group, it was five determined men who set out that afternoon, well-armed and riding hard, heading for a sometime hunting box southwest of Windsor.

Nineteen

Annabelle had no idea precisely how long she and Luke had been locked in the room. She could tell by the elongated shadows on the ground below the window that it was late in the afternoon. They had taken turns at napping on the bed.

The door handle rattled as the door was unlocked. Annabelle sat up on the edge of the bed and Luke looked suddenly alert in one of the chairs. Jake brought in another tray of food. Behind him stood Beelson. When Jake had taken the previous tray, Beelson moved inside the door and closed it, but Annabelle caught a glimpse of Chet in a chair tipped against the wall outside.

"Well, I must say you two managed to set my plans awry a bit. And I am getting mightily sick of you Wainwrights always interfering," he said darkly to Luke. "Rolsbury's interference the other night set me back a week or more."

"You! You were responsible for that incident at the Mayor's ball," Annabelle said.

"The original plan, my darling girl, was that I would take you to Paris for a honeymoon trip."

"You truly are mad if for one moment you think I would willingly go anywhere with you." Annabelle did not bother to temper her contempt to any degree.

"You need to get a civil tongue in that pretty head," he said calmly and strode over to stand next to her. "I shall enjoy teaching you some manners, my sweet." He stroked her cheek with the back of his forefinger. She jerked her head away, but he merely smiled.

"As I was saying," he continued, "I have had to alter my plans slightly, so unfortunately we shall not leave for the continent this night as I had planned. And perhaps the addition of Wainwright here was rather fortuitous, after all. In any event, I have sent to London for a special license and a friend of mine who is a sometime vicar of the Church of England. When they arrive—be it three in the morning—we shall be married forthwith, my dear."

Annabelle wanted to scream, but forced herself to speak calmly. "There is nothing in this world that would induce me to marry the likes of you."

"Oh, you will agree to the marriage, all right." His eyes glittered with triumph. "For if you do not, your friend here will feel the effects of the knife Chet so enjoys playing with. Did I fail to mention that in his own circles, Chet is known as 'the butcher'?"

Annabelle shuddered and looked at him balefully. "Luke was supposed to be your friend, was he not?"

"Ah, and he was. A most convenient friend. I was especially pleased when I knew he'd had funds from Rolsbury to pay his debts to *me*." He gave a maniacal laugh. "That was but the first installment on my revenge."

Luke looked both angry and bewildered. "Just what did I do to you that you felt such need for vengeance?"

"You? Why, nothing at all, you puppy. You are merely a means to an end."

Luke rose at this, his fists clenched.

"Tut! Tut!" Beelson waved him back. "Chet awaits—"

"He wants revenge against Thorne," Annabelle said

dully. She knew she had made a mistake when she saw
Beelson's face darken at her familiar use of Thorne's
name.

"Thorne?" Luke said in surprise. "Thorne was out
of the country for years—and then he stayed at the
Manor for even more years, recovering from his wounds.
He could not possibly have earned this sort of . . . ha-
tred."

"It goes back farther," Annabelle said. "Catherine
told me."

"Catherine? My sister told you some family secret
that even I do not know?"

Beelson looked from one to the other, with a decided
smirk on his face. "This little melodrama is interesting,
but I will leave you to it. The second installment will
come when Rolsbury's brother witnesses our marriage,
my love. Would it were Rolsbury himself, but Luke here
will have to do. And the *coup de grace* will come when
I bed you." Again he stroked her cheek and again she
jerked away from his touch.

"And you believe *that* will secure any measure of
vengeance against Lord Rolsbury?" Annabelle gave a
bitter, empty laugh.

"Oh, yes." He caressed her cheek again and laughed
softly. "I have seen the way he looks at you. Yes, indeed.
Bedding you will give me *much* satisfaction." The laugh
turned malicious.

He started to go, then turned back and looked her
over. "Hmm. Pity about the garb you have on. Not much
of a wedding dress. But never fear, love, I will buy you
lovely gowns in Paris—and the baubles to go with
them."

She jumped up from the edge of the bed and moved
out of his reach. She sounded far more brave than she
felt. "Do not be spending *my* money before you have
it!"

"It will be *mine* by then, my darling—a wife's property becomes her husband's, you know."

He was still laughing as he closed and locked the door. Annabelle sank back down on the bed and buried her face in her hands. Luke came to sit next to her and put his arm around her shoulder.

"Please don't cry, Annabelle." He sounded truly distressed. "There's still hope. Come have a bite while we think on it."

She dumbly followed his lead to the table. Cheese, bread, apples, and tea again.

"The cook has little imagination, it appears," she said, trying to create some lightness in the whole miserable affair.

"True," he agreed. "But look! They gave us knives and a spoon."

"Luke, those are only table knives. How effective would they be as weapons against that Chet person's butchering knife?"

"Not weapons. Tools!"

"Tools?"

"Tools. We might be able to loosen the plaster around those bars on the window."

"And then what? We are on the second floor. It is a long way down there."

"But there are sheets on that bed . . ."

She felt hope returning. At least they would be doing *something* to try to help themselves. They quickly fortified themselves with a few bites, then Luke set to work scraping away at the base of the first bar on the window and Annabelle began to rip sheets into wide strips which she would twist and tie together.

Thorne and his cohorts drove their mounts to the limits of the animals' endurance. They were forced to change horses at inns along the way three times. Even as they rode, Thorne's mind jumped from one idea to another. They were so sure Beelson was their culprit. What if he were not at all? What if they arrived at their destination and found the place deserted? What if they really had no idea where Annabelle and Luke were? What if? What if? What if? The words pounded a cadence in his mind to match the beat of the horses' hooves.

To offset his doubts was the surety that Beelson *was* their best bet. Marcus had informed him of Beelson's aborted attempt to blackmail Annabelle and the man's misunderstanding of the dedication of her book. Thorne knew Beelson well enough to be sure *either* incident would have infuriated him. Two such failures, coupled with that sordid business at the Mayor's ball, must have sent him over the edge.

The sun was getting lower and lower when Stimson said, "I think we are almost there."

"We are," Hart agreed. They had been lucky, for Frederick Hart had remembered a hunting trip in this area some years before. While he did not know the area well, he at least had *some* familiarity with it—which was more than any of the rest of them had.

Once they left the main thoroughfare, they encountered no traffic at all, though they had met a single rider some distance from the intersection. The rider had glanced at the five curiously, but rode on. As they came closer to their destination, they slowed the horses to a walk to cut down on the noise of their arrival.

When they came within sight of the cottage-hunting box, Thorne felt his senses heighten as they always had before a battle. "Looks like a stable in back," he observed quietly.

"Nothing else besides the house," Hart said.

They dismounted and tied their horses some distance

from the main building. They checked their weapons again. Thorne began to bark orders, which the others accepted just as though it were his natural right to do so.

"Winters, you check the stable and be sure we get no surprises from that quarter, then back up Hart and Stimson, who will come in from the rear. Wyndham and I will take the front. Pistols at the ready, gentlemen. We go in on a count of ten. Go!"

In the event, gaining entrance was easier than they had expected. Marcus and Thorne merely turned the handle of the door at the main entrance and quietly walked in. They stood in the hall listening for any sound. There was a thump and a curse from the rear, then silence. Total silence. Marcus quietly tried the door on the right. Locked. He did the same with the one on the left and it swung inward on squeaky hinges. Thorne winced at the sound. Marcus, pistol in hand, quickly stepped into the room and out of the way as Thorne followed, his own pistol in one hand, his walking stick in the other.

"Close the damned door, Jake. You know it creates a draft," Beelson snarled.

"Well, now. 'Jake' is not likely to obey that order." Thorne's tone was casual.

Beelson jumped up and made a grab for something on the opposite chair, but paused as he saw Thorne's pistol aimed at his heart. He apparently decided to go for bravado.

"Rolsbury. What the devil are *you* doing here? I do not recall inviting you to my little hunting party. And Lord Wyndham, too. I *am* in exalted company."

" 'Hunting' party?" Thorne's sarcasm was cutting as he moved nearer Beelson. "The only thing you ever hunted here were ladybirds."

"Ah, yes. And I have a particularly fine specimen above stairs at the moment."

"Why, you—" Thorne dropped his walking stick and planted his fist in the middle of Beelson's face. Blood spurted, but Beelson remained on his feet. He kicked ineffectually at Thorne's bad leg and made a grab for Thorne's gun, which exploded. Beelson grunted and put his hand to his side. Blood oozed between his fingers.

They heard heavy footsteps running above and then clattering down the stairs. Marcus went to stand near the door. A very large, unkempt fellow burst into the room wielding a vicious-looking knife. The man's grin was malevolent.

"I don't s'pose ye've had time to reload," he said, raising his arm slowly to throw the knife at Thorne.

"No. He has not," Marcus said in a smooth, icy voice from behind the bounder. "I, on the other hand, had no need to reload, and if you release that knife you will be dead before it reaches your target."

The man whirled around and apparently perceived that the game was up. He lowered his knife and it clattered to the floor. Stimson and Hart came in, followed by Winters.

"We have the one in the kitchen all trussed up like a Christmas goose," Hart announced.

"There was no one in the stable," Winters said. "You fellows had all the fun."

The round of relieved laughter that followed this was all the distraction Beelson needed. Thorne was scarcely aware of seeing him reach into the top of one of his boots and extract a very small but very deadly pistol.

"Thorne, look out!" Marcus yelled. Despite his lame leg, Thorne instantly dove away, but felt the sting of the bullet as it grazed his upper arm. In the same instant, Marcus fired his own pistol. Beelson fell with a heavy crash and lay still.

Hart bent over him and felt for a pulse. "Dead."

This took every particle of resistance out of the man

who had wielded the knife, for when Thorne growled "Where are they?" he pointed upstairs.

"Are you all right, Rolsbury?" Stimson asked, looking at the blood on Thorne's sleeve.

"Yes. 'Tis only a nick, I think. Will you keep an eye on this one?"

Stimson nodded and motioned the man into a chair.

Thorne led the way up the stairs. Despite the fact that any of the others could have taken the stairs two at a time, they held back to allow him the lead. On the second floor, there were four doors, all closed.

"Listen," he said.

"I tell you, Annabelle, that was a shot—two of them," a male voice, high-pitched in its excitement, said.

"Well, we are still locked in here, so do you not think it just might be the better part of wisdom to continue working at that window?" This was expressed in a sarcastic know-all voice that brought a smile to Thorne's lips. Annabelle had lost none of her spunk.

Marcus grinned at Thorne and said loudly enough for those within to hear, "Maybe we should leave them in there to dig themselves out."

"Marcus!" Annabelle screamed happily.

"No, too cruel by half," Thorne said, turning the key that had been left in the lock.

"I told you Thorne would come for us," Luke said triumphantly.

Thorne was the first to enter the room. He simply opened his arms and Annabelle threw herself into them, sobbing with relief. "I was so afraid," she whispered.

He hugged her to him, as oblivious to others as she seemed to be. "You are safe now, my sweet," he said softly.

He reluctantly let her go and hugged his brother even as Marcus embraced Annabelle.

Thorne looked around and spied the tray. "Maybe we can find something to drink before we start back."

"I'll go downstairs and arrange things," Hart said with a speaking look at Thorne. Thorne knew he meant he would see to Beelson's body.

"Once you take care of . . . that matter, we will put those fellows in here to wait for the local magistrate."

"Yes, sir, Major," Hart said with a mocking salute.

"What happened? How did you find us?" Luke asked.

Thorne and Marcus explained, with an occasional correction or addition from Winters.

"And Lord Beelson?" Annabelle asked. "What will happen to him?"

"The man is dead," Marcus said gently. "He tried to kill Rolsbury."

"Oh!" She turned shocked eyes toward Thorne and for the first time seemed to see the blood on his sleeve. "You are hurt."

"A minor matter. See?" He swung his arm and winced.

"All clear," Hart called from below.

They all trooped downstairs to the small drawing room, where Hart had already located a bottle of brandy and some glasses. Thorne noticed that he had also thrown a small rug over the spot on the carpet where Beelson had lain. He, Wyndham, Luke, and Annabelle took chairs in another part of the room.

Hart announced that he would look for some glasses in the kitchen and Stimson and Winters took care of seeing that Chet and Jake were incarcerated in the very jail they had assigned to Annabelle and Luke.

"We need to speak," Marcus said to Annabelle, his glance also including Luke and Thorne.

Twenty

Annabelle drew in a deep breath, afraid she knew what Marcus would say. Then he uttered precisely the words she feared he would.

"Annabelle, it appears that you have been thoroughly compromised."

"I know," she said softly, unable to look at Thorne.

"Never mind, Annabelle," Luke said, sounding very grown up and very brave. "We shall marry as soon as it can be arranged."

Her words came out more forcefully than she intended. "Luke Wainwright! You know very well that that is a perfectly ridiculous idea!"

"I have already procured a special license," Thorne said, drawing the document from a pocket inside his coat.

Annabelle was devastated. Thorne was—just willy nilly—going to marry her off to his brother? Then her temper flared. Nobody—and certainly not the lofty Earl of Rolsbury—was going to control and manipulate *her* life!

"Well, that was foresight on your part, Rolsbury," Marcus said.

"See?" Luke cajoled. "It's not so ridiculous at all."

But Annabelle thought there was little enthusiasm in his voice.

"Well, I will not have it!" She rose and stood looking into the ashes of a cold fireplace. "I have an aunt in the former colonies. She married a Boston banker. I shall go to her." Her voice became softer as she turned to look at Luke. "Luke, you and I are *friends*. You do not care for me as a man should care about his wife. I do most sincerely appreciate your willingness to protect my name, but I will not allow you to do it for me. And I will *not* marry where my heart is not engaged."

Thorne pushed himself out of his chair to go and stand beside her. "And if your heart *were* engaged, would you marry then?"

She held his gaze and spoke softly. "Yes . . . but only if the man in question loved me, too."

"Even if he also considered himself a friend?"

"Especially if we were also friends."

"Look at this license, Annabelle, and tell me it is not wasted."

She read it with a growing sense of wonder. "Thorne? It . . . it has *your* name . . . and mine."

"Yes, it does. And I meet your qualifications, I think. You will marry me, will you not?"

"Yes! Yes, I will. But . . . but . . . how did you know?"

"I read your book." He laughed softly and enclosed her in his arms. He kissed her very gently, but very soundly. "And now you are truly compromised here in front of your guardian and my brother. You will have to marry me."

She looked at the grinning faces of Marcus and Luke and then back at Thorne, who had an equally silly grin on his face. "Yes, I suppose I will."

Stimson and Winters returned, followed by Hart with a tray of glasses in which he poured brandy for all.

These three were quickly apprised of what had transpired as they were out of the room.

"I *thought* there was a distinct odor of April and May in here," Stimson said. "Congratulations, Rolsbury. And to you, dear heart, my very best wishes." He kissed Annabelle on the cheek and she felt tears in her eyes.

Hart raised his glass. "A toast to new beginnings."

Others said, "Hear! Hear!" and downed their drinks. Annabelle took only the smallest sip of the burning liquid as her eyes met Thorne's in a time-honored promise.

"At the risk of casting cold water on this happy occasion," Winters said, "I feel I should point out that it is getting late. If we are to have a prayer of making it back to town before it is pitch dark, we need to leave now."

Annabelle rode double with Thorne and Luke rode Beelson's mount to the nearest village. There they informed the magistrate of what had happened back at the hunting box and left the matter in his hands. Thorne hired a post chaise for Annabelle and himself and the others secured new mounts. She thought Thorne welcomed not being in the saddle, for he rubbed his leg rather vigorously.

"Does it hurt so very much?" she asked.

"No." He placed an arm around her, drawing her closer. "I hired this closed carriage mostly to be alone with you."

"How did you know none of the others would join us?"

"I threatened them with dire consequences if they did."

She giggled at this and raised her face for a rather resounding kiss.

"Thorne?

"Hmm?"

"Did you really know I love you from the book? Catherine told me it was a declaration of love."

"And she forced me to read it because it was."

"You were not offended . . . or embarrassed?"

"Humbled is more like it." His breath at her ear was doing strange and wonderful things to the rest of her body.

"Humbled?"

"By the miracle. The miracle that you could love me with the same depth and feeling as I love you."

This declaration was punctuated by a very long, very satisfying kiss.

"I think the sooner we use this special license, the better," he said, going back for another kiss.

She merely responded in kind.

A few days later, the Earl and Countess of Wyndham hosted the grandest ball of the Season to celebrate Miss Richardson's coming of age. Only she was no longer Miss Richardson at that point. She was already the Countess of Rolsbury—and she was contemplating a new book tentatively titled *Love Returned*.

ABOUT THE AUTHOR

WILMA COUNTS lives in Nevada. She is currently working on a historical romance set in the Regency period. Look for it in May 2002! Wilma loves hearing from her readers and you may write to her c/o Zebra Books. Please include a self-addressed stamped envelope if you wish a reply. Or you may e-mail her at wilma@ableweb.net.

More Zebra Regency Romances